Doune

DEREK GHIRLANDO

authorHOUSE®

AuthorHouse™ UK
1663 Liberty Drive
Bloomington, IN 47403 USA
www.authorhouse.co.uk
Phone: 0800.197.4150

Published by AuthorHouse 10/16/2017

ISBN: 978-1-5462-8028-6 (sc)
ISBN: 978-1-5462-8027-9 (e)

Print information available on the last page.

This book is dedicated to
my mother, who instilled in
me a love of patriotism;
to my dear cousin Kay,
who died far too young
and to all the inhabitants of
Doune: the very little place
with the very big heart;
the very cold place
with the very warm people

Prelude

Ye banks and braes o' bonnie Doon
How can ye bloom so fresh and fair
How can ye chant, ye little birds
And I sae weary, fu' o' care!
Ye'll break my heart, ye warbling bird
That wantons thro' the flowering thorn
Ye minds me o'departed joys
Departed - never to return!
-Robert Burns-

I had only gone to the doctor for a routine check-up, but suddenly he was telling me that I had a tumour and that we would have to wait for the test results to discover if it was malignant or benign. But I felt perfectly fine, I protested, feeling as if I had to defend myself. As if I had done something wrong. The onus was on me.

'Things that lurk within us do not always make themselves known,' my doctor commented dryly, while looking through me at a far-away wall. 'If it is bad news, there are still many things that can be done; all is not lost.'

I felt lost at sea.

And I felt angry with him because he told me this earth-shattering news as if he were informing me of the weather or the results of a football match. So there you are. There is the information. Do with it what you will.

I had never been ill a day in my life, apart from the odd upset stomach or backache, so I left his practice in a mild state of shock and confusion after he had pumped my hand as if I had just won an award.

It cannot be.

In the car park, I sat in the car for a while, thinking on it and then decided to be philosophical about it. I have always believed that when God wants you, he'll call you home and there is nothing you can do to change that. So I decided to leave it in His hands and have faith. I just wish it hadn't started to rain so heavily as I drove out onto the main road, as it made everything seem all the more desperate and depressing.

When I eventually got home to North London, I would never have suspected anything was amiss until I saw the lonely note on the table and even then I thought it was simply a scribble from Claire saying she would be later than usual. But when I opened it in my dripping raincoat and hound-dog face, I came to learn that she would be later than later than usual; in fact infinitely later, as she had decided to leave me. There's nothing like a double whammy to jolt your soul.

She said that I was unambitious (true) and idle (not true) and that she was not prepared to wait around simply for nothing to happen, like waiting for a bus that is not running that day. Charming. So she was going to make it happen and flit. I gave a little half-laugh through the surprise and mild shock of it all. Yet, after the other shock of today, this was nothing. A needle in an ocean. She had complained at times, but it had not been with very much conviction.

I walked around the flat, noting that she had indeed taken her personal things from the sitting-room and her side of the bedroom wardrobe was completely bare. As bare as I now felt. She had even taken her pyjamas from under her pillow. I know, because I looked. I stared at the empty space as if a swarm of moths had suddenly and un-expectantly eaten all her clothes. It was as empty as outer space.

I felt even emptier inside. I loved her so much and didn't realise she was so fed up with our relationship. I sat on the bed and stared at the floor for a while. I would not contact her, as I was too proud and believed in free-will and I could never be with anyone who did not want me there.

Two bad bits of news in one day was too much for me and I couldn't decide which one was worse.

Yet, still, I am a survivor and knew exactly what I was going to do. I had some time off work due and would go back to my mother's village where I had spent so many happy days during my childhood. That was the therapy I needed now.

Yes. I would go back to Doune.

Prologue

Stirling Royal Infirmary

-1901-

What nationality are you?
Scottish
How do you know that?
Because I came up clutching the grass
Onto the very ground on which I am now standing
-DRG-

In the soft glow of an orange flickering light, the sturdy anguished father held his little seven-year-old dying daughter Hailey in his arms. She was small for her age and had always been poorly and frail; as delicate as frozen lace. She had looked so tiny in her big, old-fashioned hospital bed and had resembled a little pebble on a vast landscape when he had walked in; lost, exposed and vulnerable. Time ticked by, heavily and ponderously.

For now, rheumatic fever had its claws dug firmly into her with the determination of a man hanging onto the edge of a cliff by his fingertips. Both precariously balanced between life and death. Her mother on one side and God on the other.

Her blonde curly hair lay damp and clammy and stuck to her forehead. It looked so healthy and yet she herself wasn't. It was alive yet she was dying. It was fresh yet she was flat and dull and fading. Her eyes had a glaze to them. He knew she was dying, but he didn't think that she knew, until she looked over his head, far into outer space and stated matter-of-factly:-

'I see the angels coming Da.'

Daniel Hocks looked down at his precious wean and slit his eyes almost shut to stop the tears from escaping; for he was a proud man and big men did not cry. Scottish men did not cry and Clan men, especially, did not cry. They were made of iron. Still, it even rains on iron. And rots it.

'They're coming, da. They're here!' and with that, Hailey splayed out a beautiful, happy smile, fluttered her young blonde eyelids shut and her dead head dropped into the crook of his arm with the softness of a butterfly wing.

Daniel Hocks had eight other children (being a good Catholic) to worry about and had to stay strong for them and his wife. He could do this because he was a hard man; a man's man; a Scotsman.

He sat there for what seemed like hours, letting the bairn grow cold in his arms because he just could not let her go. This is where she was safe and warm.

His wife sat on a stool in the corner and sobbed into her black Victorian dress, bent right over, clutching a white lace handkerchief in her blue-veined fist.

It was his job to protect his off-spring. He stared down at her wee cherubic face, taking in every detail, which he already knew like the back of his hand and, though, dead, still wanted to keep her warm and safe. To protect her. He had to protect her.

Then he suddenly got up in acceptance, just like that, passed his floppy, arm-dangling, rag-doll daughter to a nurse who had been standing quietly nearby, put an arm on the heaving shoulder of his mourning Irish wife and walked out of the room.

A nice brisk walk in the highlands was what he needed. To walk alone in the wilderness for hours, breathing in the ice-cold air into his lungs to shock him back into life and try to make sense of what had just happened and to ask God why He brought a child into the world just to kill it. What was the point of that? Suffer the little children. But please not my children.

Was God really good, or was He both good and bad, just as in the make-up of Mankind? Was He a supernatural schizophrenic? Did He really have a plan or was He just a crazed experimenter playing with human beings as a cat toys with a mouse? Bitterness is a very easy emotion to rouse, but whatever the answer, he knew one thing for sure and that was that he didn't want to see another living soul for a very, very long time.

***

Daniel Hocks had had an exceptionally hard and poor life and had dragged and fought his way along the un-ploughable fields of survival for as long as he could remember. His family was so poor that his father had had no option but to send him down the mines when he was only five years old.

But how could a five-year-old boy pick up a bucket of coal, let alone work a mine? It must have been another one of my mother's tall stories, or, at least, deviations from the truth. He must surely have been older when he went down the mines. Maybe twelve. Who knows? History grows more silent and obscure as it ages.

It's a testament to God that his lungs survived the ordeal. Yet a hard life can make you more determined, also give you a good grounding for morals and discipline, give you a stronger constitution, a hardier immune system and it can also let you appreciate the good times even more when they come along.

Once, when he was younger, though some years after he got married, his family were starving so much, that he dropped his morals and fear of God temporarily and went out into a field and stole a sheep to feed them.

He did not like having to do it, but he was desperate and at his wit's end. In those days the laws were much harsher. The farmer had seen him and reported him to the police. The judge, with a belly-full of good meat from lunch, sentenced him to twenty lashes with a cat o' nine tails and had the court's punishers squeeze lemon juice into the welts and wounds for good measure. So that he didn't forget his offence in a hurry. Something to mull over.

That's where the cruelty came in and a fellow inmate commented to him:-

'It's aye easier to be honest an' straight when yer no so embroiled in poverty.'

Never a truer word was spoken. It's alright for the rich to pass snooty judgement, for they do not have to commit any financial crime to survive in desperate times. (Though some still do anyway).

But it all made him a stronger man and then with two world wars behind him, he became stronger still. He was now the sturdy nail embedded in the plank of two by four. The sturdy nail who had been a brave member of The Black Watch *to boot.*

He ended up having ten children, probably because there was no TV nor contraception in those days and the cold weather was always tempting you to do some form of physical exercise to keep warm.

Though he lost a lot of his children, he managed to bring the rest through fairly unscathed. But no-one could measure what psychological damage was inflicted on them, as psychology was more in its nascent stages in those days and society believed that anything negative was kept behind closed doors and not discussed nor noted and ignored by the professionals.

But there was humour, too, though. Hard humour.

Like the time he had a motorbike without a baffler that was so loud that it sounded like a pneumatic drill and you could hear it starting up in Deanston; an extravagant indication that he was on his way home and for his wife to put the tea on.

By the sound of it, you would think it had fireworks for fuel, because that the engine could really suck, squeeze, bang and blow.

In later life he would become known as Grandpa Hocks, my maternal grandfather. God bless him.

Chapter One

DOUNE

-1997-

O' ye'll tak the High Road
And I'll tak the Low Road
And I'll be in Scotland
A' fore ye
But me and my true love
Will never meet again
On the bonnie, bonnie
Banks of Loch Lomond
-Anon-

Now, as I drove closer to the fabled village, I felt the fluttering butterflies of anticipation becoming agitated in the pit of my stomach. It was excitement but also fear. But fear of what? Fear of having been different? Fear of meeting people that I had known all those years ago when I was just a child and not an adult? Fear of people asking too many or too-awkward questions? Guilt by association? Guilt by gossip? But it had not been my fault. I just happened to be there at the time and you cannot blame a bystander for a tragedy. In reality, no-one blamed me and I would not have blamed myself, even if I had been an adult, let alone a child, at the time.

Yet, in the back of my mind, being so conscientious, I felt that the wind sometimes whispered suggestively, while not saying anything of note at all. Still, that air pressure got to me sometimes.

Suddenly, a sign stating *'Doune 9 miles'* loomed up at me tauntingly and I tensed involuntarily; as you do on a ghost train, in spite of an obviously-plastic ghoul appearing suddenly in your face. Or when you spot a policeman. You know you have done nothing wrong, but still…

A rupture in the road jolted me as if indicating that I had to be brave. As brave as my grandfather had been. Too late in time and years to turn back now, even if I had really wanted to. It was a bit like a horror film, really: scary yet very exciting and thrilling at the same time. Addictive. That's exactly what this village was to me. Addictive. It had brain-washed me so many years ago. Almost to the point of obsession.

When we lived in London, my mother was always selling and promoting Scotland and all things Scottish to us. So we were always hearing about bagpipes and kilts and sporrans; old wives' tales; all the edible goodies and the traditional songs, such as *'A Scottish Soldier,' 'On the Bonnie Banks of Loch Lomond,'* and…wait for it…*'Donald, Where are yer Trousers?'* I loved this last song and still do. It's a classic.

Apart from all that, our house was full of Scottish souvenirs and humour and my mother would always sit and spin us stories and whopping tall tales of Doune and all the characters in it, with the deftness of a spider spinning his geometrically-accurate web. I think the smaller the place you come from, the more endearing it is and the more you are nostalgic of it. And the bigger the stories. I remember my mother was always laughing at two little magnetised small plastic Scottie dogs she had brought back from Scotland, one white and the other black, so that when you brought them together, they would spin around with one's nose jammed up against the other's bahoohie. Oh she thought that was so funny; and as a child so did I.

Anyway, I drove over a little hump-back bridge, which ran over the river Teith, noticing the tarmacadam bandages threading the road surface from a recent repair and my pupils dilated at the logo of the crossed flint-lock pistols, the village's only claim-to-fame and thought it so amazing that such a little place on the planet could manufacture the gun which fired the very first shot in the American War of Independence. Doune and America were from opposite sides of the planet and opposite sides of the size spectrum, yet still had something in common. I wondered if the bullet had killed anyone.

I was glad to have reached my destination, as I had been plagued by slug-slow traffic at some points on my journey, especially around Birmingham. But now, rounding the bend, I saw the overly-familiar, creaky old '*Woodside Hotel'* sunk strategically into the junction at the entrance to Doune, known affectionately as '*The Gateway to the North'* and swung into its small open-air car park as the gravel crunched. So many memories there.

I got my bags out of the boot and, before I could think too much about it, strode in through the front doors. I loved the Woodside because it was an oldie-worldie aged establishment with an open wood-burning fireplace and cosy, thick green tartan carpeting.

At the reception, a very kindly-looking, white-haired lady with powder-puff pink skin looked up at me with a smile which immediately put me at ease and sent a flow of warmth through me. The sort of warmth I used to feel sitting in front of my grandfather's hearth in his flat above the Co-op.

I don't know what possessed me, but I simply and suddenly blurted out:

'Hello. I'm Anna's boy.'

Then felt like a fool.

I thought I heard some female voice in a back room say 'he's here,' to someone in a strong Scottish slant. But I was tired by the long drive from London and thought that it was just an auditory hallucination. I just wanted to steal away to bed and stare the village in the face in the morning. In the full light of day, although the full light of day could sometimes be quite dour up in Scotland. Nonetheless, I looked forward to it. Like your first terrifying kiss. You want it, but you dread it. You want it so much, but you dread it even more.

***

In the morning, not wanting to make too much noise on the incredibly creaky staircase, in the incredibly creaky old hotel, (as I had always suffered from self-consciousness), I, as-lightly-as-possible, descended it.

This was such a lovely, ancient, archaic establishment, with its welcoming fireplace; old stained wood throughout;

impossibly-comfortable, over-sized armchairs in the main lounge; a loud ticking grandfather clock (as if to remind everyone that life didn't last forever) and hunting pictures in brass frames prancing about here, there and everywhere. There were the aromas of plants and chimney smoke, old furniture and wood. My mother always used to bring people to lunch here or just for a drink.

Or two or three.

More often it was to have a good session, which was a tradition in these parts, even if you couldn't remember it. One too many. One hundred too many. Who cared how many?

But I still had fond memories of this place because I had come often as a child and because the Scottish were so friendly. I was happy to be back, now that I was here; yet it was still tinged with a sadness I had carried for so long, which I always tried to blot out of my mind.

Something hidden in the past.

I banished my negative thoughts and walked into the breakfast-room. The dining-room was at the front of the building. I was really looking forward to this and was actually physically rubbing my hands together in my mind.

I came across a sea of deeply-polished, dark wood tables set with silver and lily-white crockery, as a poet would come across a host of golden daffodils. They immediately reminded me of a period drama, like '*Upstairs Downstairs*.' The setting looked wonderful, what with the big shafts of light coming in at acute angles and splashing the whole room alive.

I targeted a table and sat down, nodding to the other few '*breakfasteers*' quietly munching away with silent decorum.

Most of them, I had been told, on some previous occasion, were sales representatives touting for business in the area and servicing existing clients in these parts. After all, you didn't get the locals staying in the hotel and you didn't get many tourists here. They all passed through to the Trossachs.

At first I couldn't see any staff, as, with all small places, they seemed to vanish. However, then this really pretty blonde woman in her late twenties came out from behind a hidden wood-panelled wall in a black and white uniform.

Not only was she pretty, but she was so cute she should have been born a teddy-bear. She spotted me with a genuinely radiant smile that would have warmed the coldest parts of Scotland and approached me.

'Good morning,' I said chirpily. 'How are you today?'

'I am very well, thank you sir. Mom said that you arrived last night.' She had the softest, musical Scottish accent I had heard in a long time and it made my heart melt like hot butter. It was the complete antithesis of the rough Glaswegian brogue. A marvellous lilt. So refined. The sort of voice you would want to hear as you are dying.

'Oh, that's your mother, really? Well, I can see you take after her, as you are both so pretty and amicable.'

I would have felt like such an idiot, giving her such a corny, cheesy, line, had it not been so absolutely true and had I not really meant it; and I was older now and didn't really care. I had always over-worried about what people thought of me.

She smiled at me modestly with a little pink blush and asked me what I would like.

'Two eggs, two pieces of sliced sausage, a rasher of bacon, a pot of tea and plenty of toast and butter, please.'

'My goodness, you've done your homework!' she replied and was gone. I regretted her departure like the loss of a beautiful dream.

Now, getting on to more serious matters, I was very excited because I loved sliced sausage, as it had such a unique tang and taste and you could only have good sliced sausage in Scotland.

I had found it in London, but it had just tasted like ordinary sausage meat. I loved a fried breakfast in itself, but in Scotland it all tasted so much better, especially with the sliced sausage. That was the icing on the cake, or the sliced sausage on the plate! They said it was because of the water.

When the banquet came, my eyeballs bulged with gluttonous glee and I savoured every mouthful by religiously chewing and not just swallowing it. I would have a bit of toast, shove in a bit of fried egg and sliced sausage and mix it all around like cement in a mixer, to get 'the hit' which fusion creates. Then I would have a sip of tea, have another bit of toast, shove in a piece of fried egg with bacon and start the process all over again, all whilst looking around innocently and with what dignity I could muster; while, at the same time, looking perfectly innocent.

I was reminded of my mother telling people that: 'Luke eats once a day…all day!' My mother loved laughing at her own jokes, much to my chagrin.

Every time I returned to Scotland, I vowed to take back a ton of sliced sausage, yet every time I left I didn't and I have never known why.

Now, eager and trepidatious to walk around my mother's village, I soon got up, thinking of what I would have for the following day's breakfast and began to walk out. I made a mental note that I would start the following day's breakfast with porridge, to celebrate all things Scottish and really go for it.

What would be my first port of call? What would attract me first?

'Thank you, sir,' a wee voice wafted up to my ears from behind me.

I turned. 'Call me Luke,' I asked of her. 'Please.'

'Okay, then,' she smiled and looked so humble, this Goddess who could so easily have been a successful model, that my heart softened. Had I been in the business, I would have given her a contract immediately. But I wasn't and I couldn't and that was life.

As I walked by the bar on my way out to explore the village, I overheard two men talking in cheerful, animated tones. One was telling the other the tail-end of a Scottish joke that I had heard many times before, throughout my childhood.

It was about a bragging American in a taxi, who was telling the driver how everything was built at superfast-speed in America where things went up before you knew it. After a while the taxi driver was really getting fed-up with his boasting and so, when the American pointed out a very tall skyscraper as they drove through Glasgow, the American asked: 'What's that?' and the cabbie had replied glibly: 'I don't know…it wasn't there yesterday!'

Well, this was Scottish humour at its best and I smiled to myself as I walked out, leaving the two Scotsmen guffawing away.

O what a glorious day!

I was reminded of '*The Sound of Music*,' as corny as it was. The sun was shining in the cold breeze as I stepped outside, half-expecting to bump into someone I knew immediately. I began to think of my childhood in the '60s here and was reminded of a little ditty I had foolishly written a few years ago:-

When the sun is shining
Our arms are intertwining
And we're rolling about the grass
with my fingers up your …
-DRG-

I didn't know why I made up these poems. Just something to entertain my immature mind. Though my family lived in London, we had come to Doune every year for the summer holidays and my childhood had loved it. Compared to London, it was so peaceful and quiet and safe. Like a hidden garden forgotten in time; like an island incorruptible and cut-off from bad influences.

My mother was always extolling its virtues and it had rubbed off on me. There were few cars going up and down the high street, so you were less likely to get run over and nobody locked their doors. Everyone else's children were in everyone else's houses, even having their tea there and at times staying the night. It was quite common for a mother to meet her child in the street the next day and ask them where they had been for their tea that night.

'Oh, is that right? Ach, well, I'll hae tae thank aunty Mae for that, will I no?'

I had so many memories of Doune and I didn't want to betray them.

I began to walk up George Street to The Mercat Cross. In the distance I saw a figure of a woman who looked very familiar. I smiled when I recognised who it was. I kept walking towards her and she to me. I was looking forward to surprising her.

There were some people I didn't particularly wish to run into, but she was certainly not one of them. She was my mother's oldest friend. They had gone to the original old Doune school together, had remained steadfast and she had always been faithful to my mother, even with all her problems. A good, down-to-earth, staunch friend. Not like the false people in London who ran away at the slightest hint of rain.

'Hello, Aunty Joan,' I said sincerely, as I smiled lightly at her.

She had been making her way by me and turned with a vague glaze in her eyes.

'It's me, Luke,' I explained.

'Och, my, Lukie! Ye aye gave me a turn! Ah cannae believe it's ye! Ah havnae seen ye fer years! Ye've grown so aye big. I didnae recognise ye. Where's all yer podge gone?'

'Melted. Well, I recognised you straight away, with yon red hair, that unique face and trim figure of yours!' I proffered, loving to tease and flatter her, as I put an arm around her, hugged her to me and gave her a wee kiss on the cheek.

I had never said her unique face was pretty.

'Och, away wi' ye, ye gowk. Er…I wiz sae sorry tae hear about her mammy, son,' she said, with a slight tear and cloud in her eye.

'That's quite alright, Aunty Joan, I know you are. I thank you for the friendship you gave me mother. I know she valued it greatly and she was always talking about you. Out of all the people I wanted to meet now, after all these years, it's you. I only arrived last night and you're the first person I've met. Is that no fate?' I added, trying to blend into the Scottish tongue. I would have felt ridiculous, had I not been part Scottish and so had the right to sound ludicrous.

Then it was the usual questions of: 'How long are ye here fer? How's yer brother and yer sister? Where are ye livin' noo? How's yer work? How's yer life?'

Fine…fine…fine…fine.

I invited Aunty Joan to lunch at the Woodside hotel, which was kind of me, yet also slightly selfish, as I loved hearing stories of when her and my mother, Anna, were young together.

As I watched her walking away, listing from the weight of her laundry bag, I thought of what a kind and humble person she was. When a child in the 60's, I was forever running into the Co-op and saying 'Aunty Joan!' this and 'Aunty Joan!' that and she never said an angry word or got fed up with me, no matter how busy she was or how naughty I was being.

She was also proud, like a lot of the Scots. As proud as a lion and, if you ever showed her sympathy or offered her money or help, she would look at you as if you had just told her you had drowned her baby.

I continued up to The Cross and up to its highest step, feeling like the Statue of Liberty, though I am sure I didn't look quite as gracious.

The Cross of Doune was the focal point of the village and sat like an 'x marks the spot,' just before a split in the road which headed either back down to the Woodside Hotel or on to the Calendar bus stop and beyond.

My mother had told me The Cross was a meeting place for all the soldiers in medieval times, and no doubt in later wars, who were gathering to fight the English. But, in reality, it was simply a Mercat-topped marker which indicated where an open market could legally take place.

It was old, though, dating before the 1700s and was described in an Act of Parliament of 1696 of having recently been erected. Not very interesting compared to the tale of the soldiers. But my mother always liked to embellish things and, as a child, I had fallen for all of her tall tales. Even when I found out they weren't true, I didn't mind, as the stories had been so rich and entertaining. My goodness! How much she loved this village.

It was early morning and there were not many people about. I looked to the right where Don MacFairlane's sweetie shop used to be and my mind reeled back to my 60s childhood:-

Little me walked into Don MacFairlane's sweetie shop sometime in the mid 60s and I was immediately surrounded by a cornucopia of candied delights everywhere. This sweetie shop really was a Pandora's box and an ultimate treasure trove to a child.

To the left, to the right, up in the air, down near the floor and behind Don, jars and breathless jars of all types of sweets, in all sorts of shapes, sizes and gaudy colours stood proud: Sherbet Fountains, Liquorice Pipes, Gobstoppers, Soor Plooms, Love Hearts, Edinburgh Rock, Macaroon bars, Snowballs, Tablet Fudge, Flying Saucers, Berwick Cockles, Hawick Balls, Liquorice Comfits and just so many others, too many to mention or remember.

I didn't like the gobstoppers much, because I couldn't chew them and my greedy stomach always demanded a quick delivery.

I remember I liked this shop because it was small, well, sort of, with two little half-moon windows each side of a little brown door with a wobbly black knob handle.

'Hello, Mr. Don,' I had called, as I had walked in. I had really wanted to call him Mr. MacFairlane, as I had been brought up to respect my elders, but Don and the other children would have just laughed, so I had found a compromise, at which they had all laughed all the more.

'Hello, Lukie, and how are you today?'

Don MacFairlane had beamed down at me from behind his huge tsunami counter. Surrounded by his wares, you could only see his little bald 'heid' sticking out of his gap-in-the-goods space, like a cuckoo in a cuckoo clock. I had never seen anyone who was always smiling so much. Could that man smile! In fact, I had never seen him without a smile. He smiled like a Cheshire cat, he smiled like a man delirious, he smiled like a mental patient on day-release from Belsdyke, he smiled like his grin had set in concrete and he smiled like he didn't realise what a horrible world it really could be. Crivvens! That man loved to smile.

I really loved Don MacFairlane because he was always so kind and spoke to me with the same reserve he held for adults and nothing was too much trouble for him, standing there with his nutty-brown face, hairless heid and hands shoved happily into his tobacco-brown store-coat pockets.

Maybe he had been kind to me because he knew I came from a wealthy family and always had money to spend in my pocket. But no. I had seen him treat everyone that way because he always tried to find the good in people.

Sometimes I had noticed that, when Don MacFairlane had to go to the back of the shop to get something, some children would grab a handful of sweets or chocolates and fill their spaces with air.

I felt very bad for Don about this. But, at the same time, I didn't say anything because I was afraid of the other children and I would have been a tattle-tale. So I had just pretended in my own mind that it had not happened. Still, I could have said something.

Anyway, I had bought some snowballs and a bar of Highland toffee. Left extra money on the counter for the other boys' misdemeanours and had trotted happily out of the shop.

'See ye again, Lukie! Say hullo to yer mam fer me! See ye on the morra!'

Even to a child, as I had been, it seemed a sad goodbye and I felt sorry for Don MacFairlane, all on his own in that wee dog-kennel of a shop of his.

Did he no hae a wee wifey to make his tea fer him?

***

Now back on The Cross in my adult body, looking at what used to be Don MacFairlane's old sweetie emporium, which was now a sad, spartan charity shop, I remembered that Don had had a limp. I do not know how he got it and had thought it was possibly an old war wound, as it was only about 20 years after the war.

However, it was more likely he had tripped on one of his delivery crates or had fallen down the cellar stairs. I wondered whatever had become of Don MacFairlane and vowed to ask someone. If he was in Deanston cemetery, I would go and lay something on his grave, because he gave so much to me and the community, just through his good attitude.

***

I decided to go and see my cousin now, but before that I wanted to have a little look around the village and get a feel of it. Though it was a small, nondescript place, it had a big heart and big memories and virtually every house and shop brought them rushing back; although I could see the changes still.

People were more mobile now than they had been back in the sixties and, in a way, this was a shame, as families didn't gel together so much and strangers were moving in.

Yes, there were people I still knew, but not as many as before. In the sixties, the village had been like one big family where everyone had looked out for each other.

In the old days, you could literally lie down in the middle of the road quite safely, as we children often did as a dare, and move when you heard a car coming. But now there was more traffic and enough noise to blot out an any approaching individual vehicle bearing down on you.

Before I turned the corner near Moray Park to go up Moray Street to Northlea and see this cousin of mine, I looked across the road to where there had been another sweet shop with an old grey-haired tall, lean, man serving in it who reminded me of a Dickensian character; especially with his severe half-moon gold-rimmed glasses. He had an angle-grinder angular face and an arête of a nose and some of the other boys had goaded and dared me to go in and ask for a penny liquorice. Only, as they were taking the Micky out of my middle-class accent, had told me how to pronounce it so that the deaf old man could understand. So, amazing how gullible one can be when young, I actually went in and said, brazenly:-

'Hello. Could I please have a penny lick yer arse?'

Being so innocent in those days, it took me a few days to realise why I had been kicked out of the shop.

'Oot! Get oot o' here at once! Ye filthy little Sassenach!'

I had not understood what he was going on about, as I had been wearing clean clothes; and what was a *sandwich snack* anyway? Thank God that hadn't happened in Don MacFairlane's shop, for I would verily have been mortified if I had ever upset and offended him.

Then I looked to the corner where *McAlpine's* bakery used to be and I miss it so much now. To me, it was the best bakery I have ever been to. In any country. Ever.

Every summer we came up, I always persuaded my mother to let me go there, as if it were a toy shop to any other normal child. This was not one of your terrible chains selling pre-baked goods that were delivered sometime in the morning. It was a made-from-scratch bakery, family-run, where the baker - I suppose it must have been Mr. MacAlpine himself, would get up at 4:30 every morning and start baking like a man possessed.

The freshest, tastiest, most aromatic bread, both crusty and soft, loaves and rolls; the most delicious and best-quality Scotch pies; Stovies, Potato scones, Oatcake, Shortbread,

Bridies, Pancakes, Scones, Fruit cakes, Black buns, Dundee cakes, Clootie dumpling, Selkirk Bannock, Border tarts, Ecclefechan tarts, Macaroon tarts; the creamiest fresh-cream cakes and a wealth of other goodies too many to mention. In fact, come to mention it, he baked an awful lot of bake-ables for such a small village. But I remember there wasn't much ever left by late afternoon. They must have come from all around. And while the other local children had their noses stuck to sweet shop windaes, I had mine stuck to the bakery window.

This was my vision of heaven. Like a girl torn between two boys, I was torn between the two shops.

In fact, when my other playmates couldn't find me, one place they would look in, was MacAlpine's. Oh, how I wish I could go back in time. Just to walk in there again and ask for six Scotch pies and a crusty loaf, if you please.

When MacAlpine's closed, it was like a loved one had died and there was no other bakery in the village. It was as if the heart and soul of Doune had been torn out of it. But all good things come to an end, that's life. Yet it was wonderful while it lasted. God bless that bakery. God bless Mr. McAlpine.

Katie was pleased to see me and I have always had a soft spot for her. She is very artistic and happy in her life, with two lovely children, a boy and a girl and a very amicable, gregarious, affable and sociable husband she met at university. She is very pretty with short black hair and a nice character and I have always felt a bond with her, even though we only see each other once in a blue moon due to where we both live.

I always thought she had a mind too big for a small village, but maybe it gives her the peace she needs to do her thing. She had no idea I was coming and asked why on earth I was not staying with her. But her house is a bit full, what with her family. They both work and I do not like to intrude on people's daily routines, being such a private person. Anyway, she understood and she knew we would be seeing lots of each other during my stay. Plenty dinners, etc.

After catching up on old times and the latest news over a cup of tea and cake, I told her I would see her later as she had to go out anyway. When we were younger we went around a lot together, but now we had tighter agendas. She has a lovely, gangly Dalmatian, which I really enjoyed playing with. Daft loping, long-legged, spotty dog, who would roll over when I got down on the carpet to play with him, with his tongue hanging out like a collapsed bridge.

I walked around Moray Park for a while, smiling to myself as I remembered the putting green, where you could *hae a gaime fer tuppence* and how, as children, we used to run about wildly, teasing the Irish tinkers (one of whom chased me right over the crossroads up towards Castle Hill) or playing *Kiss, Kick or Torture.*

I always, of course, chose the kisses. Not necessarily because I liked them, but because I was a coward and didn't like pain. Those girls could kick like mules, you know. Being so young, they were wet and slobbery kisses, as if a slug had landed on your cheek. Luckily, the girls chose kisses too, which I enjoyed donating.

One girl I remember being introduced to, was only around nine years old and yet was already an aunt. Just goes to show that there really isn't much to do of an evening in a small village, apart from breeding like rabbits or getting drunk, or, on any special occasion, combining the two. Wayhay! Is that no right, son?

Sometimes crazy Opie, the village idiot, was there telling us stories of how he had slept with a thousand women (whatever 'slept with' meant to my child's mind), or how he was a spy *doon sooth* and how he often flew planes and helicopters.

He had a hobbledehoy gait and was very awkward in his movements, as if there was an intermittent fault with the wiring in his brain: the message was simply not getting through.

He was known as the *Prophet of Doune* because he kept making predictions like: it's gannae rain when it was already raining and predicting that he would soon be eating a Scotch pie; when he was already eating one and he kept going around telling all the villagers: 'We're all aye gain' tae be here on thae morrow.' Chances are.

He wore ill-matched and ill-fitting clothes which seemed to compliment his mental condition, had short wiry hair in the most old-fashioned, conservative mode and had the most alarming and piercing grey-blue eyes which seemed to burn through you like a laser.

He made you feel very exposed but excited, because his strangeness was very thrilling and something to mock. He told taller tales than my mother, but he had an excuse. Mind you, I suppose both of their brains were frazzled in their own separate ways.

Whenever anyone spoke to him he would always say 'whit?' as if he didn't understand the simplest sentences and it became his and our catchphrase. We children were always running around shouting 'whit?' every time we met someone with all the adults scratching their heads, wondering what we were on about, as we had giggling fits. Silly I know.

I was told he was still around now, was in his fifties and had lived with his mother since the day he was born. But I had never, ever, seen his mother or his father in all the times I had been to Doune. It was as if they had stayed indoors out of shame. You blame yourself when you give birth to a simpleton. Well, he wasn't a bad man or a sad man; he was just a mad man.

'Och, he's harmless enough, right enough.'

But that didn't turn out to be quite so true.

After London, it was so nice to walk around in such peaceful and quiet surroundings, as you listened to the breeze rustling in the trees and where you only saw the odd car and odd person, Opie Cameron notwithstanding, going by.

***

When I got to the crossroads by the Protestant church, which many Catholic mothers rushed their children by, prams, toys and all, as if they were going to be cursed or diseased for being exposed to it, I looked at what used to be the '*Balhadie'* pub on the corner.

This had been a very mysterious place to me as a child, because it wasn't like '*The Red Lion*' or any of the other drinking establishments. This one had a very high front with high-set frosted opaque windows which no-one could see into. I had kept trying to jump up to the height of the windows to get a look-in, but had never managed to. I had imagined it was some experimental laboratory or where Frankenstein was made.

I knew that this place was where '*men came to do what men had to do,*' (mainly get away from their wives) and always wondered what was going on in there. Were they planning a revolution? Were they planning a bank robbery? Were they storing contraband? Were they showing naughty films? Were they pirates?

All these ideas were going on in my head from time to time; but, being a child, I soon forgot about it and concentrated on playing. How daft! But if an adult tells you it's where '*men came to do what men had to do,*' then, obviously a child's mind is going to run away with him. Almost as much as my mother's.

I looked down the road to the little Catholic Church, which nestled behind a low moss-covered half-wall, surrounded by trees and plants and gravestones. I used to run my fingers along the moss because I liked the feeling of it, soft and spongy. It was like feeling Nature's warm bosom. I also loved these walls. They were all so natural-looking, as if they had come straight out of the ground.

I thought it was quite amazing how the little church had stood staunchly there, lost in time, while so many people had come and gone, lived and died.

My mother was baptised there, married there shortly after the war and had finally had her funeral there; and God knows what else she had done there.

I wondered how long the church would stand there now, as I admired how the walls had sealed and discoloured, seemingly set and locked in slow decomposition, which actually made it appear all the stronger and all the more charming.

I wasn't that interested in having a look around inside the church, as I am not that religious; though I do respect religion and certainly believe in God, whatever God is.

But I have to admit that going to Mass bored me to tears and it was like watching the same boring film over and over again, sometimes in Latin, in slow-motion. In my subconscious, I was also probably a bit angry at the priests, who thought they were God's gift to the planet and who scared the living daylights out of us children by telling us we were all bound for Hell, over the river Styx, all in a burning boat. But I did love the wee kirk, it's history and what it stood for.

I carried on down the high street, nodding to the few old men and wee wifies who passed me by. In London you never bade hello to anyone. That would have been quite absurd and people would have wondered what was wrong with you. But here and in other little villages it was a given.

'*Helloo......helloo the noo...cheerio...cheerio the noo.*'

I saw a mother approaching, dragging her wee boy along behind her and I was attracted by their raised voices.

'I telt ye, mammy, this dug came up behind me in Moray park when I wis lying oon the groond an started makin' strange movements on me back end. I tried to shove 'im aff but he jist growled in ma ear an slobbered doon me neck. I wiz afeart, mammy, an' all the other boys were laughin' at me! The owner came runnin' up an' shooed the dug aff. But I had all this white staff on me breeks and all the other children said ah wiz gonna hae puppies!'

The woman looked at me, embarrassed and hurried the child along the road, with a firm hand around the back of his neck and with a look of incredulity and apology on her face.

'Och, dinnae be sae daft, ye big lummox. Boys cannae hae puppies.'

'Andrew MacDonald's aye git wan,' the little boy commented, defiantly.

'See you, Jimmy? I'll burn yer ear fer yer cheek! Now let's git hame. Jist wait until yer fither hears yer tall story!'

I smiled after them as memories of my antics in the park came rushing up. I was back in my childhood. The best place to be. I crossed the road just before the *'Bank of Scotland'* to look in a brick-a-brack shop and marvelled at the things it displayed in its windows, which you could not even find in London. Its stock appeared to be around twenty years out of date. Though I knew it was not old, just alternative smaller suppliers, probably all from China.

I then stood there, a silent witness, opposite the Highland Hotel, one of the most familiar and greatest landmarks in Doune and my mind reeled back as I remembered one of the funniest and most amusing days of my life.

Chapter Two

DOUNE

-1964-

Uncle Carbuncle was my uncle
And he wore a ridiculous wig
Yet, still, he proudly went everywhere
And he didn't give a flying fig
-DRG-

Uncle Carbuncle was not his real name, of course, but my Uncle Benny, who was married to my Aunty Macasa (her real name, due to her being from European descent) was so-called because he always suffered from carbuncles. Somebody said it once as a joke and it stuck like a barnacle. Uncle Carbuncle and Aunty Macasa! You really couldn't make it up, could you? My mother didn't want to get too close to him, as she said she might catch something.

Anyway, on one of our family visits to Doune, bar my hard-working father, my mother informed us (my sister, brother and I), that we were going up to Uncle Carbuncle's house, meeting him, Aunty Macasa and my little female cousin, Rae, there and all walking down together to the Highlands Hotel for High Tea.

Well, as a young rotund child, I always got very excited whenever an outing was mentioned; especially when it involved food. Especially Scottish food. So we had all trundled down Doune Main Street from Grandpa Hock's *hoose* towards the Protestant church and turned left, running alongside Moray Park towards Uncle Carbuncle's modest, yet neat and tidy home.

Uncle Carbuncle was a humble carpenter, just like Jesus, who lived in Queen Street, with a really nice disposition and a great sense of humour. He was always trying to fashion things out in his wee back shed and never really got anywhere. But at least he tried and that was good enough for me. We enjoyed playing with all his off-cut bits of wood, where we pretended they were swords or guns.

My mother, always laughing, once told us, and anyone else who would listen, about how Uncle Carbuncle had once built a wooden caravan for a client in his garage and that, when it was finished, virtually the pride and joy of the whole of Doune, he had discovered that he could not get the caravan out as it was too wide to fit through the double doors.

So Uncle Carbuncle had had to demolish the front of the garage. Not so much profit in it for him then!

Uncle Carbuncle also looked very funny because he wore this terrible, overly-obvious ginger toupee, which looked like a square of dried grass plonked on the top of his heid! It was as orange as Irn Bru on a sunny day, with the light shining through the bottle.

We children were always laughing about it. But my mother, laughing herself, remonstrated with us and had said:-

'Och, ye know, ye should feel sorry fer him. All his hair fell oot from shock when Oor Hailey died.'

'*ALL* his hair?' I had asked, incredulously.

'Aye.'

'All the hair on his chest?'

'Aye.'

'All the hair on his head and face?' asked my sister, joining in the curiosity.

'Aye.'

'All the hair under his armpits?' I had demanded.

'Aye.'

'All the hair on his legs?' my brother joined in, finally taking an interest.

'Aye.'

'All the hair on his bum-bum?' I threw in, knowing this would soon come to an end.

'Och, aye...an dinnae be sae rood, ye wee scamp!' though laughing still, 'And don't go mentioning his handicap.'

'Is he handicapped?' I had asked in all innocence.

'No he's nae,' my mother had replied, as she rolled her eyes up to the sky and hurried us along King Street. She could be confusing at times.

When we got to his house, (I knew it from his green 1959 Ford Thames 300E panel van parked outside, which I used to ride around in sometimes with my cousin Rae, as Uncle Carbuncle did his round of carpentry clients), we went to the front door and rang the bell.

Most family members and close friends always went to the back door, which was actually on the side of the house, the one without the red carpet, but my Aunty Macasa was a bit more correct than that and wanted her guests to come through the main entrance when they were calling on her in an official or more formal capacity.

Talking about Aunty Macasa, it was actually Aunty Macasa who answered the door, with an '*Oooh hellooooo!*' with her shiny rotund face and pug nose. With a nose like that, you could always see what was in it, like a pig and I was always trying to catch her out. But she was a clean woman, with no bats hanging in her nasal caves that day. Boring.

She had beady eyes, to match her vertical nostrils and had a comical face to match my Uncle Carbuncle's comical carpet sample. If he had sold carpets, maybe he could have gone around with an actual carpet sample on his head to show prospective customers how it looked; a great form of commercialism. Well, it would have been a very novel idea, anyway; mobile advertising.

Uncle Carbuncle finally joined us in the sitting-room, where I had taken refuge right beside my mother, for fear of Aunty Macasa asking me for a big, wet juicy kiss. I stared at him, trying to spot an errant hair. But I could not see even one. His arms were as bare as porcelain. There was no needle in his haystack. My eyes kept darting from Uncle Carbuncle's hirsute-forsaken body to my Aunty Macasa's pug nose. Nothing to report. If only I could have seen something fluttering in her nose.

More Boring still.

After a bit of small talk, which went right over my head, through youthful ignorance and disinterest, Uncle

Carbuncle asked: 'Right! Are we all ready then?' I could not stop staring at his rectangular toupee because, even as a child, you could tell it was false from even a mile away. Even from outer space. Especially that colour. You could even have tee'd off the top of that thatch on his head.

We all started walking back towards Moray Park, my mother and Aunty Macasa, armed with their big black handbags, as if off to war, with my cousin Rae and I giggling away like gaggling geese, just for the fun of it and because we were excited to be going out on an outing. We were only a year apart and had always got on very well together. In fact, one day she had asked her mother whether cousins could marry each other. I almost took flight. She always had had dreams of marriage and silly Sindy dolls. She always wanted me to play with her with her Sindy dolls and I was mortified. The only saving grace was that Ken looked like an Action Man figure, so I always dressed him and took on his character, while *Sindy Rae* swooned all over me in her romantic fantasies. The things you do to get on with people. *Wheeshit!*

Suddenly, Uncle Carbuncle stopped in his tracks, scraping the road with his shoes to a halt and announced that he had to go back to the *hoose* as he had forgotten something. Aunty Macasa kept impatiently asking him what he had forgotten and he wouldn't say. But still she insisted until he went bright red, which clashed alarmingly with his orange wig and, finally exasperated, said:-

'Ma teef, woman! Ma teef! I've forgotten ma teef!'

Well, we children, always looking for an excuse to titter, completely collapsed with laughter, as he ran back to get his dentures, accompanied by his big, gaping hovel of a mouth;

the big yawn. But I also felt sorry for him, as you can't really enjoy your High Tea if you can't bite into your sandwiches without your pegs, can you?

After quite a few faltering attempts at a rhyming song, my cousin Rae and I managed to come up with a passable chant about my poor Uncle Carbuncle's misfortune and we both stomped down the road, while waving our arms about extravagantly and reciting our wee poem, to the accompaniment of wide jaw movements, like a Grouper fish.

Ma teef! Ma teef!
Ah cannae find ma teef!
Ah cannae…
Ah cannae…
Ah jist cannae find ma teef!

Ma tea! Ma tea!
Ah cannae hae ma tea
Ah cannae…
Ah cannae…
Ah jist cannae hae ma tea
Withoot ma teef!
Ma teef! Ma teef!
-DRG-

My mother was trying not to laugh for Aunty Macasa's sake, as she clutched tightly onto her handbag as a distraction to her thoughts for seriousness's sake, while my Aunty Macasa looked quite mortified and rolled her eyes up to the sky in total frustration. She was always very conscious of appearances and she held a face that said she was going to kill my uncle when they got back in behind closed doors. Still, after a few seconds, she stoically walked on.

I have always loved '*Oor Wullie*' and '*The Broons*.' It's all my mother's fault that her patriotism rubbed off on me; but, every year without fail, no matter how old I became, I always bought whichever annual was out that year; and it always brought me back to my childhood memories of Doune, when I used to read them up in my grandfather's house above the Co-op, surrounded by sweets and chocolates and Irn Bru.

I mention this because, as we all entered The Highlands Hotel to have our grand High Tea, with a few other cousins and another uncle in tow, it was like a '*Broons*' event, what with all the family members of all shapes and sizes. We children were always excited by any occasion that entertained us and giggled as if we were all wearing furry underpants.

My mother's cousin, Aileen Loherty, owned the hotel and she greeted us at the doorway to the dining-room with a great fuss and bother and it made me feel like Lord Snooty. When I saw the table she had set out for us, I was delighted. All silver and crockery, as if we were visiting dignitaries. As if we were Royalty.

The room came alive with chatter and scraping chairs, as we jostled about for seating positions and I made sure I sat next to my cousin Rae; so that we could giggle all the more. But I needn't have worried because I didn't realise what our giggling would turn into. I could never have imagined it. Some of the locals were looking through the windows at us and passing comments to their companions silently, as if we were famous people. A big Doune event. Maybe they would put it in the paper.

Loads of pots of tea and milk and sugar came, followed by a big, deliciously-greasy fry-up, followed by freshly-cut sandwiches and cake. 'A rare treat' as me mam would say. (Lapsing again.)

Anyway, I don't remember exactly when it was, but our other cousin Nigel, a right unruly cheeky wee scamp if ever there was one, suddenly shoved the pepper cellar under Uncle Carbuncle's nose and shook it upwards. Uncle Carbuncle, taken by shocking surprise, gasped through his nose and, turning sharply away from the table, let out a Vesuvius-of-a-sneeze, throwing his head back at the '*Ah*' and violently forwards at the '*Choo*!' At this point - oh it all happened so fast - his orange carpet sample toupee, took off and flew off, landing just in front of the kitchen door, which was quite a distance for a first flight.

If you consider the difference in size between Uncle Carbuncle's flying carpet and the size of the Wright Brothers' planes, especially the first controlled powered flight in 1903, which flew just 120 feet; then Uncle Carbuncle's magical flying carpet actually flew further, in real terms. So there. Another world record for Doune.

As all we children howled with laughter like demented hyenas, with tears in our eyes, followed by the adults, after they got over their initial shock and disbelief, I don't know where it came from, but my mother's cousin's dog, a wee Scottie named Harry, came out of nowhere and started wrestling with the wig in its mouth!

All eyes, least of all Uncle Carbuncle's, were on the terrier as it ran around the room, left, right, up, down, diagonally, growling at the inert item playing dead in its mouth. My Aunty Macasa was absolutely mortified as she gave my Uncle Carbuncle the dirtiest look I have ever seen. Her look said that he had shamed her irrevocably and wobbled and quivered her dignity to the core. Her look stated that she would never talk to him anymore, as she was capable, at times, of being quite snooty and appearances were everything to her reputation and standing in the small community. Ironically, the smaller the community, the more people you knew intimately. Now, she wouldn't know where to look. She was to never set foot in the Highlands Hotel ever again until the day she died; even when one of her dearest friends had her wake held there.

We all seemed to stand up at once, to try and grab it off the dog, while intermittently gawping at Uncle Carbuncle's pinball head, which had gone bright red, as red as the tomatoes in the ham sandwiches, or as red as a pool ball. There weren't any traffic lights then in Doune in the 60s, apart from the one on Uncle Carbuncle's shoulders and it looked hilarious.

'Ma heir! Ma heir!' my Uncle Carbuncle groaned loudly, desperately, despairingly, as he watched his headpiece gallivanting all over the place. I think he focused on his wig because he just didn't know where else to look through his agonising embarrassment. He felt like a small child again; a fool, an imbecile, like Opie Cameron. So where he did look was the main doorway. He didn't care about his wig anymore. He just wanted to get out of there and not look any more ludicrous than he already did. So, in all the confusion, he just disappeared out the doorway and ran all the way home in his shame.

As we (children at the fore) went for the dog, a waitress came through with more hot water for the tea on a big tray. All of us darting about was like a crazy, frenetic dance movement. She screeched with fright and shock at all the commotion, the alien head, the alien thing and at the dog, who had whizzed between her legs, still shaking its head from side to side, trying to chew a bit off this unexpected treat. (Short back-and-sides, please).

Needless to say, she dropped the tray with a great clatter and deluge, adding to the scene of bedlam and mayhem which had greeted her eyes. My mother's cousin came rushing out of the kitchen and didn't know where to look. She was so upset after all the effort she had gone to to make us a memorable tea. She had made the sandwiches into crust-less triangles and had even sprinkled pepper in the ham ones. Her little touch of refinement.

Well, this High Tea was certainly memorable for becoming one of the low points in her life and later became known as the High Jinks Tea Party; once the ever-changing story went around the village. I have never forgotten it and neither has she, because I laughed so hard, with tears running down my face in rivers, that I vomited all over the table-cloth. This I must confess. It was just one unfortunate thing after another. We really caused a riot there.

It would have been the end of our High Tea Extravaganza anyway, but this end was sealed by the other event of the dog running out the front doors of the Highlands Hotel, nearly knocking other guests over like nine-pins and disappearing down towards the Callander bus stop, with all us children and some adults chasing it in vain, because you can't laugh and run at the same time. It is just not possible.

Opie Cameron, ambling along and rambling on to himself on the other side of the road, preoccupied by his washing-machine thoughts, shouted across:-

'WHA'S THON HEDGEHOG DAEIN' IN THAT DUG'S GOBBY?!'

Well, that was the end of it, it just had to stop. The laughter was just too much. So we stopped chasing the dog and sat on the pavement to recover, our faces rosy-red and tear-stained, streaked with dirt and grime.

On seeing me collapsed on the ground, a kindly villager had stopped, bent over me and asked 'Are ye alright, pal?' rhetorically, more out of bemusement and amusement than concern, before moving on. Then an old lady with her shopping bag came by and asked me: 'Are ye okay, wee man?' with more genuine caring.

Later we heard that a stranger to the village had found the wig and had known who to return it to, because inside the hirsute ensemble it had read: *'This item belongs to Benjamin Hocks. If found please return to…'* Who the hell would put that in a toupee? Well, Aunty Macasa, of course. An old habit from her school-days. How ridiculous! Still, toupees were quite expensive, you know.

***

Aunty Mary had a canary
Up the leg of her draws
She pulled a string
To hear it sing
And down came Santa Claus!
-Anon-

My mind came back to the present day with a jolt. I had a big grin on my face and a little chuckle in my throat. Some villagers passing by might well have thought that Opie Cameron was not the only strange *'un'* around. Then I remembered my cousin Nigel, the *'Pepper Pot King'* and the smile slid off my face. Poor thing. The innocence of his childhood had transmogrified into a body ravaged completely by drink and drugs and by nineteen, he was dead.

As dead as Doune in mid-afternoon.

Poor Nigel.

Anyway, that's the way it goes, the only guarantee in life is death; the only constant is change. I decided to go back to the hotel now, as I felt it was enough for one day. I was still tired from my long drive up and wanted to have a nice, long, hot bath and read and relax. I am a solitary soul, I suppose, but I love reading and writing and thinking about literature and people are always inviting me here, there and everywhere to give a speech or sign a book and I often decline. For I enjoy my own company and am a happy hermitical soul and when I feel a void in my life, I just go and see family or friends. But too many people make me unhappy.

I walked down the hill towards the Woodside and bade hello to the few people who passed by. I am sure my mother had known the older ones, but I was out-of-time for them.

'I'm Anna's boy...I'm Anna's boy. Did ye ken Anna?' echoed in my mind.

I admired the Austrian appearance of Muir Hall. To this day I have never been in there. It didn't interest me as a child, looked a bit foreboding and, not being an extrovert, it hasn't interested me as an adult. Some places just look too foreboding. But my sister, all skyscraper beehive, layer-cake make-up, garishly-painted spike-like elongated false nails, raccoon mascara and spider-similar false eye-lashes, used to go to dances there in the sixties and she once said that she saw a girl in a topless dress with her bosoms wobbling all over the place, as if pointing out all the exits! Talk about taking your goods to market! My ears had perked up then. If only I could have sneaked in for a glimpse.

My sister had also said that men walking back to their tables after a dance, had big bulges in their groins. I had thought that maybe they were just keeping a sandwich or Scotch pie down there in case they got hungry a bit later on, but she said it was their 'things.' My sister used to come out with some very strange comments from time to time. I'm sure women originally came from another planet, as they are just *SO* unlike men. They were wired completely differently.

This was the era of the mini-skirted '*Swinging Sixties*' when girls were screaming their lungs out and fainting at pop concerts and the performing boys on stage were screaming their lungs out in return. The shackles were coming off stiff society and teenagers were being set free.

This was the era when the young stopped dancing formally in suits and ties and conservative hair-cuts and dresses. This was the era when they started wearing more adventurous, avant-garde and outlandish psychedelic clothing and war paint and when they started to let themselves go wild with flowers and headbands in their hair. They were the wild things.

This was the era when they found their voices and dropped the automatic, mandatory and *de rigueur* over-respect for their elders. This was the era when they began to question what they didn't like and were determined to do something about. This was the new era, the new dawn, the new age, the new pain-in-the-neck for the authorities and parents. Remember Jim Morrison?

When I walked into reception, that lovely lady was checking through some invoices and looked up upon hearing my clomping and smiled brightly again. She had beautiful, pale, marshmallow-soft pink skin and snow-white hair, which made her look younger than she was.

'I didnae ken yer mammy, as I havenae been here fer long. But I wiz askin' aroond and everyone, well, the older generation, that is, all remember her fondly and say she was a very nice woman, very kind-hearted.'

Well, yes, I thought. Everyone who didn't get close enough to see the cracks or smell the fumes. And they were big cracks. More like a gorge, really. And very strong fumes.

'Oh aye?' I commented, feeling more Scottish with every passing hour here. 'Where have you come from?' I enquired sincerely.

'Och, well, my husband and I spent the last twenty-five years in Nepal.'

'Nepal? Really' I enthused. 'Not many Scots travel to those areas. I know there are more Scots out of Scotland than in it. But not to those distances.'

I thought she may have said Aberdeen or Neath.

'Well, he wiz an engineer working on many o' yon projects.'

'How did you find the difference in the temperature? It must have been a culture shock for you,' I commented, remembering my work trips to Africa.

'Oh it was! My husband didn't seem to be bothered by it. He was always red-faced, but I suffered a great deal because I have a condition where I cannot sweat. So I just used to swell up like a big balloon!'

I had an image of her expanding bosoms and was determined not to laugh, because I have always been taught to respect people. Yet I could feel the giggles rising. Her comments took me by surprise; and when she added that the doctor's solution to her problem was to cut her throat to modify her sweat glands and relieve the pressure, showing me the long scar across her neck, I was so flustered by this incredibly-involved and personal story that I blurted out: 'Oh, that's not so bad. It just looks like another one of your wrinkles.' It's amazing what you can say without thinking.

I then realised what I had said. At this point, there was a pregnant pause in our conversation. She looked quite stunned. I looked quite stunned and flushed red.

'I'm very sorry. I didn't mean it that way. I meant that, well, er...well, it doesn't show that much.'

I think she enjoyed my agony, because she held my deer-in-the-headlights stare for even heavier seconds, then burst out laughing.

'Och, I know you didn't; and it didnae bother me in the least. Ah wiz toyin' wi' ye.'

Now we were both laughing. Me with the greatest of relief. Still, I wanted to change the subject before something else went wrong.

'I must say that I had a lovely breakfast this morning and I must add that your daughter was very sweet and helpful. You're all wonderful here.'

'Oh, ye mean Morag. Aye. She is that.'

'I was wondering,' I blurted out, so happy that I hadn't said anything risqué about her, 'if you would be offended or take umbrage if I asked her out to dinner one evening. You are a mother who deserves that consideration.'

I was getting into the habit of blurting things out before thinking and asked as casually as possible if she might like to.

'Well, ma daughter may not mind, but her girlfriend might!'

I think my friendly female proprietor liked to shock me repeatedly; like a jelly-fish.

I laughed nervously and waved my hand in front of her and commented: 'That's it! I can't take any more tonight. I've put my foot in it twice already!'

As we both laughed, I walked away from the reception desk, taking my livid-red head with me, while the going was still good and told her I'd be down for supper later. As I climbed up the creaking staircase, I couldn't stop guffawing and my jaw was hurting from the exertion. I was hanging on the balustrade like a floppy rag doll.

However, when I got into the room, I was overcome by great disappointment.

'What a waste,' I thought.

Later on in the bath, remembering our encounter downstairs, I started a fit of hysterics again. It was just the ludicrous thought of that encounter. With all the exertion my anus erupted and big bubbles popped over the surface of the water. I laughed more and felt a bit ill. Nerves probably. What a stink!

God! It was good to get out of London.

Chapter Three

DOUNE

-1997-

'Who farted?
Me mammy
Do it again
Me cannae'
-Anon-

The Great Flood

Joan Plumly was out the back sorting through some boxes that had just been delivered to the Co-op when she heard Angus calling her from behind the counter, where he was serving a wee woman. Bread and pies and what not for tea.

'Joan! Joan! Ye hae tae git oot here the noo! Quickly!'

Joan tutted and blew hair out of the way through her pursed lips. As if she didn't have enough to do.

'What is it noo?' she demanded as she came through to the shop. 'I'm busy.'

'Aye, ah ken ye are, bot look o'er there. He's at it again. It's no right, is it, Mrs. MacKeiron? He's aye bin a naughty boy again, has he no?' The lady laughed and shook her head. So did Angus. He thought it was quite amusing, really.

Joan looked to where the frozen food was on the side of the store and witnessed a cascade of water coming down from the ceiling.

'Och, no! Will he never learn, the daft auld git?'

She rushed out of the shop, turned left and went through a big red door after almost tripping over a wee Chihuahua's lead that was attached to it and the owner.

Who the hell would have a Chihuahua in Doune? It was barely the size of a rat. And it looked as ugly as a bat.

She sprinted up the stairs two at a time and when she got to the first floor landing, she stopped in front of a glass-panelled door to catch her breath. Too many Woodbines, she told herself as she hacked and heaved.

She rang the door-bell and for a while there was more silence than at a morgue. But then she saw an amorphous shape shimmy across the glass panelling as it went to grab the door handle. The vision that engulfed her was quite disquieting. It was the mountain man.

Grandpa Hocks stood there, dripping like a thawing foodstuff, with a baby towel wrapped around his 'circumnavigating-the-globe' jelly belly, which stood out like a great slab of lard and Joan Plumly couldn't help staring at his slanting bosoms. For some reason they reminded her of the huge slices of fish she had seen on a deep-sea fishing documentary. He stared back at her with little beady coal-black eyes underneath an explosion of wispy white hair, sprouting out in all directions as if not knowing where to grow.

'Ah wis haein a baff!' he told her indignantly, spluttering with excess water.

'Ah ken! 'alf o' its doon in the shop wi' yon frozen food! Yer gannae cause a short-circuit wan dae, ye daft gowk!'

'Oh...er...right ye are Joan, ma pet. I'm aye sorry.'

'Aye, well...remember, when ye take a baff, half the wiater comes oot when ye get in! Ye've gottae put less wiater in. Ma Area Manager will bill ye if ye carry on.'

'Right ye are, then. I'll take greater care from noo ane.'

'Mind ye do, ye banana-heid and take care of yersel'' Joan Plumly called back as she descended the stairs to continue with her day's work, thinking about what she would give her man for tea, feeling a bit fed-up with the pressures of life.

***

When I came down to breakfast the next morning, I couldn't have cared less about the creaking staircase and didn't even hear the loud cracks that resounded around the place, under my weight. I felt as if I had floated or hovered down the stairs singing '*The hills are alive...*,' such was the lightness and absurdity of my well-being. I think extreme happiness can encourage you to go back into your childhood.

The stress and pressures of urban London-living had drifted off me as if *Ten Ton Tess* had got up from lying on my chest. Who was *Ten Ton Tess*, anyway? Was she Scottish or English? For someone who worked in literature, I should have known. I suppose I would look it up one day; if ever.

When I glided into the breakfast-room, I saw Morag at some other guest's table, talking quietly to him and I felt jealous and territorial. It was immature; yet it was also primal. I sat down at the same table I had occupied the previous morning, even though familiarity breeds contempt; although I do not believe that myself, and waited for the *Angel of the North* to notice me.

Presently she trotted my way and, when I mentioned that I would have the porridge to start, as well as the main divine dish of fried ecstasy, she commented on me being a growing boy. I blushed because I always thought of the double entendre and was afraid her mother might have told her about my request. She showed no sign of knowing anything, happy in ignorance. But before she left, she bent a bit closer to me, smiled lovingly and said:-

'If I wasnae, I would.'

And then she was gone, this beautiful wraith who dreamily wafted off into thin air. Or rather, into the thin partition leading to the kitchen, from where cooking smells and noises wafted flourishingly. That phrase: *'If I wasnae, I would'* kept going around in my head like a carousel, complete with music and flashing lights. It couldn't have meant anything else and I beamed across the room within myself.

***

Bounding out of the Woodside hotel, like a frisky puppy, after my gargantuan breakfast, weighed down like a ship riding an anchor, I decided that today I would go to the Castle Hill area and then on to the castle itself. It was the best-known landmark of Doune and always silently called me back. It had stood there in quiet mystery for centuries and its silence made it appear all the more mysterious. As if it were suddenly going to jump up and scream.

I had my rucksack on my back with my literary tools-of-the-trade in it and would gloat in the glory of wandering about at my leisure. Not rushing, as I did in London, but taking my time and just ambling along, encountering what I may. Oh, how great it was to be unfettered, unshackled and untied. *The slave is free.*

I walked up George Street once again, towards the Mercat Cross. I had known quite a few people who lived in Castle Hill. I had an uncle, aunt and four cousins, playmates and people who knew my mother well. Everyone knew everyone in the long row of council houses and were ethereally linked together in familiarity. No one ever locked their doors because everyone knew everyone else and a burglar would have soon been routed out. Not every single person got on or was interested in knowing their neighbours, but they all nodded to each other and bade a cheery '*hellooooo!*' whenever they came across each other. There was little animosity here. The atmosphere was too peaceful to allow that.

As I walked up the narrow entrance which leads to Castle Hill from Main Street, I remembered all the times I had spent there, playing outside my uncle's house. Uncle Billy was thin and scrawny with grey brillcremed hair and was my Uncle Carbuncle's brother. They couldn't have been more different and they didn't get on at all. Many was the story of my Irish grandmother racing down the stairs from the flat above the Co-op and having to go and break up their fighting in the *Red Lion* pub right opposite the house. The idiots acted like prize-fighters.

My Uncle Billy was a builder, quite a bit rough around the edges, drank too much in the pubs, suffered from delirium tremors, ('suffer' being a misnomer if ever I heard one), wasn't very nice to my aunt, used her as a testicle-drainer, had greasy, wiry, white hair, wore a string vest, had lecherous-looking beady eyes as penetrating as Opie Cameron's, (what was it with these Scots? Had their eyes evolved that way from staring the Highland Winds straight in the face, looking out for the English coming over the border?), spoke more like a Glaswegian, spent most of his pay on himself and Johnnie Walker and farted when he coughed. Or rather, coughed when he wanted to fart in the presence of others in a vain attempt to cover up the blusterous explosion; when he knew full-well he shouldn't.

His repertoire used to go: cough!-prapp!-prapp!-cough! Or prapp!-cough!-cough!-prapp! Or cough!-prapp!-prapp!-cough! Or even prapp!-cough!-prapp!-prapp!-prappity!-prappity!-cough!

I thought of this as his application to an anal-emitting Morse code. Could have come in handy during the war. His expellations were quite alarming, to say the least.

All the children had been perplexed by him and asked their parents why his coughs smelt so bad and the parents didn't understand what they were on about. They assumed it was halitosis. Well, in a way it was. It was halitosis of the anal region.

My uncle was such a hopeless case that he couldn't get the timing right and ended up in not a fart-cough or co-fart or far-cough (Oh, that sounds a bit rude, doesn't it?) in perfect synchronicity, but a cough trailing a fart or a fart trailing a cough, seconds apart, like a car towing a trailer. Like one twin following another at birth.

One evening, when just the family were present and my uncle started pumping away at will, my cousin Nigel just had to get up and join in the farting festivities. So he went behind the couch, gripped the back of it with both hands flat, spread his legs, gritted his teeth, squeezed for all he was worth, went red in the face, stopped breathing momentarily and suddenly let rip an almighty blast from his arse.

I swear I felt the wind of it bouncing back off their council house window panes. Nigel started laughing so much that he collapsed and disappeared behind the sofa and his dying, trailing methane gas poppings sounded just like the death-throes of a hot-air balloon I had once seen on a television documentary, crash landing.

After a few seconds of everyone standing and sitting around sniffing the air in mock surprise like rats in a sewer, my cousin Nigel, once he got his breath back from both ends, commented that it smelt 'O rotten eggs and tomatoes!'

Where he got the idea of tomatoes from, I have no idea. I never thought that tomatoes smelt. Until then. I suppose they would do if you farted on them, though. The incredible aroma really was like that of the corpse of a horse or a cow full of cow pats; and it penetrated everywhere, just like water in a leaking boat.

Naturally, I went bright red and didn't know where to look, even if I was laughing uncontrollably; because my father never allowed that sort of thing in the house. It was strictly taboo. Only difference was that I ended up going home early because the reek, stench and stink became too overpowering to bear.

So I had bid my goodbyes and had left the farty family sitting in their own gases, continuing their deep and prolonged conversations with their arseholes. I must admit, though, that I never heard my aunt break wind; perhaps because she probably thought she would not be able to get a '*word*' in edgeways. I just prayed that they wouldn't all be found dead in the morning, having been overcome by their own methane poisoning. But that's enough of the nether-regional news for now. I imagined my uncle lighting a cigarette and me having to go to their funeral the next week.

Anyway, I am going off on a tangent here, if not on a smelly one. As winding as his aromatic dispersions no doubt. I had once tried to emulate my uncle, in his gaseous exchanges, as children are so easily influenced (even by effluence) even though my father would have been utterly horrified by my lack of anal etiquette, as he was a true gentleman.

Still, I had decided to immediately retire from my new-found career when I one day waddled home with gravy in my underpants and sent my mother into a fit of despair.

In later years, someone commented to me that '*farting was an art*' and I had commented back that, if that were true, then my uncle would never become a Grand Master.

But I still liked my uncle, as he had a wicked sense of humour, had been kind to me and I had admired my mother's stories of how he had been a paratrooper during World War II, had been constantly jumping onto the enemy and who had almost been executed up against a wall by a firing-squad; yet who had managed to scale the wall and escape during an allied air raid timed to perfection, as far as he was concerned.

'Don't mention it to Oor Billy,' she would caution, 'as he disnae like talking aboot the waar,' ensuring that I would never find out if it was another one of her tall tales or not.

Maybe that is what had sent him doolally with booze.

As I now approached my uncle's house, known in the area as Billy Hocks, my mind went back to the '60s and in my mind I grew down to the child I was then, when I had encountered my little seven-year-old female cousin racing along the pavement on her old, trusty, rusty, battered, blue-and-white tricycle.

When she saw me, she cycled around and around me, singing a funny ditty I had never heard before, that had probably originated from the school playgrounds, which were not so politically-correct in those days, thank God. For Political Correctness has no tolerance nor sense of humour. She was all lips and mouth and teeth and tongue and saliva, as she had worked around the words with great gusto:

'Och, ye cannae get a hoose fer a Pakistani
I've tried so hard but I jist cannae
They gave it tae a man in a white turbani
Och, ye cannae get a hoose fer a Pakistani

They're here, they're there, they're aye everywhere
I've even been to Stirling cooncil
And said: 'I've got a problem, you see,
Is there no anything left, free, fer me?'

Och, ye cannae get a hoose fer a Pakistani!
When you see them, ye just wantae greet
They're all walking around on poppadom feet
These chapati-heids have moved into our street
Och, ye jist cannae get a hoose fer a Pakistani!'
-DRG-

Sometimes I would spend a night at my uncle's house, but didn't really like it as it was cold and dirty. Their house was like the inside of a hoover bag. But I will forever remember the taste of slices of '*Mother's Pride*' bread toasted on a brass poker in front of an open fire in the sitting-room, as night fell on Castle Hill and we were all watching '*Top of the Pops*' with Dusty Springfield and Lulu on their small, old *D.E.R.* black-and-white rented television set and wonky indoor aerial.

I kept asking for more of the delicious hot-buttered toast and all my cousins laughed at my love for food. It was the best toast I have ever had in the world, no matter how expensive the eateries I would go to in the future. Or how expensive a toaster I bought. Or how expensive the bread...

My aunt also used to make the tastiest teas of chips and fried eggs and sliced sausage and beans and mushrooms and ordinary sausages and '*Mother's Pride*' bread washed down with highly-sugared tea. Best chips are in Scotland because of the water. Amazing how something as tasteless as water can make other things so tasty themselves.

The High Tea was revitalising enough to send any Celtic warrior off to finish the English. And I would have gone with them! We children would stand there slobbering like neglected and mistreated dogs, as we watched everything spitting in the frying pans; willing everything to cook post-haste, so we could fill our bellies. I used to watch my Aunty Maisie peeling potatoes with an old-fashioned potato-peeler, (the cheapest that could be found in Woolworths), staring out the window sadly with her typical 1960's peaked glasses, when she thought no-one was looking, no matter how chirpy she appeared in front of us, standing on the worn-out linoleum floor, master of all she surveyed, which was master of nothing at all.

I used to watch her bent over the wringer, winding soaking-wet sheets through to the other side or trundling up and down the carpets with her impotent carpet sweeper (a strange sight for my family, as we all had vacuum cleaners in England) and thought she didn't deserve the hard life she led.

Children are far more observant than adults think. Then God dealt her a bad hand of cards and cancer got her at a fairly young age and, do you know, I never thanked her for all the teas she made for me. Children can be very thoughtless at times and I hope she will forgive me for that. I hope that if she is up there looking down on me, that she realises how grateful I am to her. God bless her puir wee soul. Yet another person to visit in the graveyard when I get round to it.

***

-1963-

My cousin Nigel came barrelling around the corner on his home-made wooden cartie. Just like the one '*Oor Wullie*' has in his annuals. I had never seen one in real-life before, as we were not poor and had brand new bicycles all the time.

But, even as a child, I had been impressed by the ingenuity of putting it all together, everything obtained from the local tip and the fun and anticipation everyone had building it with the help of adults. Or watching it being built by an adult. The idea of having created something out of nothing; well, scrap, anyway, filled my child's mind with fascination.

'Lukie! Look! Watch how fast I'm gaein,' he shouted as he trundled passed me, with the wonky pram wheels under great stress bending alarmingly; for they were never made to carry a baby as big and heavy as he. He stopped and came back to me.

'Hae a go! Hae a go!'

'Well...how do I steer?' I asked, getting on uncertainly.

'With yer feet. And hild on to thon stringie fer balance,' he advised as he ran alongside me. It was basic, but the more I rode it, the more I loved the wee cartie made of planks of wood and rusty nails, nuts and bolts.

'Put both feet on yon cross plank an' push wi' yer left hoof to go right and yer right hoof to go left.'

'What?'....

We had spent the whole day playing on that daft thing, with all the other children wanting to '*hae a wee gae*' too.

Poor Nigel.

***

Near Castle Hill, on the right-hand side, there was a lot of farmland in the sixties and, in particular, a very big yellow wheat field. This was something I never saw in London, so it was very new and exciting to me. I loved the long, tall golden sheaves that stood high against the pale blue sky, waving slightly in the breeze, as if they were dancing with the happiness of freedom. Yellow against blue. What a perfect colour combination. In London it was grey on darker grey.

My other playmates enticed me into the wheat field and we would chase each other around, shoving sheaves of wheat out of the way and squealing like piglets and sometimes one of the girls would suddenly stop and say: *'I'll show you mine if you show me yours.'* So we would pull our panties down, gawp at the strange things between our legs and carry on playing again innocently in confusion. I would then spend the rest of the day wondering where the girls' willies were.

We would trample down a circular area of the wheat field, so that it was like a round room, a hidden hovel among the sheaf walls and we would lie spread-eagled, staring up at the bright blue sky and the ultra-white cotton-wool clouds, just enjoying the moment.

Enjoying the moment, that is, until one of the boys said that we had to watch out for the farmer because we were not allowed to be in the fields, as we were actually ruining his crops and that, if the farmer caught us, he would thresh us alive. I wasn't really sure what '*thresh*' actually meant, but it sounded painful so, being obedient, I immediately left the area, more yellow than the wheat itself, leaving my playmates behind. *You can run, but you cannot hide.*

I remember being given some tractor rides by kind farmers, but they shook too much and scared me, so I didn't make a habit of that. And they made me feel sick to boot. And they went too slowly.

Castle Hill also brought back the memory I had virtually forgotten. At one time, my mother, well, it must have been my mother, or a kind aunt, bought me two white rabbits. I can't remember whether I had them at the same time, or one after the other. But I know that the first one I hugged too tightly and it died in my arms; its red eyes almost having popped out of its head and the second one died when I was standing with a group of other children in Castle Hill, near my uncle's house; the one who sat on the goldfish I had just won at a fair, I think at the shooting range. He sat on it when we were coming back on the train. Instead of saying 'sorry' he had just pulled it out from under his farty bottom, said '*Whit's tha?*' and had simply lobbed it out the window! I mean! Maybe it didn't die from being crushed to death. Maybe it was gassed. *'My Life as a Goldfish.'* That sounded like a good title for a story and I filed it to the back of my mind for possible later usage.

Anyway, someone said: 'Put the rabbit on the grass and let's watch it play and hop.' So I did and no sooner had its four paws touched the blades when, out of nowhere, my sister's then boyfriend's dog mauled it to death right in front of us, with an 'Oooh' and an 'Uggghhh!' and a 'Yuk!'

Even as a child, I knew that you could not stop a dog in its attack mode; so I did nothing and can only remember the blue of the sky, the green of the grass, the white of the rabbit and the red of the blood. There was a lot of red of the blood.

It happened so quickly and I thought that dog was so cruel. It is not true that animals kill just to eat. It had no intention of eating my rabbit. It just wanted to kill it. Territorial animal pig. I hate huskies.

***

-1997-

With the memories fading the further I walked towards the end of Castle Hill, I continued on to Doune Castle, where very many more memories awaited me, like a group of old friends at a bus stop. *Where are we going today, lads?*

I loved the little country lane with the twin beige tracks cut into the grass that led up to the castle, just beyond the Catholic church and iron fencing. Here was an even quieter part of Doune, where anyone could be more on their own. Most locals had already been to the castle umpteen times, so were not very interested in seeing it again in a hurry, unless they had a visitor come up from another part of the country or from abroad and wanted to show them around.

Opie Cameron had once tried to tell people it was his summer *'hoose'* but didn't get very far. My mother, in her usual, or should I say, very unusual, sense of patriotism, pumped up the importance of Doune castle and made it sound like God had stayed there on the seventh day, after having created Heaven and Earth on the previous six. She told us many famous battles had been fought there, where, in truth, the only one had been in Monty Python's *Holy Grail.* Bonnie Prince Charlie did pass through Doune in 1745, but there is no evidence that he stayed in Doune castle. Maybe he stayed at the Woodside hotel! (I must remind myself not to be so flippant, just because I'm on a happy holiday).

Doune castle is simply a medieval merchant castle with no further claim to fame. But I have always adored it, even though it is not much more than an empty shell inside, (boring for a young schoolboy who wants to see knights in shining armour, catapults, canons and buckets of boiling oil cascading over the parapets of the ancient castle walls.) Still, I did like the well, though and when the castle would come into view amongst the trees, when driving up to Doune, it stated staunchly that you had arrived. The silent signal. The silent sentinel. The quiet warning of respect. You had reached your destination. The castle marked the spot.

I passed a row of thistles, a plant I have always loved for its unusual shape and bright purple head. I liked the fact that you had to respect it, for it could hurt you upon the touch and because it was something so very Scottish.

My mother, instilling everything Scottish in us, through the love of her country, proudly told us the story of how, unbelievably, Scotland had once been part of the Kingdom of Norway (you couldn't get two more different races!) and that, by 1263, Norway had lost interest in its former colony and that it was not until King Alexander wanted to buy back the Western Isles and Kintyre from the Norse King Haakon IV, that the thought of relieving King Alexander of his riches and territories had rekindled his interest in Scotland.

So, a Norwegian force of longships was landed and legend has it that, trying to creep up on the sleeping Scottish clans, one of the army of soldiers, who had all taken off all their shoes to be quieter, so as not to alert the enemy, stood full-on a thistle barefoot and let out a loud scream; so alerting the Scottish clans, who, needless to say, won the battle of Largs and so made the humble thistle the emblem of Scotland.

And quite right too. I loved that tale, as I have always supported the underdog and to think that a nondescript plant could save a nation, fascinated me. Maybe that's where the phrase '*wee man*' came from. Fate can be so subtle at times. Apart from the scream, that is; and it's a good job he hadn't stood on a cow-pat instead.

As I reached the grassy hills surrounding the castle, my mind reeled back again, like a line suddenly pulled back by a fish on a fishing-rod. I was a child again, in the '60s, playing with other children.

There were cow pats spread higgledy-piggledy all over the place, like freckles and moles on a human body and we would find long sticks and poke them through the hardened crust and pull out a dollop of faecal-mousse on the sticks' ends and chase each other around the castle, to the high sounds of screams, shrieks and laughter.

I don't know whether the girls or boys screamed loudest, but I can tell you that the sharp, putrid stench of a stink that came from that decomposing army-green bovine porridge was enough to make you gag and resurrect the dead, get them crashing out of their coffins and send them running for the hills. Even towards England.

We all tried to find the most-recently dumped, freshest cowpat; so that when you pierced the crust, the strongest, most powerful and most putrid stench would sit the hardest on your gag-reflex and make the others run away from you faster. You could often tell the freshest ones as they were still steaming!

For a long time I had thought Desperate Dan was eating cow pat pies and not cow pies and was quite revolted by him. I thought that's what made him strong. For I was told that what doesn't kill you, makes you stronger. Popeye could have had them with his spinach.

Anyway, when we children ran away from these sticks, it was mainly to get away from the smell. It was a lot of fun, that intense thrill of fear and disgust, which always seemed to end too soon; after we got very disapproving looks and comments from the adults passing by. What? Whit? Were they never young?

Then we would go and feel our way around the castle walls for old thruppenny bits that the workmen would mix in with the mortar when they were making their repairs. It was an old superstition of good luck and one we children were very glad of because, though I did not need the money myself, we would then all race down to the sweetie shop and spend all our mortar-caked, salvaged metal discs on gooey goodies. It was satisfying to have had to work for that money. The sweeties tasted even better.

But today, though I did see a few cow pats, there were no children about. It would have been wonderful to poke a cow pat and have those memories rushing back, as I chased a couple of adult tourists around. If only. But what sort of a reputation would I be left with then?

I walked around the grassy knolls for a while, just enjoying the lovely scenery and the peace and quiet and looking up at the majestic, though humble castle, wondering about all the ancient peoples who had set foot in it ever since the day it was erected in the thirteenth century.

I looked at the little keeper's lodge near the castle and it looked like such a sweet little cottage. I had always fantasised about living there, in the seclusion of nature, just spending my days writing away and philosophising about the meaning of Life and wondered how much it was worth. It was probably a listed building now and had probably originally been the gatekeeper's dwelling. Oh, well. Some things are not to be. Some dreams are not for sale. Some dreams are not made of this.

Not being in any hurry at all, I took the time to sit under a tree and felt compelled to write some poetry, knowing exactly what the subject matter would be. I felt my spirit oozing into the land and becoming one with nature. I felt inspiration pour into me with a vengeance and I laughed to myself because I was reminded of Keats writing *'Ode to Autumn.' 'Close bosom-friend of the maturing sun…'*

I am not in the same league as such an esteemed poet, but I didn't care, as I wrote only for my own pleasure and everyone else's discombobulation, no doubt. Usually, when I wrote something, the Scottish side of my family would say: 'Whit? Whit?' and go off down to the pub, as they were not interested in that sort of frilly-writing culture. I had not intended to finish the poem at all. But I sat there as if under a spell, the victim of automatic writing, until, after many re-writes, and the sun sinking lower and lower, it was done. I couldn't stop until it was done. I was a man possessed. It had become my mission in life and I hadn't even noticed the sun dipping in the sky. I looked at my finished piece with a critical but happy eye.

ODE TO

BONNIE DOUNE

I ken a wee hamlet they ca' Doune
Tha's no even as big as an, och, so-wee toon
It has a Catholic Church withoot a steeple
Wi' no many cars and very few people

See by yon castle
Nestlin' in thae thistles and heather
Its bastions aye strong, standing firm
In a' sorts o' weather
The children up to all sorts o' tricks
Prising oot o' its walls auld thruppenny bits

Aye, this impressive landmark
Stands so bold and proud
And tho' there's nothing tastier than Mother's Pride
There's nothing greater than thon Scottish pride

And on a far-away hill
A lonely piper wails a sad lament
As all the villagers reminisce
On all the good and bad times they've kent
Of glorious days in this wee-womb toon
Which were always aye heaven-sent

Deanston an' Doune standing proudly side by side
Within the glens, burns and braes o' this
Beautiful Scottish countryside
Any problems it can and will abide
In this twee village they ca' Doune

And as you walk along the river Teith
The frigid waters rushing underneath
Will aye be icy enough to chatter yer teeth
If ye e'er go swimmin' there

A cheery 'hello'
To everyone you meet
Doon in Doune's sweet Main Street
As you amble along
Singing a song
Afore runnin' on hame fer yer tea
O' a piece 'n' jam

At night it's so quiet
Shrouded in orange sodium street-lights
Surrounded by midgies
On crystal-cut-glass frozen nights
A picture-postcard if ever there was one
A happy place to live,
Is that no right, son?

Lunch at the Woodside
And Tea at the Highlands Hotel
You'll never hear the call to the kirk
As someone's broken the bell
Och, well, what the hell,
Everything's peaceful here
Is it no?

As you walk around this village
You can smell the coal fires burning
And when you are away
You will soon get the yearning
To return here to this lovely wee nest
To the place you know and love the best

Bonnie Doune, Bonnie Doune
Bonnie, Bonnie, Bonnie Doune
I ken I've telt it so many times,
And though the bell's no working
In our voices you can hear the chimes
In Bonnie Doune, Bonnie Doune,
Bonnie, Bonnie, Bonnie Doune
Doon in Doune
Doune!
-DRG-

I always liked to finish with a flourish! As I got up as stiff as a board from my gargantuan effort, I realised I had an urge to see the river Teith. To stay and rest awhile. It was a beautiful river, even though it held a sad memory for me and the rest of Doune itself. Once I had been swimming there and only once, for the water felt as freezing as liquid nitrogen, and the waterline as sharp as sulphuric-acid burning through you; a razor blade of ice. Enough to shock even Frankenstein back to life.

I stood there, once again, a silent Witness.

***

-1965-

Scotland is not famous for having the best weather in the world, being a Northern country. But if you are lucky enough to have nice weather, there can be little more impressive or enjoyable to be a part of. And so it was today, a truly stunningly sunny morning in late May that prompted Mr. Archibald Ailbert McKenzie, (a good strong Scottish name, as strong as Edinburgh granite rock, steeped in tradition and culture) of Balkerach street in Doune, to wander down to the river Teith and go fishing for a couple of hours or so. I can't remember what house number he lived at, but it was near the Callander bus stop. A lot of things were near the Callander bus stop, as the village was so wee.

Mr. McKenzie was a fine figure of a man; tall, lean, but not puny, rugged, ash-grey eyes and an open-legged spread of a salt-and-pepper moustache striding over his upper lip, which underlined his strong, pointed nose. He also had ruddy cheeks with red running capillaries and he drove a very reputable *Princess Vanden Plas*, a very impressive car for Doune in those days. He had quite a presence, did Mr. McKenzie; and no-one had ever heard him break wind or swear, so proper was he in manner.

The very early dawning watery sun shimmering through the windows looked promising and so had the STV weather report. So Mr. McKenzie got himself out of bed very early, had a quick quiet breakfast, so as not to disturb his wife and child, got his gear together and trundled off down the road towards the castle.

The river Teith was famous for its fishing and held plenty of big, fat trout and salmon. The river Teith is formed from the confluence of two smaller rivers, the *Garbh Uisge* and the *Eas Gobhain* at Callander and flows right into the famous river Forth near Drip, north-west of Stirling. A lot of people look at rivers and do not know where they originated from or where they end up. But now you do, is that no right, son?

Translated into English from the Scottish Gaelic, *Uisge Theamhich*, means '*quiet and pleasant water*,' and the water is so pure in the river Teith, that the distillery at Deanston draws it to make its single malt whisky. And it has to be good water for that. In fact, if this water were human, it would be the Virgin Mary.

'*Quiet'* may have been a slight misnomer, for sometimes that river could really roar.

Well, as Mr. Archibald Mckenzie put down his gear on the river bank, he had to admit that it was indeed as deservedly named. Standing up and stretching his back, painful from bending over his schematics all day, he took a few moments to relish the vista and aura of the place. Mr. McKenzie was an engineer who worked hard in the hubbub of Glasgow. So it was nice to return to the peace and solitude of Doune. Especially its quieter end by the river Teith.

The river was flowing rapidly, throwing its water down towards the North-west of Stirling at a fair rate. The sun was shining brightly and strongly now, lighting everything up. Sun rays glinted on the dancing waters, giving them a silvery sheen and making them look like tin-foil in places, mainly where they humped over the bigger submerged boulders.

The whole river was twinkling like sequins on an evening dress and the trees, influenced by just a slight breeze, swayed ever so lightly back and forth so as to make its leaves shimmer and glint, so as to make them look metallic as the invisible birds sung happily in the foliage.

Mr. McKenzie thought to himself that when the sun was out nature came alive and when it was not, it slept. The sun was bright-white yellow, the trees and grass bright green and the sky a beautiful royal blue. Puffy white clouds, looking like popcorn, hung in the air, as if spilt from a giant's hands.

Archibald McKenzie sat down on the bank and put his massive green waders on, relishing the enjoyment to come. He assembled his fly fishing-rod and opened his basket to have a critical look at the flies he had bought at '*The Fishing and Tackle Tabernacle*' up Cameronian Street in Stirling.

Approving of the quality, he attached one of the chosen few and gingerly stepped into the river to win his prey. The romance was greater than the reality and that's what gave people obsessions. The anticipation of it and not just the action nor the result.

Even through the waders, the shock of the freezing water stunned him for a few seconds. But when one has an obsession, these are trivial matters. The good thing about standing in the middle of a river, was that other people could be kept away and you had the whole watery landscape to yourself. The water was so pure, that you could see the boulders, stones, fish and riverbed quite clearly beneath you; the only distortion coming from the movement of the water itself. It was a fine, fine day and he was in a fine, fine mood. Oh, what a glorious morning!...nature's alive! Alright, Let's not get carried away now.

Archibald (Arrivaderci Erchie, as my mother Anna always used to say) McKenzie looked all around him as he sucked in his wonderful day-off and flung his long, thin, delicate spider-web-thread of a refined line way ahead of him, watching the fly splatting on the water ever so lightly. It was an addictive hobby and he liked to wade-walk the river, whether he caught fish nearer to his point of origin or not. He liked to get a feel for it. Of it breathing and spitting.

It behaved differently on different days. He liked to guess where the good fish were and if he was wrong it didn't matter. It was all in the game.

Steadily, without even noticing it, really, Archibald McKenzie worked his way just past the *Ardoch Burn*, about two miles from the castle and swished his rod through the air again. It was a sensitive rod and he could feel a few nips, tucks and pulls now and then. He was concentrating so much, that at first he did not pay much attention to something that kept bumping against his calves, underwater.

But the more he kept trying to concentrate on the idiosyncrasies of the fish, the more this object, which he thought might be a piece of branch or some other flotsam - as fish did not behave that way - kept bumping against the back of his legs persistently, vying for his attention.

'Och, fer goodness sake!!!' he finally blurted out, as he reluctantly turned around and looked down to see what it was.

And there he was.

Puir wee Gordon.

White moon face, curly fire-red hair, sprinkling of freckles over the bridge of his button nose, the brightest fully-open green eyes you ever would have seen this side of Glasgow. Staring right up at his father with a frozen, alarmed expression. A dancing face under the influence of the flowing water. A grotesque manikin under no power of its own. The image mutating in front of Archibald's very eyes.

Not smiling.

Not saying hello.

Not alive.

Dead.

His little three-and-a-half year-old son as attached to him now in death as he had been in life.

Mr. McKenzie froze colder than the river Teith on a bad winter's day.

Now it was a bad winter's day within him.

A very, very bad winter's day.

For quite a few seconds, which may have seemed like hours to him, he looked down at this macabre image, which he simply could not make head nor tail of. It was incongruous. It was totally out-of-place. It was a double-decker bus on the moon; it was a tiger swimming underwater. He should not have been there. He should have been with his mammy, who had always been so good at looking after him. What had gone wrong? What was he doing there? How did he get there? Had he come down to the river looking for his daddy?

He lifted him out of the river like a giant fish, all the water cascading off him like a waterfall. The one that didn't get away. For split seconds he had thought it a doll. Yet far too familiar a doll.

'Oh! Gordi! Ma wee Gordi! It cannae be you! Wa's ganan on? Oh, NO! No, No, No!'

Gordon was as cold as the fish he caught. The eyes just as lifeless, staring out with the impartiality of camera lenses, glazed over.

I know not what I see.

Mr. McKenzie forgot all about his rod, he forgot all about his fishing. He forgot all about his day off. He left everything in a mess by the river bank. The evidence that he had been there. He completely forgot about the life he had had only a few seconds previously, as he scrambled up the bank and lay him tenderly on the grass. He had to think...

he had to think. A cold sweat came over him as he felt like a murderer who had to hide the body before it was discovered, caused by guilt.

Like an automaton, he raised his son in his arms and walked back towards his house near the Callander bus stop like a robot in stunned reflex, to somewhere comforting and familiar. He needed to get help. The doctor. The mortician. Don't say that word! His son, his creation, lay limp in his arms, with his limbs dangling dead, as the drips of water falling off his son's body became less the further he walked; the further he walked into death. Everything drying up. Including his soul.

It was not long before the odd straggly villager was asking him questions to which he did not reply, about what had happened, and exclaiming: 'Oh, dear! Oh, deary, deary me,' before quite a crowd gathered alongside him as he walked mechanically on. A lot of women were crying and those men who were wearing them, took their caps off.

Housewives doing their cleaning looked down from their bedroom windows, cyclists stopped to see what was occurring the nearer he got to the village centre and cars slowed down from curiosity and for the commotion ahead and stopped out of respect. Dogs barked and cats screeched, as if telling the animal world what had happened and, for a while, Doune seemed to stand still in a miasma of shock.

Mrs. McKenzie, who had been out looking for her wee *Bairn,* who had simply vanished from under her very nose, as she had been busy talking to a neighbour at the front door, fainted when she saw the mob.

'Ma bairn! Ma bairn!' she shrieked as she ran an incredible sprint down Doune's normally tranquil Main

Street, powered by supernatural adrenalin, fear and panic; much to everyone's increasing shock and horror. Many felt guilty and helpless through no fault of their own.

She knew instinctively that her wee Gordie was *deid.* A mother's instinct, which is, they say, simply the spirits and your soul telling you something is not quite right. Your soul knows because your life was written out for you even before the day you were born. But she did not faint just out of shock; she also fainted out of guilt and shame.

Her mind did not want to see what was being portrayed in front of it, so it simply shut down and cancelled out life momentarily.

God, in his infinite wisdom, had given Gordon McKenzie three-and-a-half years. Three-and-a-half years to bring the greatest grief to those who loved him so very dearly. He had given him just a taster of life and had then snatched it away from him so cruelly. Why, God? Why? Why so much pain and suffering in the world? Was it to make heaven appear more wonderful upon arrival?

Archibald McKenzie never ever went fishing again and he most certainly never ever went fishing in the river Teith again until the day he died and breathed his last breath in Doune and on Earth.

Years later, for some reason, Mr. McKenzie gave up his car and bought a motorbike instead. He had never given anyone any indication that he suddenly preferred two wheels over four. Maybe it is because he didn't have a family any more.

In any event, he always used his motorbike to go to work and was going around a bend on the wrong side of the road, near the *Blair Drummond Safari Park* on Lime Avenue, just off the A84, on his way to Stirling, when he slammed straight into the grill of an *ERF* lorry. Mr. MacKenzie had never gone onto on the wrong side of the road ever before.

The police commented that it was a bit strange because, upon seeing the lorry, he apparently made no attempt to take any evasive action whatsoever. Not even a hesitation on the accelerator nor application on the brakes; according to the traumatised driver of the lorry and there were certainly no skid marks anywhere. He seemed to stare straight ahead of him, as if under hypnosis or in a trance. The lorry driver, having to be held up by the ambulance crew, so as not to collapse, told the '*polis*' that it was as if his lorry had been completely invisible to him. Perhaps his mind was back at the river Teith, fishing away, with his son bobbing against his leg; the memory that would not stop nagging him. Perhaps, and most probably, he had simply decided that he had had enough of his painful life and had killed himself.

However, whatever the speculation, when he died, he went fishing with his wee son in the river Teith and they spent a very lovely day together.

Forever.

Chapter Four

-1960s-

Skinny Malinki Longlegs
Big Banana Feet
Went tae the pictures
And couldnae find a seat
When the picture started
Skinny Malinki farted
Skinny Malinki Longlegs
Big Banana feet
-Anon-

By the time I became more aware of my environment, my maternal grandfather was already an old man. I don't know exactly how fossilised, but when I was around 10- or 11-years-old my grandfather was already in his late '70s or early '80s. I identified with him because, like me, he was quite rotund (to say the least). He had a mountain of a body on which sat a crepuscular pea-sized balloon face, little bright-grey beady eyes that homed in on you like the best military missile, sprouts of white hair which stood up like un-mown grass on the side of a verge and a red light-bulb potato nose which reminded me of the character in the

'*Operation*' game. I thought that if I touched my grandfather it might light up. No such luck.

I thought he was very funny because he wore his braced-up trousers riding just under his arm pits and I imagined he had one testicle down each trouser leg because his crotch must have been right up his bahookie. I remember him always sitting in one of the big brown leather armchairs whose springs had gone flat over the years; although it was still comfortable.

He would always sit there like Popeye and suck on his pipe like a baby on its mother's teat and say *'Och aye the noo,'* or *'Ora Wora,'* or *'Dae ye no ken?'* with a long, satisfying sigh; like the one you take after sipping a refreshing cup of tea.

I only remember him ever being in his bedroom or in front of the fire wafting off all his pipe tobacco, which had a lovely aromatic aroma. If he went out, it would be across the road to the bookies for boredom-distracting titillation or to see that Mrs. Wallis in a neighbouring village. Well, you know, there's nothing like being discreet! He would always say: '*Hello Wee Diddums*,' and I would always reply: *'Hello Big Diddums.'* It broke the ice and gave us a bond. He was quite quiet, but after 80 years of listening to women talking, I'm not surprised.

One day my Uncle Carbuncle came over to the house holding a little saw in his hand and I thought he was going to do some carpentry repairs. But it turned out he had come to cut his faither's toe nails. They were so tough, thick, yellow and hard that that's what was needed; so all afternoon you could hear the sound of sawing, crunching and clipping, to the accompaniment of flying toe-nails pinging with great force off the window panes and the odd *'ouch!'* as my mother ducked to avoid the crescent projectiles getting caught in her hair or pinging off her nose.

'Dinae tak ma tae aff!' I heard him once shout at my Uncle Carbuncle. I didn't actually see this operation in progress, as I was and still am, quite squeamish and was happily cowering in another room. The sounds were bad enough; but that's what my mother told me...unless it was another one of her tall stories. I walked into the sitting-room once the job was done and, like the truly professional carpenter my uncle was, I watched as he packed away his wee saw and other bits back into his toolbox and got up to leave. He smiled at me, still sporting that ridiculous salvaged toupee and I half-expected him to tip it off at me in formal greeting.

I didn't know my grandfather when he was younger, but I did see the photographs of him. He was a very impressive figure, looking tall, swarthy and strong and I was especially impressed when I saw a photograph of when he was in *The Black Watch.* To me he looked very aggressive and warrior-like, with a face as stern as a block of granite and not anybody I would want to meet in a dark alleyway or even on the Mercat Cross in broad daylight, for that matter.

He was most certainly one of the lads. Yet, when I knew him as an older man, he was a big softie; at least with me. It was hard to believe that, not only had he led a hard life, but that he had been through heavy fighting in two world wars, had seen one of his soldier friends have his stomach torn open by a German mortar, spilling all his entrails, blood and guts onto the ground in front of him and he had actually killed many enemy soldiers, one of which was with his bare hands. Maybe that's why he was a softie now. He didn't want any of that horror back.

The Hocks family was originally of Dutch origin and, according to my mother, we did not have a tartan, so adopted the MacDonald plaid instead, which I was glad about, because it was a lovely colour and I thought it was the best of the bunch, a classic kilt design.

My grandfather's house, in the sixties, was diagonally across the road from the Mercat Cross. From the sitting-room window we could see the people getting off the Callander bus when it came back from Stirling. My mother and sister would stand at the window, real curtain-twitchers and comment: 'Oh, there's Mrs. so-and-so. Her daughter has a terrible illness, don't you know...and there's wee Alec! His dad aye beats him fairly often...Och, puir wee soul...and look...there's old Mrs. McVitie, now she takes the biscuit...' My mother would always laugh at her own jokes and my sister would smile along with her, humouring her, two old farm hens-in-arms. 'Ah dinnae see Alastair McReery. He's usually on the bus the night.' Good God!

Amazingly, we didn't have a television in the house. My grandfather, or '*grandfaither*,' as my '*mither*' used to say, was old now and had lived his long life without that '*fandangled thing*' and so, if we watched to watch *'Dr. Finlay's Casebook,'* or *'Z Cars,'* we had to go to some other relative's house and take a seat among the farting few, before being gassed out for the night. Don't blame me. I am not obsessed with natural gas; they were.

Even in the summertime, when we always came to visit from London, it could be very cold in Doune and especially in my grandfather's house. These were the days before Central Heating was rife and he only had two fires. One in the sitting-room, or front-room, as they called it in those days and one in his bedroom, which always smelt of pipe-tobacco. Out of respect, we did not go in there very often and when we did sneak a peak, it was just a mysterious mess which smelt heavily and sweetly of his pipes and other smells best left unquestioned and undiscovered.

In the sitting-room, he had two lovely studded leather armchairs facing opposite each other, right by the fireplace, which was always emitting a hot hello to everyone who entered the room. 'Shut that doar the noo!' my grandfather would always say: 'Yer lettin' 'alf o' Siberia in, are ye no?' as soon as we opened it. In London we had radiators, so we were not used to the roaring foundry-like furnace blast we would encounter with singed eye-brows, abutting the freezing cold weather front.

He would always sit there, on the left-hand-side armchair, so that he could see who was coming in to the room, smoking away on his aromatic pipe, just like Pa Broon, (only my grandfather was a lot fatter) and philosophise about Life to anyone who would listen. I did, but most of it went over my head. Still, it was lovely sitting next to the fire in those impossibly-comfortable armchairs, just watching the flames dancing happily away and the embers glowing red like Devils' eyes and hissing at me from time to time.

Often I used to fall asleep in front of the fire, by the hot hearth, before my mother made me go to bed under eleven blankets and freeze to death. For some reason, the third bedroom, by the front door, didn't have a fireplace.

The blankets didn't really warm us up that much anyway, they just felt very heavy. We were used to fridges in London, but my grandfather didn't have a fridge. He just had a larder and that was as cold as a fridge, let me tell you.

I often opened it, expecting to see something half rotten, mouldy or trying to walk out of it; but everything was as fresh as daisies and I always loved looking in there, to see what was around to eat. The shelf I was interested in was at my eye-level.

I always remember seeing a lop-sided frying pan sitting on one of the shelves with hard lard lying white in it, with little crusts of fried unidentified food remnants in it so that it looked like a dirty ice-rink. But I was very fond of that humble larder and once told my mother that I wanted to marry a scullery maid and live happily ever after in a larder. Maybe because it was bigger than a fridge.

'Dinnae be sae daft! Jist dinnae be sae daft, laddie! Now get oot o' ma road!' she would say, poking me out of the kitchen with her broom or finger, whichever was at hand.

Whenever we arrived in Doune, my mother would give me some money and I would immediately go and buy Scotch pies, Irn-Bru, sliced sausage and Mother's Pride bread.

Irn-Bru is the most original-tasting drink I have ever had and the look of it, fizzing away in orangey-golden exuberance yo-yo'd my eyes in expectancy and when my tongue hit that elixir, I came alive. Then I would feast and banquet all day.

Now, let me tell you about Mother's Pride. It was tall sliced bread with a dark top crust, almost black, wrapped in wax paper and it tasted simply divine. No other sliced bread has ever come anywhere near it and I used to pull slithers of bread off the sides and hold them above my open mouth like long worms fed to young birds in their nests. Best bread in the world. It had a particular flavour that couldn't be matched. Unique. Slightly tangy. Scotland forever!

One day, I was busy in the kitchen, being a bit adventurous and creative, after having decided to make myself a Scotch pie sandwich. A Scotch pie between two slices of Mother's Pride bread. I mean...what could be better? How could you top that?

My mother came into the kitchen at the most inopportune time and stopped in her tracks.

'Lukie! What on earth are ye daein? Whit?'

'But, mom, it's delicious, really!'

'Whit? An' wi' butter too? O MY!' She sputtered incredulously, through her horrified face, spying the packet on the table. 'All that butter and lard! Get oot o' here, you daft boy!' I took the sagging sandwich with me, biting bits of it off before I lost it all to the floor.

But later, my mother just looked at me, shook her head and laughed. 'Whit are ye like?' she kept asking me. 'Whit are ye like?' Well; that kept all the adults amused for a week or so. I became the laughing-stock of the village, but I had the last laugh like *'Oor Wullie'* when The Co-op gave me six free pies. An entertainer's fee, they called it. I'm sure Aunty Joan had something to do with that.

With the seeds of culinary creativity planted in my head, I did, a few days later, ask my mother if I could have mince and tatties...

'Aye, of course, dear.'

'Poured over two Scotch pies?'

I was chased out of the house before I could defend myself. Honestly, people are just not imaginative enough with food. You have to be daring.

Now my grandfather didn't have that many friends left, as most had died off, but, one evening, a much younger man than he, called Morris McCracken, in his 50s, came to visit him in his kilt. He was wearing the full outfit, including a ghillie shirt, the buckled shoes, a kilt-pin in the shape of a silver sword and even a *sgian dubh,* the Scottish dagger, tucked into one of his upper long socks. He was quite an impressive sight, just like my grandfather had been in the Black Watch and, in fact, I think his father had even served with my grandfather in the Black Watch himself, or something like that.

I was half expecting him to be dragging the bagpipes in, which, to me, sounded like someone stepping on ten sick cats.

'Wull ye hae a wee dram?' my grandfather had asked him hopefully.

'Aye, Daniel, I'll hae a wee swally wi' ye. Tha' wid be aye grand the noo. Och aye the noo.'

Being bored with no television and no comics to read and curious about this man and his incredible dress sense, as, even though we were in Scotland, not many people were by then wearing kilts, unless you went to the Highland Games, or were watching Andy Stewart on T.V.

I sat at the dining-room table in the sitting-room, (as he had no dining-room) looking on, as my grandfather puffed away on his pungent pipe. And when the kilted Scotsman sat down and rearranged himself to get comfortable, as would a woman, sitting on the very edge of the armchair, striking up a *Capstan Full Strength*, with his legs slightly ajar, so that my grandpa Hocks could hear what he was saying, as he was starting to go deaf (because he was sitting forwards, not because his legs were open) I couldn't believe what I saw and rushed out of the room to my sister and told her she simply *HAD* to come into the sitting-room and look between the man's legs.

We both excitedly walked back into the sitting-room nonchalantly, like two chaperones with my sister innocently saying *'hello,'* while not looking too soon, so as not to alert him to our Peeping-Tom habits.

I could hardly contain myself from giggling, but did not want to prevent my sister from witnessing this rare spectacle. So, waiting until my grandfather and the kilted guest continued their conversation of 'Och, Aye...is that a fact?...de ye ken Tam who's noo oot o' wirk from yon factory in Dunblane,' ...etc, my sister, unable to resist anymore, casually looked while pretending not to look and then locked on to his groin like a bolt being driven home, to see a frozen explosion of pubic hair, underneath the tarpaulin of his great kilt, acting as a backdrop to a big *'McGregor's'* sausage poking out and casually draped over two impressively bulging tatties, hanging in mid-air, jingling and jangling away as he breathed and heaved, swinging like a pendulum every time he shifted a bit in his chair.

Oh, my! Oh me oh my! How simply overwhelming!

She stared at his hairy, airy genitals with flying-saucer eyes. To me, his pinched foreskin looked exactly like the pinched skin you get at the end of sausages where they tie-off the meat. Someone told me that these things (willies) sometimes grew and I was wondering where it would go? I prayed it would not start growing towards the floor nor towards me, like some of the very long horse willies I'd seen and, scared by my imagination, I had had to eventually leave the room, after my own curious stare, as I had turned as red as a beetroot and felt an eruption of laughter about to invade Scotland.

I laughed all night about that, remembering the look on my sister's shocked, yet fascinated face. She had even tilted her head like a dog does when it doesn't quite understand what it is looking at. Did that make you see better? I had tried it myself once and had just felt a bit dizzy and cricked my neck.

She was at that age, you understand, where curiosity had killed her cat countless times and she had looked at it as a starving dog looks at a bone. I had this awful fear that she was going to suddenly spring up and snap her gnashers around it, crunching it!

I had always believed that the long-standing joke about *'What does a Scotsman wear under his kilt?'* to be a myth and fantasy. But now I had living proof, if not squidgy proof and dangly proof that some did not wear anything underneath their kilts at all; apart from the tools of Creation and thought that it must get cold and draughty up there and they must dribble a lot. Their thingies, not the people themselves, that is, unless they were very old. Then they would probably both dribble.

Then I thought that perhaps some did not wear underpants to save money. But I soon dismissed that notion, as I know the Scots are not as stingy as depicted. None of the ones I have ever met were. So there. Nothing but generosity in their hearts and in their pockets.

I loved my grandfather, though. We had formed a tight bond. Probably because I was always joking and laughing with him when he was bored. My mother called us *'Big Diddums'* and *'Wee Diddums'* as if we were a Laurel and Hardy comedy team and my brother teased me, as always (yawn) as to which was which, as we were both so fat. My grandfather is now not so fat, as he is dead and I am still as fat, as I am still alive. I always remember my grandfather saying, through his loose, wine-red, elastic-band lips: 'Ach! It's nice to be nice; and it disnae cost ye onything.'

One day I complained to him that everyone was calling me stupid and fat and that I did not feel as clever as other people. Well, he looked into the fire, then at me and smiled.

'It's no' the only quality of a human being, son. What ye feel ye may lack in yon grey matter (eh?) you make up in being a gud person, working hard and having the right attitude to life.'

Well, he may have come from a humble background, but I hadn't realised he was such a philosopher; and he knew I wouldn't fully understand what he said when he said it, but that I would fully understand it in the future. And that's why he had said it.

***

My grandfather had an old sit-up-and-beg black Ford Popular 103E from the early fifties, which he used to use to go and see that girlfriend, Mrs. Wallis, in. Not only was he a slow driver, but the old jalopy was only capable of a top speed of 60mph, at best, when new. Probably downhill.

Well, my mother was worried that he was going about in such an old car that he had to start with a wire on the choke, because he couldn't afford to have it fixed, or didn't bother. She thought it might break, especially with his weight. So, one day, as my family were well-off, my mother informed my grandfather that she was buying him a new second-hand car. 'Oh, grand,' he said. 'That'll be aye grand.'

So my sister, mother and grandfather set off for a fairly nearby farm, as a farmer was selling his Rover 90. Well, my grandfather, being quite podgy and having a belly that could circumnavigate the globe, sat behind the wheel of this larger car to try it out for size and his gut pressed the horn down firmly, all the way it would go.

My mother, embarrassed and alarmed by the violent blare, told him to *'git oot o' the motor!'* But he got stuck, jammed and couldn't budge an inch, with the horn incessantly blaring away like an air-raid siren. My sister, then my mother and then the farmer tried to set him free. All three were tugging and pulling, pushing and panting as my grandfather puffed and gasped, growing redder against the contrast of his snow-white hair.

'Breathe in!' my mother had screeched.

'Ah im breathin' in,' he remonstrated. 'An' if ye aw keep pulling n' pushin' I'll soon no be breathin' at a!'

The pigs started oinking and grunting enthusiastically; the chickens starting clucking in mad disapproval and flapping their wings as if wishing they could fly away from the incredible din; the horses starting neighing in the most un-neighbourly way and, finally, the cows mooed all the way back to their sheds.

With my sister by now in stitches, slipping and sliding in the mud and my mother stone-faced, ever the Scottish warrior, just like her faither, all three finally managed to prise my grandfather out with a splodgy 'pop' and groan from the driver's seat. 'Shouldae used some o'yon pig fat to unhinge ye!' my mother commented in angry embarrassment.

Still, he got his car though, admiring it with his sweaty red face, from all the exertion. Bought it for £50.00. and all the animals were then very contented to have a nice, quiet afternoon, without that strange, ball-shaped blob of a human being bobbing about and making strange animal sounds. What sort of animal was that, exactly? He later had the Doune mechanic extend the runners to accommodate his big belly.

***

-1997-

I decided to go and visit my other cousin, Janet, who lived in Keltie Place, Deanston. We have always had a humorous rapport together and were always laughing and guffawing together. But when I went to start the car, it wouldn't because of the blasted starter motor. I am a bit lazy at getting around to things, but will do it when I get back to London, because I do not want to waste time doing these things while on holiday.

I sat in the car, wondering what to do and then realised how wonderful it would be to walk there, as it was so near. I have never done so before, so thought it was a brilliant idea.

Luckily, it was a dry day and not too cold. So I ambled along the A84 and stopped at the bridge overlooking the river Teith. It was so relaxing, watching the river flow, nature's busy highway. I then crossed the bridge, turned right onto the B8032 and right again onto Teith Road and on towards Deanston.

As soon as I knocked on the door, a cacophony of five barking dogs and a squawking macaw rushed to my ears. Janet answered the door with a big smile on her face and

I said, in my terrible Scottish accent: 'I've come fer ma breakfast!' As with Katie, her sister, we caught up with all the latest news and gossip and I played with the dogs, one of which reminded me of a pregnant sausage roll. I peeked into the kitchen to have a look at her multicoloured macaw, which had lost some feathers and whose base, like an oversized pizza dish, was covered in white, chalky excrement and it was everywhere. I thought that was hilarious! What a load of crap!

At one point, Janet started talking about an event she had been to when she was in her early thirties, and I, ever the charmer, said: 'Oh, Recently then?' Oh, yes. That made her day, considering she was pushing fifty.

As we said goodbye on the doorstep, of course arranging for us all to meet, I was trying to persuade her to come out with me sightseeing. She had a habit of doing her own thing and staying close to home and I told her it would be nice for her to get out of her immediate surroundings and take a break. So she asked:

'Where are you going?'

'Callander,' I replied merrily.

At this point she just exploded with laughter and by so much that she couldn't even talk, which is a miracle for her! She was doubled-up, holding her stomach as if afraid she would pee or pump and the tears were rolling down her face. Realising what I had said, I started to laugh uncontrollably too, picturing in my mind that I should have said Oban or even Perth, somewhere a bit more exotic and not some where right on her doorstep.

Because her fit of very contagious laughter was getting so out of control, she suddenly shut the door on me! I couldn't stop laughing at that in itself. My jaw was beginning to ache and I noticed that there was an old man on the opposite side of the road, with a newspaper in his hand, just staring at me as if I were an alien. (*They're aye strange doon sooth.*)

I, still laughing uncontrollably and unable to speak, pointed to the door and he just shook his head and walked away. After a few minutes (I could see her standing at the window still laughing, she opened the door, so that we could say goodbye properly. Talking about things in general, she casually pointed to a house with a grey door in Leny Road and said it was where a young boy had killed his parents.

'What? Really? In such a quiet area?' I had replied, flabbergasted, as if it were a house in a tough part of London.

'Why don't ye go and check it oot?' she suggested, as if I were a reporter.

I was very shocked at this revelation, because nothing at all like that ever happened in innocent Doune or Deanston. So I decided I would try to find out more about it.

***

Donnach Luag Colquholn (whit?) was a very nice boy. Everyone said so. There was never a word spoken against him and there was never a complaint made against him. He was very quiet, polite and mild-mannered; although some had not noticed how withdrawn he was. His parents gave him such a Gaelic name because they were staunch traditionalists, in their own ignorant, warped way.

He did keep himself to himself, though, which made him *'No ane o' uz.'* But most said that was because of his parents. They had made him that way. What was wrong with his parents?

'Well, we don't like to say. But they could be a bit... erm...overbearin' and odd,' a Mr. Henderson, from *Deanston Gardens*, said that the parents kept to themselves, never spoke to anyone else, only returned a curt and severe nodded greeting to others' cheery hellos and always seemed to be nagging and forever shouting at the puir wee lad and at each other. *'But that was their business and not oors.'*

'They were no exactly middle of the road, if ye Ken whit ah mean,' said a father who was with his son.

'Middle o' the road? Mair like right aff the bloody verge!' the son commented, twirling his forefinger around his temple, in a merry dance.

The father glared at his son because he didn't like to hear him swearing in front of strangers; and in front of respected professional strangers at that. Quite a few locals were interviewed and pretty much said the same thing. *'Furtive,'* they all agreed. The parents were aye *'furtive.'*

Nothing ever happened in or around Doune and then this.

The parents were strange.

They kept to themselves.

The lad was really nice.

The parents were really horrible.

They were totally flabbergasted by what happened.

'Whit, here? Ye ne'er even get that drama on the telly. No even on '*Z Cars*.''

But you never know what people are up to when they close their front doors. They might be innocent on the outside and very guilty on the inside. The wee wifey you see closing her door with her bag of shopping, could be a kleptomaniac or a dipsomaniac at heart.

The labourer you see closing his door when he comes back from work with his sandwich box under his arm, could be a wife-beater or pervert. The sales representative with all his smiles and gift-of-the-gab, could have a gambling habit or foot-fetish. Sometimes, the more innocent they look, the more guilty they are. And so say all of us.

The young lad was forever being bullied at school because he was small, shy and his clothes were tatty and dirty, because his parents had never wanted him, didn't care about him and neglected him. He was the last thing they would spend any money on. He was taunted all day at school and thumped when the teachers weren't looking.

He was taunted all night at home and thumped when the authorities weren't looking.

He was under constant pressure. Very hard for a young mind to deal with.

He was constantly nagged and belittled at home and shouted at for no reason at all. He was shouted at if he left the top off a bottle; he was shouted at if he left a rare comic lying about, even though their house was extremely dirty and unkempt; he was shouted at if he went to the toilet for *Number Two* and left a smell; he was shouted at if he hiccupped; he was shouted at if his hair was not combed, even though his mother's hair looked like it was trying to escape from her head at all angles in panic; he was shouted at if he gulped down his food too quickly, even though it was because he was starving and they never fed him enough; he was shouted at if he had smelly feet, even though his parents themselves smelt like two walking cesspits; he was shouted at for no good reason and this preyed heavily on his developing brain. They blamed him for being born, but it was not his fault; if anything, it was their fault, because they were the ones who had made him in disgust and it was so easy and convenient to blame everyone else. Shouting, shouting; always shouting. *Shout at the Devil*!

Instead of being given a hug, he was given a shove; instead of being given a kiss, he was given a smack on the kisser; instead of being shown any affection, he was shown rejection, in many more ways than one. So it is not surprising that he cracked; because even a bucket can hold only so much water; even a balloon can take in so much air before bursting; even a brain can only take so much pressure before exploding.

Everything in the world was his fault. This was not a haven for him. The only peace of mind he had was when he was going between his school and his home. That lonely walk. The loneliest walk of all. Only then the pressure was off for a few precious, priceless minutes, could he feel in any way normal.

For in his home he was bullied too and made to feel worthless. He would sometimes lock himself in the bathroom, hold on to the sink and shut his eyes, as if blocking out the unsteady world, because he couldn't stand the pressure and felt like his head was going to erupt or rocket off from his shoulders. He felt like a human volcano.

A human pressure-cooker. He couldn't go here and he couldn't go there. He was stuck between two razor blades. He had no sanctuary, neither physical, emotional nor mental and he had no-one to turn to.

His parents were guilty. They were guilty of mistreating the boy, making him do too many chores, treating him with scorn, neglecting him, not feeding him properly, constantly putting him down, taunting him, slapping him, making him feel worthless and, if that were not bad enough, constantly nagging him about things that had nothing to do with him.

They locked him under the stairs in the darkness and freezing cold, so that they could have the run of the house, because they couldn't be bothered with him. Sometimes they chained him up in the bathroom and his mother served him cold food when she could not be bothered to cook him something. If he got the cold food or any food at all.

Some people were not cut out to be parents; and they were certainly a prime example. They had such a hold on him that they even made him sit between them on the small couch when they watched television, so that they could keep an eye on their valued possession. Or valued *obsession.* Not valued because they loved him as a son; but valued for all the slave labour he could carry out for them while he was meant to be studying or playing or just living a normal, carefree childhood life.

Out of all the appalling variety of mistreatments, there were the two that made him snap. It was the nagging and the shouting. *'When are yer grades going to improve? Why can't ye be like so-and-so? Why can't ye wash the dishes properly? Why do ye always spill some of the rubbish when ye take it oot? Why have you no got a girlfriend yet? (what? At eleven years old?) why are ye not talented?* (Dunno, must get it from his parents). Why? Why? Why? Why? WHY? WHY? '*Yer face is stupit, yet ears are aye stupit, yer hair is stupit, everything aboot ye is stupit...'*

Resounding, resounding and resounding in his head like Chinese water torture or somebody scraping their nail eternally down a big blackboard or voices shouting down a long, deep well. Or standing in a belfry right next to a ringing bell. I have to stop this. I am at my wit's-end. Even a child knows the limits to pressure and abject abuse.

So, one night, without saying anything at all, or giving any indication, as he sat between his two parents, his mother smelling of sweaty armpits and his father of pee on his groin, at a moment when they were distracted by laughing hard at a slutty comedy show, which really reflected their mentality, with the knives pointing backwards in his hands, he stabbed them each thirty-seven times as he laughed along with them, his arms moving to and fro, as in a skiing motion. The sort of motion that couldn't stop once it started; like perpetual motion or magnetic attraction.

But he wasn't laughing at the comedy show; his laugh was a maniacal one born from the release of his pent-up emotions and the final psychological and physical escape from his captors. His brain had finally blown a casket.

His laugh was built from the freedom he felt from getting rid of his parental shackles. From the torture. From the immense, unbearable pressure, as if you were a thousand feet down in the ocean, about to implode. From the screaming in his head.

It seems that some people's relationships can be too close for comfort. He had no idea what he was going to do now and he didn't care because he knew he didn't deserve to be treated that way and nothing in store for him could be worse than what he had already gone through. All his emotions were now completely depleted and expended. He was finally at peace. There was nothing left: he was a husk.

And if someone had said *'why didn't you wait until you were old enough to leave home?'* well it just didn't work that way. The strain would have been too unbearable. The mind has a mind of its own and knows when it had reached its limit and they had already bent his mind and sent him do-lally.

The boy wandered around Deanston in a red-rag daze until two workmen found him and called the *'polis.'* The expression on his face had begged them for help. They thought he had been beaten up. So did the police. Until they went to his house, found the bloody smudge on the partially-open front door and found the massacred couple with the wild, laughing grimaces on their faces within; like abandoned fun-fair characters and blood absolutely everywhere. Static hyenas.

It was on the walls, the ceiling, the carpet, the door, the cat, under her sweaty, bat-wing armpits, on his pee-stained groin, in their cups of tea, on their broken biscuits, on the lava lamp, on the furniture, on the newspapers and on anything else it could land on, even itself. There were layers and layers of it. It had been a spray-away day beano party extravaganza.

Not that the police would have said the following in public, but someone overheard a policeman telling a colleague that *'the sitting-room was like the inside of a tomato ketchup bottle.'*

There was a mini traffic jam of cars outside the unassuming, humble house, made up of two blue-and-white Ford Anglia patrol cars, a divisional black Ford Zephyr, with its radio aerial swaying in the sad breeze and an ambulance, all with their blue lights spinning, looking like lost lighthouses in a misty sea, as the day came to an end and darkened in more ways than one.

The boy, after seeing social services and a psychiatrist, ended up in Belsdyke. No one has heard of him ever since; though it is said he is much happier there than the madhouse he originally came from. They say he just watches television and smiles out the window, lost and far away in his own mangled thoughts. He loves comedies best. God bless him.

I was thinking that perhaps my mother might have met him there sometime, when she went for her electric shock treatment against alcoholism. I visited her in Belsdyke once and it was a very gothic, dour building and a depressing experience, even though she was happy and smiling away, as if nothing was wrong. As if we were at a fun-fair.

Candy-floss, anyone? Cuckoo!

***

My mother also had a male first cousin named Matt Mallone who lived in Castle Hill right next door to Uncle Billy, who also did not get on with the rabble-rouser. I don't remember him being around much, but when he was, he was nice, though more formal and distant with us children.

I remember he had a fairly oval head with black hair and a moustache. He was still nice, though. But his wife Hattie was the real gem. The sweetest, kindest lady - and I call her a lady - you could ever hope to meet. She was small by normal standards, with delicate features and hands, a small curious round face, like that of a squirrel, tightly-permed black hair and a Jimmy Durante nose (whit?).

They had two children, a girl, Lucinda, and a boy, Ryan, who would have been my second cousins or cousins twice removed. (Or removed right outside the front door, for all I understood about more distant relative phraseology.)

They were more refined than my rough diamond uncle, *Billy the Kid* and I never heard a swear word in their house. I think a lot of people swore in Doune to warm up the cold winter nights. Like Joan Plumly, my Aunty Hattie was always smiling and pleasant and would do anything for us.

We were always there and she just took it for granted that we were. I'm sure they had problems of their own, but perhaps not big ones, as the atmosphere in their house was always very cordial, happy and relaxed. I remember that Lucinda had long, wavy, carrot-red hair, green eyes and freckles and we were always playing together. Funny how children always get around to kissing. We could only have been nine or ten and we used to invent these games where all us children, along with all the other neighbourhood children, would close ourselves away in the entrance hall and see how long we could kiss for. With closed lips of course. Lucinda and I always seemed to end up together. (No doubt, a conspiracy between her and all her other girlie friends).

I must admit I enjoyed the electrical charge I felt passing through our lips (between all the giggling!) and the tangy-tarty taste. Once, Lucinda organised it for me to lie with my eyes shut on the couch and have a string of her girlfriends kiss me in turn. I thought it was quite amazing and flattering to have all these eligible girls kissing me sweetly. I remember feeling their wet pecks before opening my eyes un-expectantly and realizing that they were simply pressing their wetted forefingers against my forehead or cheeks. Cheeky besoms! Wait until the next time I go to Don MacFairlane's; they'll not be getting any sweeties affa me!

Aunty, as we called her, Hattie, must have known what we were up to, but obviously put it down to the innocence and natural exuberance of youth. Come to think of it, a lot of the Doune girls used to chase me for a kiss and I don't think it was because of me. I just think it was just the daring nature and curiosity of growing up.

I got on well with Ryan, too. He was a well-behaved little boy with a Beatles haircut and big grin, who once saved my life in the *Ardoch Burn*, when I froze, when trying to cross it by stepping on the boulders. I was a ridiculous coward then and if I had said boo! to a mirror, I would have frightened myself to death! But Ryan just took my hand and guided me back to the bank, through the 8 inches of water. I thought he was very brave and I told Aunty Hattie so too.

'Ryan was very brave,' I enthused to her, while she served us our tea at the kitchen table, smiling.

'He saved my life!' I exclaimed with exaggerated gratitude.

'Oh, I did not,' Ryan had countered, with a big grin and a modest wave of his hand.

'Yes, you did,' I retorted as we both sat there happily munching away, swinging our legs under the table, impatient to go out and play.

My brother, Juan, (God knows why my mother gave him a Spanish name! Maybe there was something we children didn't know about) was also always round Aunty Hattie's and had a soft spot for her. Even as a child I felt that he had a special fondness for Aunty Hattie, as they were always talking together. Whenever I couldn't find him, he would be in the kitchen, talking to her quietly.

I don't know whether I was jealous of their more adult conversation, wanted the attention or just wanted to embarrass my brother for all the fast ones he had pulled on me, but, one day, as we were all standing in the kitchen, the Communications Centre of their wee council house, I suddenly blurted out very loudly:-

'Aunty Hattie, Juan has got a lot of bushy hair between his legs.' Obviously, I didn't mean on his bottom, although I don't know about his bottom. Not the sort of thing I would ever have wanted to see.

There was a deadly silence for a moment and then Aunty Hattie burst out laughing, as she scraped her spatula around the frying-pan, with her little chicken chuckle and my brother went even redder than he already was. I could feel the heat off his glare more than grandpa's fireplace or the sun itself. He was at that age, I suppose. But I was only relating a fact. What was wrong with that? Did I ruin his Cliff Richard image or what?

A few times I stayed there the night; and while Lucinda and my Aunty Hattie slept in her bed, Ryan and I slept in his. We giggled, read comics, pretended to be whispering about Lucinda, much to her chagrin and showed each other each other's jelly-beans. I can't, for the life of me, think why, as I didn't even know what to do with it, apart from going for a pee-pee. And neither did he. (Thank God!)

I remember Mr. Mallone coming into the house one day and announcing that we were all going for a drive, as he had just picked up his new car. He was in a very happy and positive mood and I remember clambering in with my two cousins and Aunty Hattie.

As a child I always liked to go for rides and play in things. Everything was an adventure for me. We waved to everyone we knew, as we passed by regally in his brand new, sparkling, pale green, halo-topped Morris Minor. I liked the car because it was shaped like a bug and we all laughed every time he blew the horn, grinning greatly with pride.

In later years I came to realise that it is not the value of the item you buy, that makes you proud or happy, but just by the fact that it was *yours*. He even took us on the motorway for a short spell, which was very thrilling because everyone kept overtaking everyone else. It was a bit like being on a racing track. As I loved cars, it was as good as a car show, trying to spot all the different ones. Over the hill, toot! toot! and far away. Yahoo!

***

Once, I was in for the evening, after a busy day playing in the streets and around Castle Hill. I was often bored if I did not have enough comics to read or pies to eat. So, one evening, after getting fed-up of watching my grandfather sitting in front of the roaring fire (yes, this was in the summer!) on his sagging, over-sized burnished-brown studded-leather armchair, as he watched the embers of the coals falling and spitting red and orange sparks upon the hearth, I hit upon the idea of writing an accolade to something.

I had taken to writing essays, compositions and poems in English classes back at school and I found that I enjoyed writing, creating something out of nothing and was getting quite good marks for it. It was certainly much better than mathematics, which I had given up on at around the age of five.

So I looked around the room, thinking of what to write about, when my mind wandered around to food and I knew then exactly what I was going to write about. Everyone has some good qualities and my mother's was that she was an excellent cook and gave me the incredible appreciation of it because hers was all home-made. I remember always laughing whenever she said she was going to make *Cock-a-leakie* soup because I always unfailingly imagined a dripping willy.

Anyway, she was old enough and her mother had certainly been born long ago enough (when ready-made food wasn't available and when women didn't go out to work) to stay at home and cook all day the recipes which had been handed down to her over the generations.

To cut a long story short, my mother would spend hours in the kitchen making home-made mince and tatties with little pastry domes, lentil, potato and vegetable soups where every mouthful was heaven at its most divine and a myriad of savoury pies and cakes, all with the best natural ingredients, of course.

I got some paper and a scrawny pencil from God knows where and, with the tip of my tongue sticking out like Charlie Brown in concentration, I began.

After a while, my mother poked her head into the sitting-room.

'Keeping Grandpa company, eh, Lukie?'

'Yes mom.'

My mother stood there wiping her hands on her apron, trying to land her eyes on my piece of paper.

'Whit are ye daein'?'

'Hey, mom! I'm writing a poem. A dedicated poem. It's called an ode.'

'O aye? And whit's it aboot? Is it aboot one o' ane bonnie lassies frae the village, son?'

I looked at her as if she were crazy.

'Girls?' I said, as if she were talking about some horrible disease, as I had no interest at all in them. 'Oh, no. I am writing a poem in honour of a Scotch pie.'

My mother stood there for a while with an expression on her face as if she had regretted having me.

'Oh…er…right ye are son…weell…goodnight. Dinnae ye git yersel' to bed too late then.'

'No, I won't mom. Goodnight.'

I wrote and re-wrote until my grandfather had fallen asleep by the fire and then I suddenly jumped up shouting 'Eureka!!' I'd heard that word somewhere.

My grandfather suddenly snorted up and asked in alarm:-

'Whit's wrang? Who's Eureka? Whit?'

But I just ignored him and ran to my mother's room and burst in breathless. She was reading a *Woman's Own* magazine with a *Titbits* on the bed next to her and munching on a *Mars* bar.

'Whit is it, Lukie? Ah'm readin'.'

'I've finished it mom. I have just written the whole thing! Isn't that great?'

'Och, aye, so it is,' she commented genuinely, because the one thing she did have was unconditional love for me, pride in me and was always promoting me. 'Tell ye what. Tomorrow night I'll get the family in and you caen read it oot lood to everyone.'

'Aw, mom!' I protested, because I was shy. But at the same time I did want to share it with everyone because I was proud of it and wanted to spread the good word, as they say in the church. Even bashful people like to show off and get attention sometimes.

I wanted mom to read it first, but she said she wanted a surprise, so I just agreed. It makes life easier for a child.

So I was both dreading and looking forward to the exciting event and it wasn't long before I heard the family traipsing up the stairs and chattering excitedly, as if they were coming to a cinema. By the family, I mean my Uncle Billy, my cousins Nigel and Bunion, my Aunty Macasa, and my cousin Rae. There is no way my Uncle Benny, aka Uncle Carbuncle, would have come, as, as I said, he didn't get on with my Uncle Billy, which was a shame, as they were both entertaining in their own ways.

Anyway, talking about entertainment, we were suddenly all gathered in the sitting-room and when I say all, I also mean my grandfather, mother, sister and brother as well. I was not happy about my brother being there, as he was always teasing me and after this he would have a field day. Still, my love of Scotch pies came first and foremost.

Everyone was standing around chatting and, for a moment, I thought they had forgotten what they had come for. But then my mother clapped her hands as if she fancied herself a *Flamenco* dancer.

'Hush the noo, a'body. The reason ye're a' here is to hear oor wee Lukie (good God!) recite his poem to ye a'. He's told me it's called an 'ode."

'What's an '*odd*' Da,' Bunion asked her faither…er I mean father, pulling hard on his trouser legs and looking up at him expectantly.

'Er...ask yer Aunty Anna,' he advised her, looking very unsure of himself. Most villagers were not into highfaluting poetry.

'It's no an 'odd,' hen,' my mother told her. 'It's an 'ode.' It's a sort of poem, a rhyme.'

'Oh,' Bunion replied, still not really understanding. She was wearing a very nice flowery dress and white socks to hide her spindly legs and knobbly knees.

At least all had made an effort to dress well for the grand occasion. I had hoped my mother was going to forget about it; as now that all these people were here I was beginning to have serious doubts and bouts of severe trepidation.

'Off ye go then, son,' my mother encouraged me, much to Nigel and my brother's smirks.

So I stood near the centre of the room near Grandpa with my scrap of paper and podgy, sweaty hand, looking aghast. But then it was their turn to look aghast when I read the title.

'My poem is entitled "*Ode to a Scotch Pie.*"'

'Whit?' my Uncle Billy exclaimed, before he could stop himself.

'What's that?' asked my cousin Nigel, while Bunion just stared at me with a dropped jaw before sniggering away to herself. 'Oooh, I like them,' she added.

'Shhh! Everyone. Go ahead, son,' my mother urged me with one of her maternal smiles. So I did.

'O Scotch pie. Shall I compare thee to sliced sausage?
Whatever the answer you give
I shall admire and remember
You for as long as I live...'

With that my brother let out a raucous laugh and shook his head.

'Shut up, Juan!' my mother berated him. 'Let him get on with it.'

So my brother just didn't say anything, while trying not to laugh. But with our cousin Nigel there, it was hard not to. But I ignored them as best as I could and carried on.

'...I'm going to eat very many of ye
So please forgive me.
I'd even hae ye in a stew
Because you are as tasty
As anything could ever be...'

At this point, quite a few people, including my dear grandpa, frowned at the reference to a stew. Maybe I'd just invented a new Scottish dish!

My cousin Nigel was beginning to get a bit restless now and that indicated trouble, for he was wont to start doing silly things.

I began to walk up and down the sitting-room as I read, to get the flow of things and Nigel began to walk behind me. But I had to ignore him and carry on with the reading.

'...I could eat one of you as easily as seven
And I know gluttony is a sin
But only then could I really be in Heaven
And nothing would end up in the bin...'

Everyone started commenting at this point, in the middle of laughing and it was becoming a comedy; so, like one of Shakespeare's jesters, I decided to fight fire with fire and turn my rendition into a farce. So as I read, I started to move around the room in exaggerated postures and Nigel had not needed much encouragement to monkey me. So we both started cavorting around the room.

'...O to feel your warm juices running down my chin
Makes me feel so grateful for the satisfaction you bring
O How I love your mince-meat and spices
Ye ken it is yer central hole that so entices...'

I started to wave my arms about now and wiggle my bottom at everyone with Nigel following suit and trying to out-do me.

'...Yer so valuable, they built double-crust pastry around ye
But all I want is for my mouth to surround ye
To sink my teeth slowly into your soft, warm mutton-meat
And revel in all your aromatic heat
Your flavour and consistency are aye hard to beat
And that's why I love you so very much
My very dearest Scotch pie.'

As I had read the last lines, things went a little quieter as the meaning of the words sank in and there was a bit of a stunned silence. But, of course, there is always someone who has to ruin it and, inevitably, my brother asked:-

'When are you getting married?!' to the accompaniment of great laughing, guffawing, jeering and booing. The monkeys were coming alive and my Uncle Billy couldn't help quipping in:-

'Aye. Ah ken jist see the twa o' ye walkin' up the aisle!'

I laughed along with them because it was a ludicrous poem really and because I had achieved my aim; even with all the teasing. I had got the attention I had subconsciously craved.

My Aunty Macasa came up to me with a loving smile and held both my warm and sweaty marshmallow hands in hers and said I should enter my poem into a contest. She thought it was very good and imaginative.

We all mingled about for a while like people at the tail-end of a cocktail party and then Uncle Billy announced that he had to take his wee rascals hame.

'As they say in Bulgaria…' he began, as he stood his children by the sitting-room door, '…cheerio!' How trite. Oh, how original.

So he shepherded his little flock out of the sitting-room and down the narrow corridor towards the glass front door. There was a lot of animated chatter between the three of them over which I could hear his bahoohie barking happily away, relieved that it could finally have a word.

Well, he had been very good at not upstaging me during my monologue, so I made allowances for him now.

Even going down the stairs to the street-door his bahoohie barked at sharp intervals as if forewarning the traffic below that he was coming and my mother, Juan, Diana and I got the giggles, especially as Aunty Macasa kept saying: 'Oh, my!' and 'Oh, dearie, dearie me,' and clutching her chest every time he did so.

She had, of course, known him for a long time, as he was her brother-in-law. But it never failed to shock her, as she was really quite prim and proper and it was just a pity that he had left us all in such bad odour.

Well, I think that was enough entertainment for one evening.

Give me a television any day.

For those of you who really appreciate poetry and the exertions of the underdog, here is the poem in its entirety; perhaps to read out to someone yourselves.

Ode to a Scotch Pie

O Scotch pie
Shall I compare thee to sliced sausage?
Whatever the answer you give
I shall admire and remember
You for as long as I live

I'm going to eat very many of ye
So please forgive me
I'd even hae ye in a stew
Because you are as tasty
As anything could ever be

I could eat one of you as easily as seven
And I know gluttony is a sin
But only then could I really be in Heaven
And nothing would end up in the bin

O to feel your warm juices running down my chin
Makes me feel so grateful for the satisfaction you bring
O How I love your mince-meat and spices
Ye ken it is yer central hole that so entices

Yer so valuable, they built double-crust pastry around ye
But all I want is for my mouth to surround ye
To sink my teeth slowly into your soft, warm mutton-meat
And revel in all your aromatic heat
Your flavour and consistency are aye hard to beat
And that's why I love you so very much
My very dearest Scotch pie.
-DRG-

***

The local children could usually hear the lorry coming up from the direction of Bridge of Allan and would rush up to meet it and run alongside it as if the circus had just come to town. Today it trundled passed the Catholic church, grinding its gears somewhat, as it was an old lorry, struggling up the hill. This was a '*Foden*' flat-bed coal truck that serviced Doune a few times a week and was heavily-laden with around 80 bags of coal on it. It was a mechanical ass.

It stopped outside The Highlands Hotel and the coalman, Brodie MacAvoy, jumped out swarthily. He was quite an impressive sight and, at first glance or impression, was not someone you would wish to get on the wrong side of. Just like Grandpa Hocks when he was a younger man in *The Black Watch*. That stern face was enough to send you running for the hills; and there were plenty of those around here.

But then his face would break into a massive smile and his bright blue eyes, in contrast to his coal-blackened face, would light up like the water of a swimming pool in brilliant sunshine. He had cauliflower ears, a big potato-like nose, chimpanzee head hair, hands like mallets and a stooped poise from all the years of lugging the very big and heavy coal bags on his back.

Whatever children were about when he came, would immediately surround him and start chattering away ten-to-the-dozen to him because he loved children and had time for them. Sometimes he would let them help him throw a load of coal down someone's coal bunker or climb onto the back of his lorry, sit in the driver's seat and pretend they were driving it or dance on its flatbed. People were not so health & safety conscious in those days and it was for a bit of a laugh. It killed Brodie MacAvoy's boredom, monotony and entertained the wee 'uns at the same time. No-body minded and even the adults were amused.

But today Brodie MacAvoy the coalman had a great idea. An idea he had got from watching a programme on television. As the children stood around him, all talking at once and vying for his attention, he held a lump of coal in his hand teasingly.

'Now, would any of youse children like to pretend yer on the stage? That youse are all part of a play?' he asked nonchalantly, knowing full-well what their answer would be.

To a shrill of delight and grabbing hands, with all the children shrieking 'aye!' all at once, he got down on his haunches and started to pass the lump of coal over a little girl's face. All the children laughed and watched, enraptured, until the wee lassie's face was completely black.

'Now yer in a stage musical and ye can sing away, hen!' Brodie MacAvoy the coalman told her. So the little girl, whom my cousin Nigel knew quite well, started singing and dancing around the coalman and in front of the shops, to the great amusement and delight of the few adults who were about on the street at that time of day.

Soon Brodie MacAvoy the coalman was daubing every child's face and they were all running about Main Street shouting and screaming and mock-fighting and sticking their faces in shop doorways to scare everyone inside. A few adults were not really that amused, but most thought it was really funny and sweet.

Don MacFairlane was in stitches and it gave him an idea for future amusements. It certainly brought the village to life and out of its slumber for a wee while and it momentarily shook off its reputation for being dead-end Doune. While all this was going on, Brodie MacAvoy was still carrying out his deliveries and the job was still being done.

The children also liked him because he had the time to chat to them and ask them what their favourite subjects were at school, etc and he would tell them outlandish stories of adventure. He even told them that his name, Brodie, literally meant *'from a place in Moray'* and that he was a member of the famed and wealthy regional family and that he had been disinherited because he wanted to be a coalman, which the rest of the family looked down upon. Of course, half of the children believed this whopper and so, too did Brodie himself, as we all have our dreams.

Anyway, one day Brodie MacAvoy the coalman came no more. The adults were told that he had jumped down from his lorry and been run over by a car whose driver had suffered a fatal blood clot at the wheel and had thus killed two birds with one stone. Brodie MacAvoy had gone up in a puff of soot. Such a stupid, unnecessary accident of being in the wrong place at the wrong time and the new coalman who came to service Doune was gruff and uninterested in the children or anyone else, and constantly shooed them all away, to the point where the children would just stop and stare after the lorry when it went by with uncertainty and fear, like the citizens of a town being invaded by a foreign army.

Still, they say that things never last forever.

Is that no right, son?

***

'Lukie! Hurry up fer goodness sake. Ye'll make us late!'

My mother was shouting for me again, which was nothing new. But it wasn't that I was ignoring her or being obstinate. It was simply that I was afraid.

Afeart? Afeart of whit?

Today we were going to visit my mother's Aunty Anna, her namesake, who lived near Blairlogie, just beyond Bridge of Allan and a few days ago I heard my mother telling a neighbour about how we were going to visit her and of how she had a glass eye, which she would sometimes take out and show visitors.

The thought of that eye coming out of that black or red hole in her head made me feel very queasy indeed as I was a timid, delicate boy at heart and that sort of thing made me want to hide under a bed or scream. I imagined her brain oozing out of her eye socket.

But I was also an obedient boy and so when my mother called shrilly for me and when I remembered that we were going to have a big tea at her house, I quickly tore myself away from my fearsome over-imagination.

On the journey to her house I tried not to think of her wayward eye; so wayward it came right out of her head.

Yet now that my mother was suddenly ringing her doorbell and my sister was standing expectantly beside her, my fear started to well up again and I would have run and scampered had the door not opened then.

There were the usual greetings of *'O, hullo,' 'How are ye hen,'* and *'Oh my and who's this fine young laddie?'* as I tried to hide my gargantuan body behind my mother's. Had I done physics at school I would have known that was not possible.

So I just shook hands with the alarming old lady and asked her 'How do you do?' politely, as I looked at her face warily. I must admit that, had I not heard my mother mentioning that her aunty had a glass eye, which she used to throw about as a party piece, and shout: *'Dinnae step on ma eye! Dinnae step on ma eye!'* then I wouldn't have known she had one. She looked quite normal; unless her good eye decided to suddenly look left, right, up or down, or even spin.

Still not trusting her fully, I was nevertheless quite happy to be sitting in a chair out of the way while the three of them chatted away about everything under the sun, including the weather and handbags.

Having the privacy to look around the room, I noticed a big, long table over which a light cover hid a load of bumpy things underneath and I guessed they must be for our tea. I wondered with great curiosity what was under there and was daydreaming about food, when my mother's Aunty Anna suddenly turned round to me.

'Ach, where are my manners? We've bin ignoring ye, ma wee lamb!' My wee lamb? I wasn't a baby.

'Ye must be a bit boored there with oor conversation and nothing tae play wi'. Now, ye jist come alang wi' me son.'

So I followed her to a door at the bottom of the stairs, where she pulled out an old box with a loose, torn lid on it.

'I keep these toys here for when ma grandchildren come tae visit. Ye can play wi' em while yer here, laddie.'

'Oh, great! Thanks!' I exclaimed gratefully. Anything not to have to keep looking at her glass eye, which, of course, even though I could not help looking at, as curiosity killed the cat, but while the cat still looked nevertheless.

Inside the box were a myriad of Corgi toys and toy soldiers and I busied myself playing with them carefully, as my father had always taught me to respect other people's possessions. I think the hens were quite grateful too, that they could talk in peace without my disturbing them. Great symbiosis, actually.

As I was voom-vooming and zoom-zooming the toy cars along the carpet, a cat suddenly loomed up at me and tried to grab one of the cars with its fat paw.

'Och, dinnae worry, Lukie. That's just Rabbie. Dae ye like cats, Lukie?'

I just said I didn't mind and went back to playing with the toys.

After a while, my mother's aunty got up and went to get all the tea things ready and my sister went politely with her to give her a hand, talking about all the latest fashions and hairdos. My sister Diana had a habit of doing that, even if no-one was listening. Well, I never listened anyway.

As my mother's aunt took off the table covering, my mother chatted away to her while puffing away on her *Capstan Full Strength* and turning the air blue with smoke (and not her swearing, for once).

I must admit my eyes did widen when I saw the fayre in front of me. There were many lovely sandwiches and cakes and a few spreads on little plates. As I continued playing, I kept glancing up at the food longingly, praying that the kettle would hurry up and boil, when I noticed Rabbie jumping up onto the table and gingerly walking stealthily around the plates, while eyeing everything with great interest. I froze and said to myself: *please, cat, don't eat any of my food*!

But before anyone could have done anything, if they had even wanted to, Rabbie stuck its paw right into one of the spreads and onto one of the sandwiches before suddenly meowing in alarm or disgust and hopping off the table again, leaving a trail of gunge behind her. It sat on the carpet licking its food-infested paw.

'Hey, mom…!' I started to say in protest, but then stopped politely as my sister and the old Aunty Anna walked in carrying the teapot, milk and sugar.

But at the end of the day, we all had a nice tea and I laughed quietly to myself with a gleeful smirk as my sister had some of the delicious spread the cat had pawed in. I'm sure I saw a hair sticking out of it as she laid the gunk on her bread. I could not wait to tell her when we got home and see the look on her face! My sister was always going 'Yuk!' and 'Ugh!' at anything on the planet. I just count myself lucky that it wasn't my mother's Aunty Anna's false eye which rolled back and forth over all the fine fayre. If it had rolled towards me, I would have kicked it away in panic; probably straight back into her eye socket.

Chapter Five

Snippets

There was a soldier
A Scottish soldier
Who wandered far away
And soldiered far away
There was none bolder
With good broad shoulder
He fought in many a fray
And fought and won
-Andy Stewart-

...When I was a bouncing baby boy, around 1955/56, my sister, Diana, was pushing me in one of those oversized, over-heavy *Silver Cross* prams around the braes and burns of Doune castle.

At one point there was quite a steep downward brae and Diana couldn't manage to keep hold of the gravitational pull on her skinny arms and the increased weight of the perambulator tore lose from her grasp. Not only that...the pram was flying down towards the *Ardoch Burn* and my sister panicked, thinking I would drown.

She had terrible visions of facing my mother and so chased the pram with a warrior's vigour; along with all the other screaming children, some thinking it was a game. Luckily, there was a boulder which arrested the pram, though a bit too enthusiastically, as I was catapulted out in a gliding arc and came back down to earth with a big bump and bounce. But I was already swathed in white woollen clothing and a big shawl anyway and they helped to cushion the blow, aided by my soft baby body.

All the children stood agape, scunnered, with their mouths wide open like black-hole tunnels and all were exclaiming (apart from those who were collapsing with squeaky laughter) 'Whit?' 'Oh, MY!' 'Och, the puir wee bairn, the puir wee lamb' and 'yer gaunny git intae awfy bither from yer mammy, Diana!'

My sister Diana thought that perhaps she would be able to avoid telling my mother about my tumble. But all the other children saw it happen and were bound to tell my mother all about it; especially as they could not help but bump into her in such a small village. Thank God that boulder was there or else I could have gone straight into the river. My sister was very conscientious, so could not but help telling my mother about her lapse of care. I always thought the bump on my head affected me mentally…

*

...Sometime in 1966, before England won the World Cup, I was surrounding Opie Cameron with a group of other local children, some of whom were my cousins. We were attracted to Opie Cameron because he had the same mental age as we did, or at least appeared to, and because he told us the most fantastical tales which we believed, or, at least, half-believed; whilst the adults walking by would just look on in disapproval or unkindly twirl their fingers around by the side of their heads with a sneer and utter: '*Looney*!' The problem with the adults was that they didn't have the patience to listen to his ramblings and could be nasty, but I liked Opie Cameron, apart from his steely-grey snake eyes, because he was amusing and I felt sorry for him. It was not his fault he was like that. His parents must have had guilty consciences.

Opie Cameron was being very amusing now as we all watched in awe as he attempted to shove a whole Scotch pie into his mouth after just having told us that his ancestors were Boa Constrictors! Nobody saw the connection there. He was daft enough to try to keep on talking while he was attempting this delicate procedure; but all he made were gagging sounds. If serpents spoke, they would have sounded just like him.

We pretended to be highly interested in his *World Record* attempt; but we were just laughing and nudging each other in the hope that he would choke. And choke he did!

With both hands trying to shove this fabled pie up his head, it quickly reached a terminal point and refused to go any further. Instead, it reversed and half of it shot out of his mouth and spattered onto the pavement; a dark brown, grey and beige mangled mess of meat and pastry sludge. Oh, what a laugh! We had tears in our eyes and so did Opie. But his was from the strain of the strain. I'm amazed he didn't get locked jaw.

My cousin Nigel said: 'Aye, that wis a stoater right enough, Opie. But mebbe ye should cram it in upright next time!' And he laughed himself silly at his own sense of infantile humour.

'Jings,' added a wee three-year-old, who had been trailing along with us. I think his name was Callum, but I had no idea who he wis; I mean, *was*.

'Ach, well, ye got maist o' it in,' consoled one of the girls amongst us, who was tall with long auburn hair, who lived in *Hall Lane* and who was very pretty and on whom I had a crush. But that was only a passing phase, a temporary titillation, as my real passion was for food and I was very faithful to it.

'That wis braw,' squealed a little curly-haired blonde girl, who looked like the wee girl from *The Broons*, and who started hiccuping. We all laughed all the more.

'Och...I might try it with a Stovie on the morrow,' Opie conceded, as he wiped his teary eyes with an old grey hankie, put it back into his checked jacket (God knows where his 'mither' had got that from), cocked a big leg up at right angles, and shot off down the road like a cavorting gazelle. People deal with embarrassment in so may different ways.

Opie Cameron never just walked away. He always suddenly shot off like a sane man who had just remembered an emergency; or like someone chasing a thief; or like someone with the trots or like someone running for the Callander bus as it was leaving from the Callander bus stop.

Yes, there wasn't much to do in Doune, so we had to rely on the local talent...

*

...I used to love going to play in Moray park because there would always be someone there I knew and although

I was quite shy, I was interested in meeting new kids, especially girls, as I didn't know much about them.

They were a strange, mysterious breed to me and this is all because I had always gone to a boy's school. I know that this was done so that there would be no '*distractions*,' but it just served to alienate us from the girls, as if they had two heads and were from a different planet. Sometimes they certainly *acted* as if they were from a different planet.

You would often see a lot of little girls pushing prams around Moray park with either dolls or real babies in them; with a trail of other little children following them like sheep; some looking as they had not long been out of prams themselves and I loved to watch the little girls with their motherly instincts.

My female cousin, Bunion, my cousin Nigel's wee sister, once introduced me to a pram-pushing little girl, who could barely see over the handle and said that she was the baby's aunty! So there you go, nothing else to do in a small village.

I remember this small girl was a little hostile towards me at first, until she saw what impeccable manners I had and how sincere I was as a child and just how generous I was by buying her a handful of *Cadbury's* chocolates. Then she started to mother me too! Please! One mother is enough in any one lifetime.

By the end of the day she wanted to kiss me among the haystacks and I just kept putting her off by saying 'wait a minute…wait a minute,' in the hope that she would forget all about it. But she still kept chasing me.

But in the years to come I wished that I had taken her in my arms and kissed her on the lips because I really did like girls (from a safe distance) and was curious about them and was a lonely little boy because my mother had neglected me so through her *illness*.

Luckily, she gave up in the end and thank God she wasn't any older or she would have wanted a baby of her own to boot. Somehow I had ended up in her bedroom. Perhaps I went there to see if she had any toys. Anyway, I was still worrying about what her intentions were when she had suddenly blurted out: 'My brother's coming! You'd better get out of here' and I flew down the stairs and out of her house just like a jet plane, glad to be away from her and her brother. It could have been a choice of a kiss *on* the mouth from her or a smack *in* the mouth from him.

We used to do a lot in Moray park. We used to play putting; we used to play '*hide and seek*'; we used to chase each other around all over the place; we would share sweeties and chocolates; we used to tell each other fantastical stories; (I wonder where I got that from?); we used to play on the swings and carousel roundabout and sometimes even annoy the adults, just for fun. I remember one little boy went and sat on a car bonnet just across the road from Moray park and a man opened his sitting-room window in his string vest and shouted out: '*Get aff ma motor*!' As far as I remember, they even had a little tennis court there...

*

...My sister, Diana, had a raunchy Scottish boyfriend, with the musical name of Alec MacCanish, who looked like one of the characters out of '*Rebel without a Cause*,' but who had a really nice personality. Well, he was nice to me, anyway and he had this massive side wave of hair that went right across his head, all shiny and oily, spanning it like the Forth bridge; almost looking like an ebony table-top. I mean, you could go surfing on it. A surfboard could have been jutting out of his hair and it would have looked quite at home. It was such a big wave; every surfer's dream.

You would be quite right to imagine that he had a flick-knife in his pocket, but he didn't. It was actually my brother who had the flick-knife and my mamma Anna was always borrowing it to peel the potatoes because it had a nice, sharp blade! Well, no street cred there then.

What? Did she not think of asking my brother what he was doing with a flick-knife? Luckily my brother Juan (tan-a-mera, as I used to call him, when I wanted to get my revenge for one of the many unkind things he used to do to me) was not at all violent. He just loved the sound of it clicking and swishing open. It was cool, man, cool; really cool.

I thought my sister's boyfriend was also really cool, as he was always strutting around in a white tee-shirt, jeans, a black leather motorbike jacket, which was smothered in shiny zips all over it, and Beatle boots. Sometimes he even wore the full regalia of complementing leather motorcycle trousers and motorcycle boots with more zips and he looked the coolest. Really the coolest. He was cool because mainstream society disapproved of his maverick style and demeanour.

I remember once, we were driving down the little alleyway leading out of Castle Hill to Main Street, on the rare occasions he drove a car, when the door of the Austin A35 suddenly sprang open and, as I started to fall out, he grabbed me, not by the scruff of the neck, but by the fat of my neck and I realised afterwards that it was sometimes beneficial being 'generous in proportion.'

But, still, I wanted to be like him when I grew *up*, as opposed to growing *sideways*; as I was now. I wanted to be cool too.

He had a ready cheeky grin, was very friendly with my brother and my sister and was kind to me, just like Brody MacAvoy and my sister was totally mesmerised by him. She saw him as being surrounded by hearts, stars and fireworks and they were all going off all over the place in her love-dream rose-tinted mushy-slushy world.

She went all ga-ga and gooey over him like a dribbling imbecile and I will never understand silly girls. Her behaviour changed around him as if she had been hypnotised or zapped by an alien laser gun. He often used to come up and see us in my grandfather's house above the Co-op. Diana was only sixteen when he seduced her and from then on she was totally smitten by him. As if she had sat on a live wire. So she spent most of her time around his house, gawping.

He had a very stylish and throaty 1961 BSA A10 motorbike, which looked really cool, with low handlebars. Alec's mother was always fed-up and going on at him about leaving his motorcycle engine lying on the driveway in bits or on the kitchen table when he took it off the bike to strip it, service or repair it; with oil dripping everywhere. But I thought that was quite funny. (*What's fer tea, hen? Fancy a casket on toast?*)

My sister Diana went everywhere with him on the back of that bike. Without helmets. You could often hear them roaring around the inner and outer perimeters of the village and far away over a brae.

At times they were even chased by the police through hedge-high country lanes. But it was only because our *'Rebel without a Cause'* was speeding and had not committed any crime per se. They always managed to outrun the police in their underpowered Ford Anglias (at least that's what they told me when I pumped them for all the information and details) and it brought a thrill to their lives. My sister said that being a bit naughty was delicious. Well, I don't think my father would have thought so.

When you are young, you just think of the thrills and the immediate gratification and not the consequences of what could be. They were tasting life at its rawest and they wanted to taste it strong. Like the strongest cup of Scottish tea with a cow's hoof in it. Diana also told me that they would go out, get roaring drunk, as roaring as the motorbike and then she would come back home and eat toothpaste. *Whit? Toothpaste*? What is wrong with girls? How can toothpaste compare to a nice Scotch pie or some sliced sausage?

Whit? Some girls are just weird.......Whit?...

*

...I wanted to see how much *Highland Toffee* I could fit in my mouth when I was around ten years old, so I charmed my mother into giving me some pocket money and I immediately went to Dan MacFairlane's sweetie shop and bought ten bars of it. He thought I was buying all those bars to share with my friends. But I just didn't say anything. I then just stole back home and went into the toilet, telling my mother that I had a bad tummy and she was quite happy to leave me alone, as she didn't want to get in the way of a little boy and his smells.

So I sat on the toilet, watching a daddy long-legs in the bath, breaking bits off and chewing away like a mad, BSE-infested cow. I must admit it was hard work and I had to take frequent rests as my jaw began to ache as much as a gossipy old wifey hiding behind her net curtains. I felt like one of those toy skulls you buy with wind-up clattering teeth.

I shoved more and more in, as the toffee became more malleable and the amount in my mouth grew and grew with a load of spew. It started to be fun and I tittered to myself with silly school-boy glee as I saw the humour in it. I started to drool and wiped it all away with toilet paper. I was determined to break a world record.

As I was concentrating on my grand experiment, there was a sudden knock on the door.

'Whit are ye daein' in there, Lukie? How lang are ye gonnae be exactly?' my mother asked with concern and impatience. 'Other people hae tae use the loo the noo.'

The loo the noo?

'Mmmppppfff!' I could only mumble.

'Ach, weel, as lang as yer no in pain,' my grandfather added. I had heard his footsteps padding up the hallway and stopping outside the door. I managed to get out 'I'm coming' in a very garbled way, with the big ball of toffee in my mouth, now about the size of a generous horse-dropping; which was ramming my tongue down onto the base of my inner mouth.

I had room for just a little bit more toffee and, after slow washing-machine movements of my mouth, like a camel I had seen on a television documentary, tried my best to make as much room as possible for more sweet and gooey sludge. I realised that it had now jammed my mouth completely open with a small hole around my lips as I attempted to keep all the toffee and juices in and breathe at the same time.

I had no option but to tilt my head up to the ceiling. I had to breathe through my nose and must have looked like a beaver. My round mouth looked like a bum-hole with dysentery.

I put the very last bit in that could possibly, at a great strain and stretch and creak, fit and chewed very slowly and gingerly, before suddenly grinding to a halt. My jaw couldn't open any more. It was at full lock. My mouth was completely crammed and jammed; the toffee had embedded and glued itself deeply onto my teeth, all my teeth, my gums, along with the roof of my mouth and had spread out along the floor of my mouth to boot; just like slow-moving lava solidifying as it cooled down.

With a big brown glistening ball in my mouth, my cheeks pushed out as far as they would stretch and my eyes rolling around in my head, wondering what I could do, I realised, with a cold sweat, that my mouth was stuck fast and I couldn't even gulp to swallow.

And, of course, I panicked and began to cry, leak, drip, drool and sweat.

And I couldn't breathe. I imagined drowning in Highland Toffee. What a way to go.

So I jumped off the toilet, grunting like a bull with a thorn in its side and rushed out the door like a crazed caveman, being only able to speak in grunts.

My mother screamed mildly when she saw my sweaty red face and grotesquely swollen mandible, bulging eyes and desperate monkey noises; while drooling insanely like a man possessed or a rabid dog. Of course I had been trying to talk normally, but it didn't come out that way.

I grabbed hold of her pinny and started rocking her backwards and forwards in a desperate attempt to get her attention and kept pointing at my mouth.

'LUKIE!!! Whit on earth is up wi' ye? Whit's wrang wi' ye? And whit's that in yer mooth? Spit it oot this instant!' I shook my head.

My grandfather had silently sidled himself up behind my mother and, after a moment of astonishment (amazing he was astonished at anything after having gone through two world wars) he had a big grin on his face and started sniggering when he guessed it was not serious. Still wasn't sure what it was, though.

My mother *tsked* with a Scottish accent and poked her finger into what little there was of my vacant mouth, but it just slid everywhere on the juices and there was not enough room to get two fingers in to try and pull the offending article out. My grandfather disappeared and came back with the poker from the fire but then turned around again when he saw the alarm on my face. It was stuck fast and would have been as hard to get out of my mouth as a big lump of hard wax out of someone's ear.

As the last of the juices ran out of my mouth and my mouth dried up, the toffee started to harden like cement and it felt heavier in my mouth. It was like a cue ball, only bigger. I breathed heavily through my nose and looked askance at my mother with a pleading face; a contrite face. A stupid face. I am a so-sorry-face.

'Oh, Lukie! Whit *are* ye like?' It was now becoming one of her familiar phrases. She had seen the wrappers in the toilet and what looked like very watery diarrhea in pools on the floor and toilet seat. She just could not stop shaking her head.

'Whit got intae thon heid o' yours?'

'Mmmpppfff..fff.'

'Och, I'll hae tae tak ye te Doctor Lomax,' she said, sighing, 'C'mon the noo.'

And with that she took my podgy sweaty hand and dragged me down the stairs to Muir Crescent where he had his surgery. I walked along beside her, bent over double like an old man with a bad back because I was afraid of swallowing the ball (though tasty) and because I didn't want the villagers to see me. In hindsight, I don't think I could have made myself look any more conspicuous.

The great thing about a village was that there was no queue to see the doctor and I was ushered straight in, breathing stentoriously, to the disapproving and frowning countenance of the receptionist. She clutched her chest as if she were having a heart attack when I dribbled all over her counter. My nose was shoved so far up my face that I looked like a curious rat smelling for opportunities in a sewer.

Doctor Lomax was a very nice man. Your typical country doctor, who was relaxed through not being under city pressure and he just smiled calmly when he looked into my mouth.

'Well, this is a new wan to me, I must say! So ye like yer sweeties, wee man?'

'Mmmmppff!' I could only reply.

'Weel, dinnae ye worry, ah'll soon hae thon gobby ball oot o' yer mooth sooner than ye can say *Stirling Albion*.'?!

And Doctor Lomax was as good as his word. He worked away with his little implements by cutting little bits of toffee off the ball and pulling other bits out with a small pair of tongs until the last bit of the carcass rolled out and straight into his bin. I suppose it was too much to expect to ask for it back.

'There ye are, son. All out the noo. Ye'r done.' He looked at my exasperated mother with a look of happy amusement on his face.

'Boys will be boys!' he offered philosophically.

'Not my boy willnae,' spouted my mother, shoving me out the door.

'Thanks very much doctor. Ah'm sae sorry to hae bithered ye.'

'Ach, nae bother Mrs. Garland. That's whit ah'm here fer.'

I had managed to shove eight and a bit bars into my mouth and was quite proud of that; although I decided to give up on that silly idea for now...

*

...During one of the sixties summers, I remember a lot of quarry lorries driving in and out of Doune and trundling up and down Doune Main Street, with their engines roaring under the strain of weight. Children are always fascinated by big mechanical machines and no less so was I. I saw a lot of children getting rides, like at a fun-fair and I wanted a ride too.

So it wasn't long before I found myself climbing up the metal mountain and being dwarfed by the massive interior of the cab and sat there like a small pea sitting on a fat potato and was thrilled by the way it sounded, with its roaring engine and by the way it vibrated so alarmingly. So much so that I was shaken about like a nut on a vibrating plate, or a fault line. It made me laugh.

Sometimes the drivers would talk to me in their strong brogues, explaining what they were doing, or sometimes they would just concentrate on driving; but they were always kind. I would always watch, fascinated, as the driver slammed his foot down on the clutch, pumped it and fought with the gear-lever.

Getting to the destination was even more fun, as he tipped the whole back of the lorry up, to the great sound of an earthquake rush. When I think back now, I was very lucky because, though Doune was a very safe place in those days of innocence and wonder, a lot of these drivers were outsiders and I could so easily have been abducted, assaulted and killed. You may laugh, but it was the era of Ian Brady and Mira Hindley and I could have been found buried somewhere (or not) on the Scottish moors. My father would never have forgiven my mother...and he would have killed *me*...

*

...One day during the week, my mother, sister, brother and I went to Stirling on a shopping expedition as we had all been invited to the wedding of one of her friend's nieces and my mother bought me a new suit and light-blue clip-on tie, because she always wanted to show me off to her friends.

She had once made me wear a whole kilt outfit in London, which had made me cringe into a dried grape because everyone laughed at me, called across the street and jeered.

'Jist ignore them, son,' my mother had advised. But that had been easier said than done. 'They're jist aye jealous when they see a true Scot,' she added proudly.

I liked riding the bus to Stirling because we always passed *Wallace's Monument* and I could fantasise about sword-fighting. I hated going shopping with my mother or sister because they went to boring women's shops.

But, to cheer me up, we all went to *'The Gateway'* restaurant for lunch. It was around the corner from the train station, opposite *Marks and Spencer's* and, as far as I remember, it was on the first floor. It wasn't a fancy place, but I remember having Dover sole with boiled potatoes and lashings of salad cream, which I thought was the best thing since sliced bread; especially *Mother's Pride* sliced bread. I liked the tanginess of it and could have eaten it until I felt sick, which was not such an infrequent event in my life.

Anyway, come the day of the wedding I was finely dressed with my new suit, tie, highly-polished shoes and steam-rollered, greasy Brylcreemed hair plastered down all over my head, like an oil-slick in the middle of the Atlantic ocean, as was my father's habit and demand for respectability.

We sat in the Catholic church awaiting the bride, with the priest beaming away as if he had done something exceptional and I got bored. Maybe he had just farted.

As the wedding ceremony droned on, I began to fidget and had nothing to play with, so I took off my clip-on tie and absent-mindedly started to play with the spring-loaded mechanism. My mother had not noticed my lack of decorum, as she was so cryingly rapt in the nuptials and going *'Ora-wora'* under her breath and holding her chest in emotive admiration of the bride. Or perhaps she had heartburn from all that black sausage she gorged on.

As the priest droned on, like a far-away plane in his voluminous alb, feeling very important indeed and hoping he was going to be invited to the wedding reception so as to receive his manna from heaven, I distractedly and thoughtlessly clipped the tie onto my lower lip, jerked violently, as if I had sat on a live wire and shunted my mother across the pew half into her neighbour and screamed *'ArrrggghhH!'* very loudly as the clip bit into my soft flesh.

Quite a few people were startled and everybody turned around during the temporarily-halted service to see what on earth was going on. Some with a look of disgust and others with expressions of care and concern. Or amusement.

Now that I had their attention (the last thing I wanted, of course) I panicked with this alien thing hanging off my face and ran around the inside of the church, trying to prise it off with my chubby, podgy, butter-soft, nail-bitten fingers. People started to laugh, whatever their ages and I noticed that my sister was in floods of laughter tears. The laughter resounding in this amazingly-acoustic church was really quite impressive and, as I contagiously tried to laugh with them, I screamed again in pain as the clip dug deeper into my stretching inner-mouth flesh.

A few adults started to chase me. Not to chastise me, as I had thought, but to try and help me and a teenage girl, one of the blue-clad bridesmaids, finally cornered me and, whipping out a long steel spike-pointed comb, slid it between the clip and my inner lower lip and prised it off like a burglar with a crow-bar.

I was so relieved, that I started laughing uncontrollably along with everyone else. There were literally howls of laughter, brought on, no doubt, by ceremonial nerves. People always laugh loudest and best when they know they shouldn't.

I looked across at my mother and noticed that she was sadly looking down at the hem of her skirt. Sometimes she seemed to go into herself. I did not know whether it was because of me embarrassing her in front of everyone she knew in her home village or whether it was because of her *illness*. Maybe she was the one who felt the true outsider in her own den; in her own territory. The pariah. That I will never know. But your spirit can sense these things.

Anyway, I managed to upstage the bride (not that I looked as pretty as her, apart from pretty ridiculous, especially if I had been wearing her wedding dress!) in the most ludicrous way, but she didn't mind at all. In fact, she didn't mind at all to the point where she came up to me to check that I was alright and to say that I had really broken the ice with such stiff formality and made her day.

I was quite overcome with that, even if I didn't quite understand what she was going on about. But, of course, in later years I often thought of her with gratitude for not having barked at me. I often thought in the future of how her life had gone.

During the reception, held in a big marquee, it was all anyone talked about and people kept coming up to me and patting me on the head, or sticking their tongues down to imitate the errant tie. Some people even gave me some money. O happy days…

*

...As a generous person, I always spread myself around Doune like a pat of butter, going to my various cousins' houses on different days. I used to like playing with my cousin Rae, as girls held a mysterious and curious fascination for me. They were creatures that always appeared to hide something. Like the monsters on TV. You didn't want to see them, but you still wanted to look.

I knew that my cousin Rae liked me. She just pretended not to by being aloof. Maybe she was just the type who expected boys only to chase her if she played hard-to-get; and I am not talking about hard-to-get as a girlfriend, but just hard-to-get as a friend.

Anyway, one day I remember I went to fetch her out to play and I had a Corgi toy pipe-carrying articulated low-loader lorry. It was beige with about eight black plastic pipes on its rear end. I don't know what I was thinking of, but, for some reason, I also had some cigarettes and matches on me for the thrill of being naughty.

In those days cigarettes were not considered so harmful for your health, so it was quite easy to get a shop to sell you a couple of the coffin nails, especially me. But, being a good boy I didn't buy any...I took two from my mother's packet. Big mistake.

After playing on a stile for a while, seeing who could climb up it and jump off it the quickest (girls are very agile, aren't they?) Rae and I went into a field a bit of a way behind her house and we sat down hidden from view. It was so thrilling to be naughty. I showed her my lorry, in which she showed little interest; but she did show interest in something deep in the field.

'What are you looking at?' I asked, always curious as a child.

'The Tattyboggler.'

'Tattyboggler? I don't see anything,' I said, looking down the field expecting to see…I don't know…a tinker or a rabbit or a potato seller.

'The scarecrow,' she told me, rolling her eyes up to the sky.

'Oh, is that what it's called? I never knew that. It sounds more like a potato burger.'

'Lukie! Yer aye thinking' o' food. Stoppit stupit!'

A bit miffed at being chastised by someone I really liked deep down, I pulled out the matches and the cigarettes and dared her to take a puff. Well, she was a very competitive person and would never back down on a challenge, nor show any weakness whatsoever.

To make it more fun (as I had seen many adults on TV smoking through cigarette holders) I jammed our cigarettes on to two plastic pipes that were on my toy lorry and shoved one in her mouth and one in mine and we pretended to be aristocratic, with exaggerated movements. We giggled. I lit hers and mine and then took a deep breath; as I had seen all the adults do. The first sensation was shock, followed by a knife-blade slicing down my throat, followed by uncontrollable, spluttered coughing, followed by a red face, followed by tears and not being able to breathe or see anything for a while. The sky above me spun in alarm.

'Aye…that'll dae it,' she commented, as she lay back on the grass, propped up by her elbows, studying me with the disdain of a lady with a tramp, a boss with a skivvy and a head waiter confronting a customer with doggy do-do's on his shoes. She hadn't even taken a drag of her cigarette. That was obvious from her demeanour. She had just waited for me with glee.

'Best not to get *Capstan Full Strength* the next time ye nick ony fags.'

She made up for it later, though, as she lay in the grass and kissed me on the lips for a long time, while pretending not to be interested and all the while threatening to tell our parents. Obviously, we were too young at around nine years old, for French kissing, but the electrical thrill I felt on her velvety lips soon resuscitated me.

You know, even children are always seeking love. We lay there until we heard her mother, my aunty, calling us in for tea from far away and we scrambled up the hill as the twilight drew in.

Years later she died suddenly in her thirties of a blood clot. Ah, well, it's *a sair fecht*, as they say up in Scotland. You just never know in life, do you? Poor Rae. God bless her puir wee soul. So sad, so sudden…

*

…I always knew right from wrong because my father had drummed it into us at an early age, telling us once, for example, that if we ever stole anything, the police would come and lock us away in a high tower, never to be seen again.

So, one day, with this in the back of my mind, but probably from boredom and lack of excitement and then, yes, greed does come into it; when my mother was in one of her drunken stupors, I brazenly stole a £5.00 note from her purse, which, in those days, was a lot of money.

Anyway, I ran to the Post Office, which is near the Callander bus stop (whit, again?) and gawped at the Corgi toys he had on display in a cabinet higher than my head. The post master knew me and that my family were well-off and so did not think it strange that I had that amount of money on me. He must have thought all his Christmases had come at once, because I stood in front of the cabinet and pointed incessantly.

'I'll have that one...and that one...and that one...and that one...and that one... and that one...and oh, I'll have that one as well.' And so on to a final tally of around twelve toy cars. I was so excited with my bumper purchase that I grabbed the lot and rushed out the door. I knew I could not go home with this illicit loot and was on the way to Aunty Hattie's house up *Castle Hill* when the postmaster ran up behind me.

'Ye forgot yer change!' he blurted out, panting and puffing, red-faced from the exertion. As my hands were full, he shoved a few notes and coins in my pocket.

'Thank you,' I had called back, as I kept on walking.

'Yer welcome. Say hello to ye mammy fer me.'

'Och, aye, ah will,' I assured him, trying to blend in with the scenery. Why did everyone want me to say hello to my mother for them? Could they not do it themselves?

When I got to my Aunty Hattie's house, I showed her my new toys and went to play with them guiltily in the sitting-room. Aunty Hattie didn't seem to say much. Soon after, my brother walked in and asked me where I had got them from. I think I made up a story at first and then, because I am basically honest and conscientious, I confessed.

I cannot remember if I left those toy cars hidden behind the settee or if my brother ever told my mother; but I know that they never were returned.

I felt especially guilty, contrite, doomed and remorseful not because I had stolen from my mother, but because I had betrayed my dear father's trust.

Chapter Six

I've just come down from the Isle of Skye
I'm not very big and I'm awful shy
And the lassies shout when I go by
'Donald, where's yer troosers?'
-Andy Stewart-

Due to some rare warm and sunny weather, my Uncle Billy sent a message with one of the village lads who worked with him on building sites, to Grandpa Hock's *hoose* to tell me that my cousins were going for a swim in the river Teith and for me to come along and join them in the fun holiday atmosphere. What? Swim? In the river Teith? I might as well have sat in the freezer of a fridge in my birthday suit! Still, being a child always thirsty for adventure, I did not hesitate for a second. Instead I badgered me mam...er...I mean my mother, to give me some money so that I could take a picnic for everyone with me. I always connected events with food and always wanted everyone to be well-fed. Especially myself.

Being a big softie at heart and rather than spending the time preparing it herself, she handed me a large, oversized blue five-pound note and told me to *get oot* o' her hair.

So I ran to MacAlpine's bakery and, red-faced and puffing like a suet, I bought an assortment of little cakes and a dozen Scotch pies; explaining with embarrassment that they were not all for me; much to their amusement. I next ran to the Co-op and burst through the door.

Angus was serving an old man at the counter and was asking him for '*wan poond please*.' I interrupted in my haste.

'Four bottles of Irn-Bru please, Agnus... I mean Angus,' I blurted out to the assistant behind the counter, whom I knew well. Both men looked aghast.

I spotted Aunty Joan stacking shelves near the back of the shop. She had not heard me come in as she was going a bit deaf.

'Aunty Joan!' I cried far too loudly through the natural exuberance of youth and infantile impatience. 'I'm going sinking in the river...er...ah...I mean, *swimming* in the river Teith. You know I could never sink; I'm too full of gas!' I added cheekily in my happiness and subconscious desire for attention, with the most innocent of faces and broadest of smiles.

I had startled Aunty Joan so that she nearly dropped a tin and I had befuddled her with my gibberish. Anyone would have thought I was raising a fire alarm.

Before Aunty Joan could say anything, Angus quipped: 'Aye, well here's something to give ye even *maire* gas,' as he slammed the bottles down on the counter. Everyone tittered, including a wee auld wifey who lived quite a way beyond the Callander bus stop.

'Er...aye, well, I've got to go now,' I left some money on the counter and disappeared up and over the Mercat cross before Aunty Joan could make any comments. No doubt she would make them to my mother. No doubt they would have a laugh over tea and fags, turning the air blue conspiratorially.

At Don MacFairlane's I bought a big bag of mixed sweets and Highland toffee and was finally ready for the big event. ('say hello to yer mammy fer me.')

I must admit the bag was very heavy by the time I had loaded it up with goodies. I had amused Don MacFairlane with the excitement of the big afternoon on Doune castle's banks of the river. He humoured me when he knew full-well all along that the local kids only went in for a very quick challenging dip before scuttling back home for their tea.

It's quite a long walk to the river for a fat kid, when you are laden down like a donkey and the sun is beating down on your bare head like a soldering iron. I was sweating buckets, was bright red in the face (there were no traffic lights in Doune in those days or even now, but the locals could have mistaken me for one) banging the pregnant bag against my left flank with my inner thighs chaffing themselves together and causing red welts in protest of my weight and gait. Once my father had treated the welts on my inner thighs and had commented on the unpleasant smell and, at times, through the shaky journey through my childhood I had literally felt like nothing more than an unpleasant smell.

You know, sometimes a child can feel very lonely and neglected and sense that the world is too big and overwhelming for them to handle. But we are born alone and we die alone and no other human fill-in can alleviate that.

Finally, over the last Doune castle hill, I spotted a small group of people cavorting about by the river. My Uncle Billy was standing slightly away from the others, watching and chatting to two anglers standing waist-deep in the water, with their elongated wellies, casting their rods with spider-thread-fine fishing lines glinting in the sunshine. Thank God he had a light tee-shirt on and not one of his horrendous string vests, which were very popular in the sixties, especially among the hoi-polloi. You know, the ones that made men's nipples stick out through the little holes like some horrible pigs' snouts.

I noticed that, apart from my cousins Nigel and Bunion, my Aunty Macasa and my cousin Rae were also there, sitting on the grass very primly, simply enjoying the fine climate of the day.

They waved when they saw me.

'Whit on earth hae ye got there, Lukie?' asked my Uncle Billy, in blunt amusement with arms akimbo.

'Just something for our picnic,' I replied politely, gasping from the exertion, as I put the load down heavily on the grass next to Aunty Macasa (the most trust-worthy one of the bunch) and gratefully sat down with a thump, not wanting to appear too conspicuous. They didn't have earthquakes in Doune. Yet.

My cousin Nigel was taking off his trousers to reveal a garish bathing suit underneath and stood there in his spindly lily-white legs and knobbly knees. I didn't think I had knees, as they were covered in too much subcutaneous fat.

'C'mon Lukie, let's gae in thon watter!' he suggested as he gingerly felt his way over the pebbles, the soles of his feet completely unused to the bareness of it all.

Bunion was wearing a one-piece silly frilly girl's thing and was already in the water, squealing and shivering with delight and fright at Nigel splashing her. Well, of course, that is the sort of thing he would do, being such a naughty wee scamp. In fact, he even called himself 'The Scampion of Doune.'

As I shyly undressed to take the plunge as a personal dare to myself after being used to the beaches in the south of France, I asked my cousin Rae if she were not swimming and she said *'no'* because it was the wrong time of the month for her. Wrong time of the month? How could it be the wrong time of the month when it was such a gloriously hot day with the sun shining so brightly? Girls sometimes said the weirdest things. So I just blinked back at her.

The anglers were watching with no little amusement as I daintily ventured into the frozen unknown and felt just how icy the water in the river really was, after my Uncle Billy had informed them I was a visiting Sassenach '*from doon sooth.*'

I bravely managed to get in up to my waist before screaming with shocking dramatics and acute cold discomfort. The two angling men didn't moan about all the ridiculous noises we were making, like chickens set among a fox, because they were laughing too much.

The waterline felt like the edge of a razor-blade and so, after splashing about a bit with Nigel and Bunion, I decided enough was enough as I remembered the picnic bag. I got out of the offending water and rummaged through the goodies, pulling out a Scotch pie and held it up like a trophy, asking Nigel if he wanted one. When he saw it, he made a bee-line for the bank and started to scurry up it on all fours like a beetle; just as one of the anglers mis-cast his line and accidentally hooked the top of his bathing-suit, pulling it all the way down when he tried to pull the line back, as Nigel clambered up further. I must say that I have never seen such a snowdrop-white, flat and scrawny-looking bahoohie in my life before! Everyone, especially my Uncle Billy and the anglers, burst out laughing uproariously as Nigel went as red as a tomato and as angry as a bull to a red flag, as he struggled to unhook the line from behind him; *'behind'* being the operative word.

'Ye'll hae tae throw thon ane back. It's too small and scrawny!' my Uncle Billy shouted at the angler, with great glee and amusement, much to Nigel's chagrin.

Once released, he swore under his breath and gave me that all-knowing evil-eye-intent look. I knew he was planning something, though he couldn't do anything against Bunion; for he was already in trouble for that.

As he climbed up from the bank, I pretended to ignore him, as, had we made eye-contact, he would definitely have executed some evil deed on me. So I turned towards my Aunty Macasa, whom I now noticed was talking to one of the local village teenage girls, who had sauntered up to blether with her while out for a wee walk.

She was the butcher's daughter, Fiona Arbuthwaite and I distractedly heard her telling Auntie Macasa that she had just had her hair done in Callander special-like as she had a very important date with a popular lad she had been dying to go out with for ages. She was wearing one of the most stupendous golden towering beehives I had seen in a long time. Even taller than my sister's ones. Impressive, I must admit; but to me as a child it still looked ridiculous. Like a cheap Indian souvenir, like a rocket waiting for the countdown.

Most girls were, on average, 5'5" but with the beehives they soared to around 8 feet tall and were like *The Wild women of Wonga* or *The Giant Women from Planet X.*

Enough to frighten even a sturdy and staunch member of *The Black Watch* or a mighty Angus cow.

Out of the corner of my eye, I noticed Nigel rummaging through the bag after having wolfed down one of my precious pies and I just knew he was up to no good. I thought that if I just ignored him he would just get fed up and drop it, but then he suddenly shoved a huge dollop of salad cream on a table-spoon right towards my face and I instinctively threw my forearm up to block it and knock it away.

Well; knock it away I certainly did, with my big, fat ham-hock arm and the gargantuan amorphous blob of glistening, fatty substance went sailing through the air and landed on and straight into the artfully-prepared network mesh of Fiona's date-special beehive hair-do.

For a few milliseconds there was complete stillness and silence before Fiona screamed out at the top of her lungs so loudly that one of the anglers lost his footing.

'Ye wee bastard, Nigel! Wait 'till ah git me hands on ye!'

And with that Nigel took off as if he had just sat on a hot gas ring, with panic and laughter. Fiona took off after him like a powerful night train and began chasing him all around the hills of Doune castle as all of us and I mean the whole lot of us, were in absolute stitches, guffawing after them. Better than any TV show. It also took the ridiculing attention away from me.

Then Fiona unfortunately tripped on an uneven clump of turf, just before we witnessed her landing face-first and beehive-second, into a huge cow pat and saw spurts of cow dung from the sides of her face spraying all around.

The weight of her face had broken the crust! We laughed even louder, if that were at all possible, before remaining silent out of respect and sympathy for her. With bated breath we all looked on as she very slowly got up onto her hands and knees, doing quite a good impersonation of a cow herself; especially from the back. We were looking at the eye of the storm. We were waiting for the eruption. But it was the burp that never comes; the tremor in place of the earthquake. Fiona gradually stood up in complete silence, burst into tears and simply ran back all the way home; like a little piggy. Rather apt, as her father was the Doune butcher.

'I'll go after her,' my Aunty Macasa said and, grabbing her cardigan, was off.

The rest of us stayed behind and shared my bounty of goodie*s* with the two anglers. They were very happy to join us because we had amused them so with our frolics and because the fish were not biting much the day anyway. We all sat there, munching happily away without a care in the world, as the anglers told us some fishing stories; and that was what village life was like; everyone was a friend.

Another tall story? Perhaps I take after my mother.

***

'The Little Bunion,' (Whit?) Binnie the Bint's other nickname, who was my cousin Nigel'*s* wee sister, my female cousin on my mother's side, stood outside Don MacFairlane's sweetie shop sucking the lolli-pop I had bought her. She was aye sookin' it so hard, that her cheeks were sunken-in. Like someone out of *'Night of the Living Dead,'* which made her eyes goggle and I had to laugh. She had nut-brown hair and a sprinkle of freckles over the bridge of her nose, which were like seeds on a bun or a spray of stars in the night sky.

Somehow these freckles encouraged her eyes to seemingly shine a brighter hazel.

She stood there on her skinny legs and knobbly knees like a cartoon character, looking as if the wind were going to blow her away at any minute. I stood beside her with my thumbs tucked into the top of my dungarees, shooing away my long and unkempt hair with puffs of breath. I loved my little cousin. She was so twee and sweet that I felt very protective towards her. She was kooky-looking; and kooky people need protecting; that I understood.

The other boys I was with, my cousin Nigel and the rest of the gang, were prating about on the pavement, pulling silly faces and doing silly walks as if they had just invented these antics. Anything to stem the boredom of a quiet village afternoon.

'Is sae!'

'Is nae!'

'Is sae!'

'Is nae!'

Silly childish talk. Even arguing over nothing killed the ennui.

Suddenly Nigel rushed up to the kerb as a car rolled passed and he shouted: 'Yer tyre's doon!' expecting the driver to stop and check his wheel so that all the lads could have a laugh. But it just carried on going. The driver probably didn't even hear him.

'His window was rolled up, Nigel. He wouldn't have heard you if he was shutting out the cold,' I advised.

'Aye. Ah ken that right enough,' he replied, trying to mask his embarrassment.

'Whit are ye waitin' on the noo?' one of our gang asked him, as he stood dead erect on the kerbside, with his spine arched backwards and his arms folded across his chest with extreme pride.

'Anither victim,' he smiled back at us, looking our way from the corners of his eyes with the cold-steel shiftiness of two coins in the slot of a slot machine and back to the dead road again.

Presently, we all heard the chug and rumble of an engine as it came up George Street and he pointed at its undercarriage with an expression of incredulous shock on his face. The driver ignored him and then one of the others who passed by shouted 'eejit!' out his car window. Nigel went as red as a traffic light in Stirling, but he didn't give up; I'll give him that.

Finally a driver did stop after one of Nigel's screechy hollerings and stole a cursory glance under his chassis before striding up to Nigel, who was laughing like a rabid hyena and gave him a thick ear for making him late. The rest of us then began

laughing like rabid hyenas ourselves, as Binnie the Bint peeked out from behind me.

***

On an especially dire and damp Wednesday afternoon in the dead-quiet village, Don MacFairlane was idly standing in his shop, staring out the front windows in the hope of some passing trade. He loved nothing better than to be serving the community and chatting to everyone. It made him feel less lonely. For, having a lot of people around him killed the loneliness.

For wont of nothing better to do, he went over to a stack of '*The Daily Record*' newspapers and straightened them up with the care of a mother with her baby. He loved historical things, the newspaper having been established in 1895, as it gave him a sense of belonging where he could the better feel his roots.

As he was carrying out this task and looking forward to all the children coming out of school and coming in to buy sweeties, he looked up, still ever-hopeful for some trade and spotted Opie Cameron standing outside, dead-still, head dead-straight like a zombie manikin, with his eyes looking straight up into the sky like a lunatic-asylum-sedated patient and he watched him for a while, perplexed. Opie never ceased to amaze and amuse him. He was wondering what on earth he was up to when he heard a slowly-grating, grinding squark and decided to go out and investigate. He could contain his curiosity no longer.

'What are ye daein' Opie?' he asked as he opened his front door; shut because of the raw cold. But Opie stayed silent. So Don MacFairlane simply followed his gaze and saw that he was staring at the old rooster weather-vane stuck on the roof of my grandfather's house above the Co-op. It was a flat, but we called it a house because it was a home.

He looked back at Opie Cameron and Opie, instead of saying anything, as a normal person would, just put a finger up to his pouted lips and then tapped his right temple three times.

Don MacFairlane was intrigued and just shook his head.

Then Opie went to a near-by parked car, an old *Standard 10* and spread his arms across its roof as if he were preparing some black magic ritual.

'Ah've hae'd a great idea,' he commented with a dim bright spark.

'Weather-vanes on cars to tell which way the wind's blawing.'

Don MacFairlane just tittered and walked back into his shop. He didn't like to be away from his nest for too long. Opie Cameron padded in after him in like a loyal puppy.

'Ah could mak' thoosands o' poonds with ma invention!'

'Opie!' Don MacFairlane stopped him abruptly, 'when a motor is gaein' alang the road, the wind is only blawing one way, is it no? Ye daft lummox!'

'Eh?'

'See ye later, Opie,' Don MacFairlane said, as two quarrymen came in for their baccy and chews.

'Oh…aye…er…right ye are, then,' he replied uncertainly before shooting off again like a gazelle out the door and down the village street. One thing's for sure: he would have made a great inventor in a crazy world on some other planet.

***

My mother wanted to get me out from under her feet, although I don't know why, as I was out playing in the village most of the time. But I must admit I sometimes stayed in and annoyed her because I was bored. Boredom is a funny thing because, although there was always plenty to do, being in the state of boredom made you feel like not wanting to do anything. Even if it were something you really loved.

So, one evening, my Uncle Billy came up to the house.

'Whit are ye daein' wi' yersel,' these days Lukie?' he asked me with his arms folded in front of him.

'Dunno,' I replied sheepishly, 'playing.'

'Playin'?' At yer age? Oh, no! ye waint tae be a man, laddie! Get some grit unner yer fingernails. (ooer!) Do some hard graft. Tomorrow ye'll come wi' me tae the building site and help me tae build the new school. Ye can lay bricks.'

Umm. I thought it would be just like playing with my Lego set.

My mother stood over both of us, smiling away. I was both a bit frightened and excited, because it would be something different to do and my cousin Nigel would be there working away as well, learning his father's trade, as is the norm. So, out of respect for my mother and uncle, I agreed to go, even though I would have to get up early and was too afraid of adults to say 'no' anyway.

So the next morning, my mother packed me a little lunch-box with pieces and jam in it and packed me off up the street. The new school was being built just beyond the top of Castle Hill and as I neared the site I was quite awestruck by all the burly men toiling away on half-finished buildings and I felt a bit intimidated, as I could be a very shy, delicate young thing at times.

As soon as I spotted Uncle Billy and my cousin Nigel, I waved madly and ran to them before any of the swarthy men could growl at me, which, of course, they would never had done. You know, a child's mind can be far more imaginative than an adult's.

Nigel was his usual happy and silly self and started to prat about before my Uncle Billy told him off and shooed him away so that I could get down to some serious work. Work? It was such an alien thing to me. All morning I stood by Uncle Billy and handed him bricks for the wall he was laying, mixing a bit of cement here and there and generally acting as a gofer.

But at one point he gave me a brick, which felt rough in my hands, showed me how to lay a bit of cement on the top of another brick and lay my brick on top of that, levelling it off with a trowel. My Uncle Billy made a big show of placing a spirit-level on my freshly-laid brick (as if it were an egg) and the praise for me that rained down from the heavens was quite unique. Even at that young age, I knew that he was humouring me, but was still chuffed at the same time.

Of course, not wanting me to have all the attention, Nigel started going around the building site with a long strand of builders' gunge under one nostril and asking everyone in turn if they had a hankie. I thought that was very funny, actually. But the other builders just shook their heads and carried on with their work.

Even though it was summer time in Scotland, it was still fairly sharp and breezy. So, at lunchtime we all crammed into the little workmen's hut and sat in a semi-circle in front of a fiery-hot brazier, battling to keep the ill-fitting, flimsy wooden door shut.

That scene has always stuck in my mind. Probably because it was completely different to what I was used to down south and in later years I read a comic strip of '*Oor Wullie*' where he was actually drying off in a workman's hut after having fallen in a pond and it took me right back to the day I spent with my Uncle Billy and my cousin Nigel.

What I loved about '*Oor Wullie*' were the two-line ditties at the top of the page, the accompanying different postures of him next to them and I always looked down before I read any of his particular stories to see if he was happy or sad, grumpy or glad, at peace or mad, at the end of them. I also loved the antics he got up to and he reminded me of me, although a lot of people would disagree with that. Especially my brother. For one thing, '*Oor Wullie'* was skinny.

I felt famous now that I had laid a couple of bricks for Doune school. Okay, I exaggerate, I think it was only one. It was a very small thing; but it made me feel more a part of Doune. More a part of the Scottish community. It was nice to know I had contributed something, in my silly child's mind.

At the end of the day (probably early afternoon) my Uncle Billy told me my day's work was done and I ran home to tell my mother all about it (and because I was hungry) and then forgot about the whole thing.

But a couple of days later, my Uncle Billy came up to the house and gave me my wages of £1! I didn't have the heart to tell him I got five times that in pocket money each week and I knew that wasn't the point. He had been very kind in trying to teach me the value of money. Which didn't work.

***

'C'mon! we're gaein' scrumping, Juan!'

'What is 'scrumping?' my brother asked, sounding like Prince Charles, as he caught up with the small gang of local lads, one of whom was our cousin Nigel, the dubious leader of the pack; and another of whom was sporting a *stookey* on his arm with the pride of Wallace holding his sword.

'Apples, pal, apples,' explained one of the other lads.

'Well, why didn't you say so,' my brother asked rhetorically, trying to sound cool.

'He's nae from aroond here,' Nigel explained to the others, 'he's frae sooth o' the border.'

'Whit? Frae Bogieland?'

'Aye.'

'A Sassenach?'

'Aye.'

'Fram the other side?'

'Aye.'

'Well, I am half-Scottish, though,' my brother defended himself.

'Yer a line across the border,' Nigel stated, not knowing exactly what he meant.

'Aye?'

'Aye.'

'Still half-Scottish,' my brother asserted as he walked on.

'Och aye. The best pairt,' Nigel commented to my brother with a mischievous wink as they strolled on doon the road.

As the gang walked down Doune's Main Street, one of the other boys, Stewart Robinson, suddenly spotted another colourful local resident and the tease was on. He nudged Nigel in the ribs.

'Mountain Madam,' 'Canon Lady,' and *'Ten Ton Tess,'* as she was better known by her three aliases, which the more unkind and cheeky children of the village had given her, appeared on the horizon, like a big aircraft carrier at sea.

Her bazooka bosoms oozed around the corner before she did, like Tomahawk missiles. Her belly bulged out more than her gargantuan, bloater-floater bazooms, if that was at all possible; like one lava flow following the other.

She was engulfed in great swathes and slabs of fat and sagging bat wings and she had hair like the coil springs sprouting out of an abandoned mattress and wobbled on elephantine legs. Poor woman. Such a bulbous soul. So amorphous. Apparently she lived up Park Lane. (Oh, aye? Yon side street's big enough fer ye tae pop through, is that right, darling?)

'Dinnae swing they massive bazoolies onywhere near uz, or we'll all hae tae duck!' Stewart shouted, with one hand cupping the side of his mouth and they all laughed immaturely, even my brother Juan, to feel part of the gang, once he had got over the shock of such blatant disrespect for an elder person. Apart from that, people in London didn't shout out like that. In London, people were just unfriendly and aloof. Rude in a quieter way.

But my brother always thought fat people were funny and that's why he was always laughing at me. It seems that, when some people don't fit perfectly into society, it becomes open-season for the hecklers.

As my brother looked at the fat lady waddling towards them like an Emperor penguin, all a-huffin' and a-puffin', taking her cumbersome body for a walk, he did notice that she was not wearing a bra (probably no shop in Scotland sold marquees of her gargantuan size) and further observed that her water-melon bosoms were swaying precariously back and forth like two bladder-bags about to burst.

('Village Flooded in Sudden Downpour.')

He laughed anew until he realised that the pendulums of doom were headed straight for him. Maybe the lady would use them in retaliation to their insults.

'Away wi' ye, ye rampant radgees! Have ye nae respec' fer an auld besom?'

'Ach, away an' bail yer heid!' Nigel shouted back at her, which I think is a very funny expression.

'Ye mean 'an auld bosom!'' suggested Stewart, cuttingly.

'Flubba-lubba-loo-la!' another one of the gang members shouted back at her inanely.

'Flubba-lubba-loo-la!' he repeated to stress tauntingly, with jiggling movements, to imitate her loose fat.

My brother could see that she was upset about the piercing and final insult; it showed through her anger and he felt a pang of guilt and pity for her. So much so that he turned around, as they were walking away from her now, spread out his arms in a conceding gesture and pursed his lips in apology. But Stewart was having none of it.

'Ye're enough to make us all boak!' he shouted back, 'Ye auld crabit!'

And with that the gang all ran off. Who knows who ran off first, but everyone else followed like the silly sheep they were. Anyway. Taunting became boring after a while.

'Hang on a mineet lads!' shouted the smallest gang member and when Nigel looked back, he spotted him walking gingerly in his wee pair of shorts with a long brown lumpy river's streak running down the inside of his left leg.

'Whit's tha'?' Nigel asked him, pointing perplexedly.

'Ah hae'd tae much mince and tatties last night. Cannae keep it in.'

'Aw that's disgustin'!' commented Nigel, as everyone else laughed and made sounds of revulsion at the same time. 'Get yersel' away hame and clean yersel' up, ye wee dirty bastard o' yer aye no cumin' wi' uz anymaire!' He thought he spotted a bit of potato 'slidin' doon' under the influence of gravity; if ye ken whit ah mean.

Our cousin Nigel then entertained the rest of the gang with an encounter he had once had with *Ten Ton Tess.*

'Och, aye it wiz sae foony. Sae I wiz walkin' doon this really narrow alleyway when she came frae the top end. It wiz like seein' a whale in the neck o' a bottle. As we eyed each other warily, I turned sideways, ye ken, tae let 'er pass; but she just kept rollin' around me and we suddenly got jammed together! I wiz stuck fast between her and the wall and felt like a sandwich fillin' and could only look up at her heavy breathin' an' rivers of sweat as she struggled to free herself.

'Weel, the mare we struggled the mare we stuck fast! Luckily, she had just been tae thae shops for her messages and I pulled oot a bottle of washing-up liquid I found in her bag and squirted it all o'er us and then fizzed it a' up with a bit o' Irn Bru and wi' a bit o' squelching and covered in soap suds, like twa rabid dugs, we baith squelched free. Thank God! Ah couldnae imagine bein' stuck to 'er fer eternity!'

There was a dead silence and everyone just stared at Nigel incredulously, before bursting out laughing like a pack of wild hyenas. It was one of the best stories they'd heard yet.

'C'mon, let's go and get those apples,' my brother suggested, once the gang had calmed down and got their collective breaths back.

That was another tall tale to rival those of Mama Anna; only, my brother was getting a bit old for them now. It was a funny story though. And, after all, Shakespeare started with people going around small villages telling tall stories. Maybe Nigel would become a bard. Or perhaps not.

They approached a fruit shop not far from Don Macfairlane's and my brother started to walk into it. 'Juan! Where are ye goin?' Nigel asked incredulously. 'Whit are ye daein?' he asked, standing with his hands on his hips.

'You said you were going to buy some apples,' my brother protested.

'No ah didnae! I said we were gaeing scrumping to get some apples, ye English dunderheid tart!'

All the others laughed aloud like the daft lads they were and my brother went bright red and trotted out of the shop like a dog, or 'dug,' as they say in these parts, with its tail between its legs and a sheepish smile.

On the way to the orchard in Northlea, all the boys explained to Juan that they were going to relieve a smallholder of some of his apples. Yes, they could have bought some apples. But it would have eaten into their pocket money and apples, Nigel reminded everyone, always tasted better when they were free. My brother Juan was a bit dubious about this affair, as he never did anything improper, illegal or taboo, but still wanted to appear as one of the lads. And there were no other lads he hung around with anyway, apart from Ryan Mallone.

So, as they crouched down by the orchard wall and discussed tactics and ways of avoiding the smallholder; like soldiers discussing their imminent attack, my brother Juan gave our cousin Nigel a hand up over the wall, once they were confident the smallholder had disappeared elsewhere: usually for a cup of tea in his little, 'awa' frae the wifey,' shed. Unfortunately, my brother heaved our cousin Nigel up a bit too enthusiastically and he went flying right over the top of the wall and hit the ground with a thud on the other side.

'Ach! Fer goodness sake, Juan! That really hurt me erse!' Nigel complained with muffled controlled anger, while remembering to try and keep a bit quiet, so as not to alert the smallholder.

For, to the smallholder, if any apples fell off the tree and landed outside his wall, then it was a free-for-all for all. But if anyone came onto his land and took any, then it was outright trespass and theft, so heaven help any young boy or man who took such liberties.

Mr. Cuthbeart Cattenach, the smallholder, was very old-school and to him everything was in black and white, right and wrong. There were no grey areas around here.

My brother looked up as the other boys started to fill their pockets with the pleasingly-plump apples they were picking directly off the tree and their pockets were bulging like bunches of grapes. One boy, Conall Macgillivray (God! Where did they get these names from?) was shaking the branches too much. So much so that they twanged and rustled too loudly when released from the anchor points of the guilty apples in question and everyone said *'shhh!'* amid all their giggling, while crouching down as low as they could go, for fear of being spotted.; even our cousin Nigel, who was still rubbing his arsey backside.

Too late.

'Hoi!' You lot! What dae ye think ye little monkeys are daein' in ma tree? I'm scunnered, scunnered I telt ye! Thon apples wurnae fer youse a'! Get away! Get away! I ken yer parents an' I'll tan yer hides fer ye!'

The old man came running towards the tree with a walking stick held high in his hand. All the boys scampered like cockroaches when the light goes on in a kitchen, and rained down on my brother Juan, as they made their great escape.

All the boys flew out of Northlea, dropping some apples as they panicked and my brother and one of the other boys both felt a sting of their legs from the small pebbles the smallholder was throwing after them. 'Ow!' And 'Oooo!' could be heard as they raced towards safety.

Of course it wasn't long until our cousin Nigel and my brother Juan were up against my mother, who was looking down at them both with her wagging nicotine-stained forefinger, angry face and bull-snorting expression.

I mean, how daft really. It was obvious they were going to get caught, as everyone knew everyone else in the village and there was no hiding place to be had for those familiar; not like in an anonymous city.

'Ye dinnae need tae rob frae guid honest folk. Ye can jist go oot and buy them. They're no dear, ye ken,' my mother said.

'But they wiz only apples,' my cousin Nigel protested while absent-mindedly fingering the tear in his troosers and twisting a foot on the floor.

'Whit? It disnae metter whether you steal apples, one penny or thoosands o' poonds! Stealing is stealing, thievin' is thievin'. Whit's right is right and wat's wrang is wrang. It's no the value of anything you take, 'cos onything ye take withoot permission is A CRIME!!!'

'Och, aye, right ye are, Aunty Anna,' he conceded as he stared at the floor.

So then Aunty Anna felt sorry for him and handed our cousin Nigel two shillings. Her soft heart always came through. Our cousin Nigel thanked her as he pulled at his torn rear pocket contritely. More trouble for him when he got hame, I mean, home, I shouldn't wonder. I shouldn't wonder, but I do!

***

As with in a lot of small villages, boredom got the better of us. So, when, one day, my cousin Nigel suggested we have a look around the inside of our Catholic church, we all trotted down there for wont of nothing better to do.

My brother wasn't there that day, because he was now getting into girls (whit?) and was canoodling somewhere up in Castle Hill. I later found out he had spent the afternoon lying on a couch, kissing some local hopeful. It hadn't gone further than that, but he had come out feeling like Elvis.

So Nigel, two local lads I can't even remember the names of now, and I, gingerly crossed the threshold of the God-fearing kirk. We were silent and wary at first because, although the door was always open to God's children, it was not these particular children the diocese had in mind.

It was a quiet early midweek afternoon and we didn't want to come to the priest's attention, for we were not there to apply for jobs as altar boys or to pray.

We were not going to do anything naughty; it is just that we had no business being there. Everyone separated and looked around different parts of the church, prodding and poking, pointing and commenting, with everyone cracking jokes; such as Nigel commenting that Jesus was always '*hanging aroond*,' much to everyone else's guffawing and braying like donkeys, or rather the asses they were.

Once we were certain there was no-one aboot, er…I mean about, one boy climbed onto the pulpit and gave a short sermon on sinning and the absence of sweeties if you were naughty. Trying to sound like the priest, he sounded more like Louis Armstrong, as we all giggled with glee.

I walked around with a bit more respect, looking up at the painted eyes all looking down upon me in Judgement, boring through my soul. But, after a while I ignored my guilty feelings, which had been instilled in me since the day I was born. I looked in one of the prayer books and found a line I simply had to impart on my fellow intruders.

'Hey, listen to this lads,' I commanded as I looked at the page. "and Jesus rode to town on his ass." 'He must have had a sore bum for a week!' I commented in mock seriousness, to howls of laughter. Like all good Catholics, I felt slightly guilty, for Catholics are born guilty; though never really knowing of what. Actually, I complimented the Church by feeling very guilty.

'Aye, that's a good 'un right enough,' shouted Nigel from somewhere behind a column. I was about to say something when I heard a loud squeal. Feedback. One of the other two lads had found the '*On*' switch for the microphone and began telling us all, very loudly, with this electronic booster: 'I believe in the Lord!!' The three of us sat in a pew near the front, ready to listen to the sermon and ready to comment when, suddenly, there was a loud eruption, which momentarily shocked us. I was preparing to leave the premises when I suddenly realised our pal had farted into the pulpit microphone.

Prrrrrrrraapp!! The heavens shook!

The guilty boy was holding onto the pulpit with one hand and held the microphone to his rear-end with the other. (...and now a word from our sponsor). He was laughing from the strain of it all and nearly collapsing. Thank God the pulpit was there to hold him up; for there is nothing more debilitating than laughter. Then he let out another one and my cousin Nigel commented that that lad was 'full o' beans!' with a sly grin on his face.

'Aye, tha' wiz a right stoater, right enough! On ye go, laddie!' one of our other gang members chipped in, relishing in the atmosphere; but not the smell, no doubt.

We then all rushed up onto the pulpit as it creaked alarmingly and took turns at trying a repeat performance of his most original act.

Prrrrrrrraaapppp!

I managed a big long one because I was famous for creating a lot of gas with the amount of food I ate and Nigel managed a full-bodied one and some others were wet or just petered out.

Ffftt!

But it sounded so funny in its alarming loudness, the acoustics enhanced by the hollow shell of the church and just as the second of the other lads was in a boisterous mid-flow of gaseous exchanges, which did actually sound like an earthquake or even thunder, a baritone voice rose above it all, penetrating through any and all other loud noises.

'HOW DARE YE DEFILE THE HOUSE OF GOD?!!! YOUSE BOYS GET DOON FROM THERE AND GET OOT O' MA CHURCH THE NOO!!!'

We all turned around to see the priest, father Alec Drummond, approaching us as if he were facing the Devil himself. And that's when the pulpit dropped with a loud crack under our (not only my) weight. It was obviously old, perhaps woodworm-worn and couldn't take the strain. For a few seconds we were all in surprise and shock, looking around as if we had just arrived somewhere, but couldn't remember where exactly.

Now Father Drummond was wagging his finger and spluttering like an old kettle. It was as if a World War II bomb had just hit his church.

His plough-furrowed face was ravaged by anger and rage and age and from the effects of listening to too many sins over the years. He had a spinnaker of a nose and teeth like a portcullis, under a halo of puffy white-cloud hair. His indignant face was as red as the beetroots my mother used to like eating and his eyes bulged out like two boiled eggs on heat. I don't mean to be disrespectful to him, but that's how he looked to me. His black cassock flowed out behind him, ever the reluctant follower.

'...and you, Lukie Garland! You should know better than this, as ye've had opportunities in life and ye've been aye privileged. Wait 'til yer mither hears aboot this. Ye'll pay fer me pulpit. Ye'll pay! YE'LL ALL PAY!'

'I'm so very sorry Father,' I apologised, just above a whisper, engulfed by a large dust and methane cloud. But the still-working sensitive microphone caught my sibilance. I was almost in tears as I struggled to extricate myself from the debris and blew out the door like award-winning flatulence.

'Nigel! You're always getting me into trouble!' I barked as we walked back towards the village.

I was so mortified at having been caught. One thing my father had taught me was to respect others, especially your elders; let alone the highest elder of them all.

The rest of the gang tumbled out, a bit shocked, but still laughing and making comments in their bravado. But I bet they were not as shocked as Father Drummond had been when he had unexpectantly (to say the least) encountered the highly-offensive noises from Hell in God's House and the even more highly-offensive smell which, even though the church was quite large and high-ceilinged, managed to permeate and penetrate a vast area, making one imagine they were standing in a barn full of cows with bad stomachs.

Some say that the Devil's appearance is accompanied by the smell of faeces and I prayed that he hadn't influenced us to do this.

I was very worried about what my mother would say about this escapade and wondered if all would be well by the time of the evening Mass.

'Michty me,' commented Nigel, as we all separated to go home, as we had had enough for one day. 'We hae tae face Fither Drummond at Sunday morning Mass lads!'

No doubt my Uncle Billy would be very proud of his son, his wee apprentice, following in his father's footsteps (or rather, in his faither's underpants and string vest). It was very funny, though, you have to admit! Let us just hope (and pray) that God has a sense of humour. Well; He did create me and gas too, after all, so He must have one.

Chapter Seven

-1997-

Our antecessowris that we suld of reide
And hald in mynde thar nobille worthi deid
We lat ourslide throu varray sleuthfulnes
And castis us ever till uther besynes
-The Wallace-(Blind Harry)-

I was very excited today, because I decided to take a trip down memory lane by riding the Callander bus into Stirling; to have a look around and have my hair cut, as I had a lunch date with my Celtic cousins.

I remember, with the fondest of memories, always taking this bus from the Callander bus stop in Balkerach Street, near the post office. I remember excitedly waiting for the bus to arrive with my mother or sister and brother. The bus, which was more of a luxurious coach, was long, cream and blue, with a blue swallow stamped on the side, as if saying: 'Alright! Let's take flight!'

I liked the interior of the coach too, because it had these orange skylights in the roof - three of them - which spread a relaxing and soft ambience around the inner sanctum of the Pullman. I also remember loving the feel of the red and black tiny patterned seats, whose material felt quite firm but cosy, not wishing to sound like quite an old fuddy-duddy, even though I was a young child. But even children like the comforts of home. It's funny how the little things in life can please you so much. I also very much enjoyed the adventure of the ride, not knowing what was waiting around the corner.

Now, as I sat there, a much older child, I was just as excited for the off. As we drove out of Doune, I admired the low flint walls and the pale sun flickering through the trees. I caught glimpses of Doune castle through its wonderful natural surroundings. This would be a good place to come and die in peace. Is that no right son? (Whit?)

I had purposefully sat on the left-hand-side of the bus so that I could admire *Wallace's Monument*, as it stuck up in the sky like a mighty warrior's sword against the steel-grey clouds of invading England and I thought about the history of Scotland and its oppression at the hands of the English. What's right is right and what's wrong is wrong.

The Throne belongs to Scotland.

But there you go. All is unfair in love and war.

When I got to Stirling I had a look around and then found a quaint little barber shop in King Street. Being in a buoyant, holiday mood, I chatted casually with the girl hairstylist and told her I was tired of my side-parting and wanted something more avant-garde. I suggested, 'perhaps swept back like Clint Eastwood.' She was a bit young for the name, I suppose, but understood when I drove my hand from the front to the back of my head and went red. I must admit, she did a good job and made me look quite stylish (whit? Are ye' a'right, son?).

I left the hairdresser's in a strut like a cockerel and proudly walked down the windy street, feeling younger and more attractive than ever; although I obviously didn't look it because, when I happened to look in a shop window and saw my reflection I, shocked at first beyond any description known to Man, saw that my hair had risen like a cake, the wind having teased it up from underneath with its wispy fingers. It was so high, it looked like a top hat! I laughed all the way back to the bus station, laughing my head off. I just had the image of myself as a poncy Liberace. The locals obviously thought I was yet another strange tourist. I got this terrible fit of the giggles and wondered whether I should go back to Doune or carry straight on to Belsdyke and book myself in.

***

When I got out of bed the next morning, I pulled the curtain aside and looked out of the window to see what the weather was like. It was a grey yet dry day and I saw birds lying and flying about. When you live in a Northern country, as long as it's not raining, it's a good day. Believe me.

I was not one obsessed with the weather; it was just that today I had invited Joan Plumly and my cousins Janet and Katie to lunch here at the Woodside Hotel. For me it was the best and the only place to have a good, honest home-made meal without having to leave the village and I didn't want the event ruined by torrential rain. My attention to the weather reminded me of a poem I had read as a child and somehow always remembered.

'Whether the weather is cold
Or whether the weather is hot
We must weather the weather
Whatever the weather
Whether we like it or not.'
-Anon-

I had really irritated my parents by constantly repeating this ditty throughout my childhood. In fact, so much so that I had ended up making them feel completely under the weather from its effects; but that is a another story and I may only have the time to write the one.

I had another delicious gargantuan breakfast, because I had the time to do so. Because back in London I would not be having breakfasts like these and because I had a voracious appetite here in Scotland. Must have been the sharper climate here. While other workers had an expense account, I had an 'expanse' account. I seem to be the only one who understands my jokes. How elite.

I then went up George street and had a little stroll around the village to kill some time (not that I wanted the time to pass too quickly on this wonderful holiday, in this wonderful village). I looked up at my grandfather's house above the Co-op, bade a silent salute and remembered all the good times I had there as a child. It was only a small place and sometimes it was very cold; but still, it had been full of loving warmth.

I then returned to the Woodside hotel, having bought a newspaper at a new sweetie-shop, which was nothing like Don MacFairlane's, even though the lady in there was very nice. I mentioned that my mother was from Doune, but she had just moved to Doune from Alloa and didn't know the locals very well yet. Oh, well, at least she didn't know my Uncle Billy.

Talking about my Uncle Billy, I had this sudden memory flash of him having to drink his pint out of a straw because he had the DTs and couldn't pick up his pint because his hands were shaking so much.

Apparently, once Nigel had tied a scarf to one of his wrists, fed it over the back of his neck, down the other side and gave him the other end to hold; so that when he pulled, his other hand came up with the pint in it so that he could '*hae a wee drink*' without shaking and spilling the precious liquid all over the bar. Another tall story? Probably not. That one was quite believable. The trouble with a small village was that there wasn't much else to do.

It was very late morning by now. I pottered around in the room for a while and then put on some smarter clothing and went down to the lounge to read the local paper while waiting for 'the girls.'

The lovely lady proprietor was there with her soft, squidgy and cuddly bean-bag face and she couldn't have given me a warmer welcome if the hotel had been on fire. She was so lovely I could have taken her home. She was the model mother I never had.

As I waited, I thought about Joan Plumly as I stared at the newspaper blankly. Friends since school, she had been my mother's pal until the day she died. My mother was smaller than Joan and was a bit frail because of her poor upbringing and distorted bandy legs and malnutrition. She had even had to wear a leg-brace for a while and stood out like a sore thumb. So Joan took it upon herself to be a motherly-figure and look after 'Mama Anna,' (as she later became known as) and she had never asked for anything in return. Only her friendship.

Right up until the day my mother married my father and left the village, they had been stuck together like Siamese twins and had gone everywhere in each other's company. Not only to dances and around the shops, the hairdresser's and the dressmaker's; but Joan would also go with my mother whenever she had to go to the doctor's or the dentist's.

She would go with her for the unpleasant things, as well as the pleasant things; and she never asked for anything in return. She was a true friend who never said a negative thing about my mother, even though there were many negative things that could have been said about her. Joan was as discreet as a doctor, priest or solicitor when it came to my mother. I suppose that's what you call unconditional love. Something I lacked, I'm afraid.

Suddenly, I was sharply thrown out of my reverie upon hearing a very familiar voice.

'Heellooo, Lukie. We're aye here.' It was my cousin Janet, who always liked to do most of the talking. She could talk as much as Don MacFairlane could smile; and that's saying something. If the world were to end tomorrow, you would still be able to hear her talking.

I stood up and hugged and said hello to everyone of them as they whisked their coats off - engulfing me in the aromatic yet overpowering stench of their various perfumes. Gag.

They sat down all in a flutter like hens on their eggs and nestled in quite contentedly. We had a drink and a laugh as I told them about my experience at the hairdresser's and my cousin Janet laughed so hard she had to go to the toilet and pee because she had a habit of leaving a trail everywhere behind her if she didn't catch it in time. I used to think there was a puppy somewhere. Oh, well, it certainly broke the ice.

Then we went in for lunch. I always looked forward to walking into the dining-room here, because I love oldie-worldie restaurants and this one was certainly no exception. It had wood panelling half-way up the wall, traditionally-laid tables, big windows that let as much light as possible in and a spongy green tartan carpet, which added greatly to the cosiness of it all. The hunting prints on the walls made it feel all the more homely. They were the icing on the cake. What I love about the Woodside Hotel is that they have done very good, no-nonsense, home-made Scottish food there, for as long as I can remember.

The female proprietor came to take our order and, of course, knew Mrs. Plumly and my cousins and so ended up chatting about everything and nothing for about 20-odd minutes. But it didn't matter as I was on holiday and time was of no consequence. You certainly don't get this warm reception in London. All you get is a cold front and a grey slap.

I was very glad to see that *Scotch Broth* was on the menu, as I love that barley and it reminds me of my childhood. I then had a steak pie with peas, mashed potatoes and gravy. If the world had no gravy, it would be a dire place indeed. As dry and barren as the Sahara desert on a bad day.

We all talked ten to the dozen and Joan Plumly talked a lot about my mother and their friendship since childhood, with a little tear in her eye. I was interested and gratified because she brought out all my mother's good points, which had been buried deep in my sub-conscious mind and I was myself responsible for her long diatribe, because it was me who was asking her a lot of questions about my mother and not the other way around.

I wanted to see the human behind the whisky bottle.

Over an Irish coffee (don't make the mistake of stirring it!) we discussed what I was going to do while in Doune and I suddenly threw my arms out towards them, to their thrilling alarm and said that I wanted to take them to Loch Ness for the day, on me.

Katie said that, unfortunately, she could not go as she was too tied up with preparing a backdrop set for work, (as she was artfully involved in a lot of school plays) but said that her kids could go. She had a son called Domino (don't ask) and a daughter called Bella. I told her I would be extremely glad to take them, so that we could gel and that I loved taking kids to these places because you see things through kid's eyes.

'Och, aye. Well, at least we're no gaein tae Callander!' Janet interjected, making us all laugh boisterously once again. She will never let me live it down.

***

So today was the day for our big outing to Loch Ness and I was really looking forward to it because I had always wanted to go there yet never got around to it. I cannot believe the amount of times I have been to Scotland and never been there. It was shameful really. But I always had a focus on Doune and never went elsewhere. I was very happy to invite Joan, Katie and Janet to go along with me; but it wasn't only through altruism: I wanted someone to go with, as it was always more fun in a group.

So, in the morning, Joan Plumly and Janet came to the Woodside and from there we drove in my car to Northlea to pick up Domino and Bella. I had got into my car at the Woodside trusting in God and cursing myself for being so lazy as not to fix the starter motor. But I admit it was all through sheer idleness and I didn't want to spoil my holiday by having to do 'responsible' things, such as hanging around a garage while they fixed my old jalopy. Luckily the car started without any problem and so we were away.

Katie's house has a massive garden with a huge monkey-nut tree in it. Her lolloping Dalmatian came to greet us excitedly and equally excitedly Domino and Bella gathered their rucksacks together for the big adventure of the day. They were having a naughty day off school to boot. Katie tried to give me some money for their expenses but I flatly refused.

'How often do I come and see you?' I asked her, 'It's my duty as a cousin!'

So she smiled, we hugged each other and we were off.

We drove to Callander on the A84 and then at one point turned left towards Loch Lomond and the Trossachs, Fort William and Loch Ness.

I loved the road because it was all hilly and windy, with very little traffic and I just stayed in fourth gear all the way, accelerating and decelerating over all the humps, bumps and little hills. You couldn't go fast enough to stay in fifth gear; so it was perfect for when you needed that little extra bit of oomph, to stay in fourth.

We were very lucky with the day because, although it was a bit chilly, the sun was out, shining away hopefully and I have never in my life seen such a thick carpet of the most beautiful patchwork of incredibly shaggy scenery on our way there.

It looked as though nature was taking over the planet. The colours were astounding. All shades of the brown: tawn, russet, chesnut and filemot blending in perfectly with the reds of goldenrod, terracotta, sorrel and rufous as the greens splashed sprays of apple, antique bronze, celadon, olive, and citrine all over the landscape like rivers of paint. I was driving on a veritable palette.

The way the trees contrasted so alarmingly with their brunneous barks left me agape. We witnessed small lochs and waterfalls untouched by the greasy and grimy hands of Man and a double-rainbow diving into one of the bigger lakes. It was truly a magical sight and the perfect place for you to believe in God, because the making of this beauty was by no accident. There simply had to be an intelligence behind it. I sat there wondering why on earth I lived in a city and momentarily thought that perhaps I could get a job up here. Perhaps…

We stopped in Loch Lomond for a cup of tea and cake because my mother had always spoken of it. Then again, she spoke about everything to do with Scotland. I love people who are so patriotic and I think everyone should be proud of where they are born, regardless of where they are born; for you can find good in every place.

Loch Lomond was very nice, but all I could see was a big flat lake with a desolate café and some logs floating in it and nothing else there. Had I had the time, I would have walked a bit around it and prepared myself with the necessary booklets, but we had to get on.

In the car we were all talking and laughing and pointing out all the different points of interest. Domino was getting carried away with all his silly but funny jokes and I matched him joke for joke and laugh for laugh. I felt like part of a family and that I really belonged, even though, through the English side of me, I felt a bit different to them.

'I mind yer mammy and I came up tae Loch Ness in '36 or '37 on a school trip.' (1936 or 1937? Whit? Was she that old?)

'They were sponsoring some of the poorer children in the area and yer mammy wiz picked as one o' the lucky ones (or unlucky ones). We had a grand day oot and laff?! Och how we laffed! Whit a laff! Did yer mammy no tell ye aboot the story o' yon Irn-Bru?'

'Irn-Bru?' I asked distractedly as I concentrated on negotiating a hump-back bridge.

'Aye. It wiz sae comical. A'body else had brought lemonade, but yer mither an me couldnae afford it, so we pinched a bottle frae the back o' the bus when everywan else went into a café fer refreshments. We aye drank it wi' great gusto as we giggled and hiccupped away. Then we felt guilty and panic set in. We didnae waant tae get intae bither, so yer mammy suggested we pee into thon bottle o' Irn Bru, put the cap back on and put it back as innocently as wee lambs. Whit a' laff!'

I was quite shocked at such an intimate description coming from an elder.

Aunty Joan then proceeded to continue laughing until the Woodbines made her cough and splutter like an old aeroplane with engine trouble.

I laughed at this, but, of course, I didn't believe it. It was just another tall story. I'm surprised my mother never told me this one, as she was always looking for any excuse to amuse us. Perhaps it was one of the few that really was true.

Oh, the trees and the lochs and the sky and the puffy white clouds and the happy yellow sun glittering through it all was very magical. It was like being in a parallel world with everything negative removed from it. Your typical corny film day out.

After following all the signs to Loch Ness, we found ourselves at a big tourist building with a restaurant, café and souvenir shop. We were all happy to get out after such an uplifting yet long drive and everyone milled about. Some went to the toilet and I went into the souvenir shop with Domino. He is a very lovely boy with an openly alert handsome face and endearing personality.

We had a little laugh in there, pointing out all the funny tourists and souvenirs to each other, especially the ones of Nessie. I bought him a ceramic one in four bits, so that when you put it on a flat surface, it looked like it was coming out of the water. He was so happy with his little present that it made me happy. We were soon joined by the rest of the gang.

We wandered down to a part of the loch and everyone gingerly put their hands in the water. Not because they thought it would be cold, which it was, but because we all imagined that Nessie would rear her massive head and take a bite! Silly I know, but I have read quite a few books on Nessie, as I work in literature, as I said and believe it is highly possible that a forgotten dinosaur, most likely a plesiosaur, locked into the loch from both ends at the time all the other dinosaurs became extinct, escaping the destructive forces, could have survived and had continued to breed ever since. Stranger things have happened.

A lot of people just don't realise how huge, gargantuan and colossal this loch is and it is so deep that it will crush anything that tries to get to the bottom of it. Some researches sent a spherical sea-mine down there once, the ones they used to use to blow up shipping with during the war, and it came up as flat as a pancake!

So if you cannot explore such a big loch, how do you know what's in there? On the other hand, it could have been something that was thought up to help the Scottish tourist industry. I personally do not think so because many people of the highest repute and stations in life have sworn blind (pardon the pun) that they have seen the Loch Ness Monster and you would not risk your reputation or career just to impress someone or for the sake of a silly tale. I wouldn't have been surprised if my 'mither' had made up the Nessie story herself! I smiled to myself at the thought.

On my insistence, I then took them all to lunch and we enjoyed ourselves very much. Probably because our spirits had been lifted by the outing, by God's beautiful scenery, all His garden and because the atmosphere was so electric around such a happy place. The thing is, when you go away on holiday, you are leaving all your problems behind temporarily.

In the afternoon we went into a little theatre which told us the history of Loch Ness and at the end a vast curtain suddenly opened aside to reveal Urquhart Castle in all its ruinous glory. Luckily for us, the sun was shining and it glowed with all its soul. What an effect it had on us. It was a very impressive sight indeed. To think that someone from so many centuries ago was looking at the very same thing, sent a rooted thrill down my spine.

This impressive ruin dates from the 13th century and played a role in the *Wars of Scottish Independence* in the 14th century. When I was younger, I had no interest in history at all; probably because I had so little of my own, (!) but now I just stood there and imagined what it must have been like with all the soldiers fighting on it over the centuries and all the stories it held in secret, close to its bosom, taken to the grave.

I marvelled at the majesty of this rambling ruin, crumbling before my eyes with having seen so much in its lifetime. It naturally seemed to rise up from the undulating land as if it were part of it and a growth upon it; like an old, browned and broken tooth. It was a hat on the headland. It blended in so well with the earthy scenery and we gladly spent some time respectfully milling around it.

Domino, Bella and I went up to the top but Janet and Joan, who was sucking on a Woodbine like a toothless man sucking a sweet, couldn't be bothered to. She would rather suck away all day.

I told myself that one day I would come back and actually go boating on the loch, hoping not to be capsized by one of Nessie's fins. I could imagine myself with my face glued to the water's surface, straining to see if I could see any ominous shadows lurking underneath, before panicking and back, not wanting my head munched off.

We saw that there was a Visitor's Centre nearby, so decided to have a look and see what was in it. The ladies all went in first as Joan and Bella needed to spend a penny. Janet decided to wait in the main foyer for them as it was a bit windy and chilly, but I hung back with Domino, grabbing his arm and telling him that I had terrible wind and had to pump before we went in, to which he began to titter quite enthusiastically.

So, being both men of the world and for a laugh, I expelled this rancid, noxious, gaseous hot ball of methane into the atmosphere with a superheated 'hiiiisssssssssptt!' a silent but deadly, fart. As deadly as having a silencer on a gun or the hiss of a snake coming out of its basket.

The heat which passed through my anal aperture took me aback and took everything else aback as well, I shouldn't wonder. After Domino and I giggled uncontrollably for a few seconds, I walked straight into the Visitor's Centre with all the decorum of innocence I could muster before anyone else came along.

The problem was that, as it was such a windy day, when I opened the big swing door, the fetid fumes from my pungent flatulence sprang forward and wafted into the foyer ahead of me and surrounded Janet with a putrid stench of farmyard liquidised fecal slurry; an invisible cirrus cloud of green gas.

It smelt like a burst sewer. It was like a knock-out draught. Real curry-gas. Domino and I both laughed uncontrollably anew when we saw a man standing next to Janet, screw up his nose like a rat smelling the air and giving her the filthiest look I have seen in a long time. Domino and I both went bright red. Not from embarrassment, but from the exertion of laughing so hard and from trying to keep it all under control. Lest any more gas should escape.

I must say that Janet was not very amused when I told her about my gaseous exchange and the man. But Domino said that he was really looking forward to telling his mum Katie about it and that he couldn't wait till he got to school the next day to tell all his school chums! Bella just looked disgusted. I think her estimation of me has plummeted somewhat. Whit?

All good things come to an end and so when we were walking back to the car to go home, I suddenly heard someone calling me by my surname. Here it was really out of place.

'Mr. Garland! Oh, Mr. Garland, have you got a minute?'

I turned around, stunned, not imagining for a moment who on earth it could be, especially with an English accent, as nobody knew me around here. I was almost embarrassed in front of everyone else. When I turned around, the face was very familiar, but I still could not place it as it was so incongruous here by Loch Ness.

'It's Doctor Overwright.'

'Oh, my goodness me! I didn't recognise you without your white coat on (and bad news). What on earth are you doing here? You are the last person I expected to see!'

'Even we humble doctors go on holiday sometimes, you know,' he explained, almost guiltily. 'Might I have a word?' he asked, looking at Domino and the girls in a greeting of apologetic interruption. Must be quite urgent if he had to do it here, now.

'Afternoon. Good afternoon,' he bid them politely.

'Gud Efternoon,' they all replied in unison, like marionettes.

'Of course,' I said, suddenly panicking inside. First of all I did not want my relatives to know of my potentially fatal illness and then I was very afraid of being given further bad news. I felt like I was being taken away to be shot. I imagined not seeing my relatives and friends ever again and I felt a heavy sadness.

'Look, Mr. Garland, it is not within medical ethics to discuss cases in such casual surroundings and an appointment always has to be made. But I have never been very obedient nor conventional when it comes to the correct bedside manner and this is urgent. I have always been a bit of a rebel and a maverick.'

'Oh, God…' I thought, going completely cold inside. '…don't deal me this card.'

'I saw how much you were enjoying your day and felt I just had to tell you that you are in the clear. Your growth is benign; you're fine!'

For a few hour-long seconds I just stared at him, as if he were an enigma I simply could not work out.

'Really?!! Really?!!' I blurted out, holding my heart.

'Yes, Mr. Garland. You're absolutely fine,' he assured me, smiling sincerely. 'There's nothing wrong with you whatsoever. Just come in and see me when you get back to London. We'll still have to remove it, just to be on the safe side.'

When I shook his hand I must have pumped it a thousand times, like drawing water from a well in a poor African country and he laughed.

'You're my saviour and my saint. What a wonderful man you are! I cannot begin to tell you how happy you have made me. I am so relieved! You have no idea!'

'You're very welcome. It's always nice to give someone good news for a change!'

Changing the subject, through some embarrassment I shouldn't wonder, he commented to me:-

'Isn't this wonderful scenery?' he asked me as he looked out at Loch Ness in all its brilliantly natural, deep-pan glory.

'Oh, yes!' I agreed. 'It is the most beautiful scenery in the world, Doctor,' I added, over-enthusiastically after the good news. Everything was enhanced now and I loved everyone. 'Enjoy your holiday, you deserve it,' I shouted back as I ran to join my gang.

In fact, I ran so much with elation and the lightness of relief that I whizzed straight passed them, yahooing all the way. They all looked at me as if I were mad. Which was nothing new.

'Sorry, the natural exuberance of youth!' I explained.

'Ach, Lukie,' my cousin Janet commented with a laugh. 'Yer no that young, son!'

'Well, I feel like it,' I shot back at her, with laughter and smiles. They were all wondering what on earth was the matter with me.

When we all climbed back into the car, it wouldn't start and I turned around to them with a huge smile on my face and said 'Hey, it won't start! Isn't that hilarious?'

I then started laughing until the tears were rolling down my face and, being so contagious, the car was soon rocking around through all our heaving diaphragms. Perhaps some people thought we were having a massive love-in!

They had no idea why this little set-back was so amusing to me. I just got out, once I had regained control of my emotions, with Domino following me out of curiosity and with the anticipation of more fun. I grabbed a hammer and chisel from the boot, opened the bonnet and attacked my poor starter motor with the enthusiasm of a demented blacksmith or sculptor making his masterpiece; his opus.

I then turned the car over and it started immediately. Oh, what a glorious day!

I sang all the way back to Doune as I just had to get all this pent-up energy out of my system, as everyone else looked on in sheer bemusement and I eventually had to explain to them why I was so deliriously happy. Then they all smiled with the greatest sympathy and understanding and congratulated me and my cousin Janet just keep saying 'Oh, my. Oh my goodness, oh my! Oh, Luke!' (Oh, God!)

When we got back to Doune, Katie invited me to *'The History of Doune.'* An Open Day at Domino's school where parents can sit in in class as their children have their lesson and learn about their school environment.

It was implemented by the school's governing body so that parents could better understand what teaching was all about and what their children went through. I thought this would be quite fun, actually and so, with Domino hanging onto my arm, like a monkey off a tree branch, pleading with me, I happily agreed to go. Even the dug looked satisfied and lolloped around with a ridiculous grin on its face, getting in between everyone's legs.

Er…yes.

Chapter Eight

-1997-

O flower of Scotland
When will we see your like again?
That fought and died
For your wee bit hill and glen
And stood against him
Proud Edward's army
And sent him homeward
Tae think again
-Roy Williamson-

'Ye can sit wi' me!' Domino said as I walked into Katie's house to meet them and go on to the '*Doune School Historical Special Event.*'

'No, you'll be sitting with your school chums. I wouldn't be allowed to sit at your little desk, is that not right, Domino-head?' I asked, teasing him affectionately.

'I'll be sitting at the back of the class with all the other grown-ups. But you can turn around and make silly faces at me if you want,' I suggested mischievously.

He grinned as he grabbed his satchel and urged his mom to hurry up. Katie was very proud of her son, and so she should be, because he was also getting good grades.

So out the door we went. Just the three of us, as Bella was at her own school and they were not having any special event today.

On the short walk to the school, not my mother's old one, which had long since closed down, but to a modern new one, the one I had laid a brick in, Domino was jabbering away ten-to-the-dozen about anything and everything that came to mind. I wondered where that brick now was, exactly. He had now latched onto me like a limpet and I was fairly interested in what he was saying, only pretending to be more so, humouring him, as I liked children really.

When we got to the school building I was very impressed by its clean, modern and well-maintained appearance, with its very big glass windows. Okay, it did look a little bit like a building on an industrial estate, but that's because it was utilitarian, as all these buildings had to be.

A lot of pupils were milling about the teachers outside in the playground, excitedly waiting for the bell to go off.

Katie said to me: 'Oh, there's Miss Ferguson, Domino's teacher. Come and I'll introduce you.' So we ambled up to her and her face lit up when she saw Katie.

'Oh, hello, Katie. Glad you could make it.'

This Miss Ferguson was in her late twenties, pretty, with small features (i.e. nothing stuck out too much). She had short-ish blonde hair, a nice simple flowery dress that cascaded over her body like a waterfall; over all the appealing bumps and humps and her outstanding feature was that she was wearing multi-coloured spectacle frames. Very avant garde I must say! I suspected something else too, more's the pity, as I was free and single now.

'Anita,' Katie said, waving a hand towards me, 'This is my cousin Luke, up from London. But his mom was born here.'

'Not a real traitor, then?' Anita commented to me mysteriously and perhaps a bit over-familiarly. But she had such a nice smile that it washed away any offence I might have felt. And I knew she was joking, anyway.

'Perhaps to the South, but not to the North,' I replied determinedly, wanting to be so much a part of my Scottish side.

'In that case, we'll allow you in,' she teased and led the way to class with another one of her sunshine smiles and little girl in tow. She had lovely white teeth…she had lovely…

'Is she gay?' I asked Katie, as we all trundled down a corridor into a very big room with a lot of chairs facing a big board; a bit like a makeshift open-air cinema.

'Whit? Anita? Oh, no! She loves men. In fact she just finished with one,' she laughed and put an arm around me. Then she leant forward and whispered in my ear: 'Why dinnae ye ask her oot?'

'Er…well…er,' I said in mock modesty. I didn't have time to say anything else because Miss Anita Ferguson was clapping her hands for everyone's attention. *That's what I like, a room with a view*, I thought as I looked at her.

'Come along, children. Hurry up and sit doon, because we hae a lot tae get through this mornin' and with the way I speak, we'll be 'ere a' dae!' (laughter).

'Should we hae brought pieces wi'jam?' called out a parent a row behind where Katie and I were sitting. Everyone tittered.

'Parents are here to observe and not disrupt the class!' Anita said to the woman, wagging a finger jokingly, but assertively, at her. 'All questions and…er…comments, Mrs. Patterson, at the end o' the lesson or I'll gae ye detention!'

Everyone laughed anew, breaking the ice. Especially the students who loved nothing better than a parent or any elder showing themselves up.

Anita went straight into it.

'First aff, dis onywan ken whit the word 'Doune' means?'

'Dung,' suggested a big boy quite loudly and everyone laughed with shocked amusement. Someone let out a loud 'Ha!'

'Not 'Dung,' Hamish, but 'Dun.' It's the Gaelic word for 'fort''

There was a little hubbub of interest and most were commenting 'Oh, right enough. Well, that makes sense, is that no right son?'

'Now Doune may not be Paris, London or New York,…..'

To this information there were a lot of derisory sounds and some pupils even issued a 'Boo!'

'…but even if ye look in the most seemingly insignificant and, aye, smallest places, ye will find yer hidden gems…'

At this everyone, adult and pupil alike, started to listen a bit more intently.

'…now the one thing that Doune is famous for is well known. And that is what, Brian?' Anita asked one of the little boys who was sitting in the front row, a scrawny wee thing.

'Cow pats, miss!' Freckled Freddy shouted out loudly, proud of himself. (Roars of nervous laughter)

'Dinnae be sae daft, ye silly wee boy,' Anita retorted, with a slight smile.

'Pistols, Miss,' a boy replied in little above a whisper, the puir wee shy thing.

'That's right! Where examples can still be seen in *The Museum of Scotland* in Edinburgh. And it wiz ane o' thon pistols that fired the first shot in the *American War of Independence.* All that way. That's amazing, is it no?' she asked the class, very proudly.

'Wiz it fired frae Doune, Miss?' another small boy sitting next to Domino asked?

The whole class erupted with laughter. I saw Domino nudge his pal as he tittered.

'Dinnae be daft, ye bampot!' Miss Anita Ferguson rebuked him lightly as she laughed along with all the others. The boy blushed alarmingly, made worse by his bright ginger hair and pale, greenish freckles.

'…now, there's another thing Doune is famous for. Can anyone tell me what that is?' she asked earnestly, looking around the room.

'Doune castle,' miss,' a little pony-tailed girl with glasses suggested, putting her little long hand up.

'No, Patricia. We'll come to the castle later. But that was a good answer.'

'…though less well-known, Doune is famous for its Roman remains.'

'Whit?! Yon tinkers, miss? Did they find a body?' a fat girl with a tight cardigan shouted out.

Miss Anita Ferguson looked at Aggie as laughter erupted again. I thought it was very funny and shook with laughter. I just love school humour. Katie nudged me. Being a girl, that pupil was probably being totally serious and not trying to be funny.

'Romans, Aggie, not Romanies. Frae the days o' Julius Caesar and the Roman Empire. Even Doune castle is built on the site of a Roman fortification and the remains can only be seen undergroond…'

'I didn't know that,' I commented to Katie with a surprised expression. Doune was becoming more interesting than it seemed at first glance.

'Neither did I,' Katie replied, looking on at the teacher with admiration.

'…and there was a mound known locally as '*Round Wood*.' Here a coffin was uncovered which contained the bones of a six-year-old boy with a stone axe and he belonged to the Beaker people of the early Bronze age of 1800 B.C. and the remains of a Roman fort were excavated where stone bread ovens were found.'

'We've got beakers at hame, Miss. We drink oor Ribena oot o' them. Did the Beaker people make these plastic cups?' a pretty blonde girl asked very seriously, to more laughter and embarrassment, blushes and flushes.

'No, Moira. Plastic didn't exist in thae daes. That wiz jist the breed they were,' she added kindly.

'Another building uncovered is thought to have been the fort's hospital; and fragments of Samian ware and amphorae were recovered, dating from the Flavian period (whit?) and the first Roman incursion into Scotland by the Romans in AD 79-80. So ye see, we dae hae quite a bit o' history.'

'Aye!' both parents and pupils replied in enthusiastic unison, their pride beginning to emanate, chests subconsciously sticking out. The attention and interest in the classroom was quite intense now and I have to admit that I myself was very interested in what Anita...sorry... Miss Ferguson, was relating. Perhaps we could discuss it more over dinner. What? Well, you never know.

'Ye micht be interested tae ken that Bonnie Prince Charlie passed through here in 1745.'

'Wit? Passed wind through here miss?' a naughty pupil asked cheekily, to another wave of laughter.

'I think a'body should just pass through Doune, Miss, and keep on gaein!'

'O, how very funny!' Anita said to the manny almost right at the back of the classroom. 'That's very gud,' she conceded. 'I'm sure I've got a gold star here somewhere fer ye. And I know just where to pin it!' The classroom erupted into waterfall laughter, ending in a tinkle. School-boy humour strikes again.

'Now, finally, as far as Doune itself is concerned, there is another point Doune is famous for and that is that it is strategically-placed (just like the island of Malta was during the second world war. Whit?) and is known as the '*Gateway to the North*,' tae thon Trossachs and beyond,' she added with a flourish, as if she were Buzz Lightyear.

Even I felt I was bursting with pride and everyone applauded uproariously. She was really rousing the audience now. Miss Ferguson talked on for about another half-hour before holding her hand up and smiling demurely at more applause.

'I've no feenished yet,' she informed everyone in mock offence. 'Somebody mentioned the castle before and there's plenty to tell ye aboot that. But we'll all hae a wee break the noo. Drinks or tea and biscuits fer fifteen minoots and then we'll get ane with it.'

Katie and I didn't get much of a chance to speak to Miss Anita Ferguson as a crowd of parents had cornered her; full of pride and wanting to know more about their precious wee village. She was the heroine of the moment and the life and soul of the party. I must say that a lot of radiance came out of her. The sort of radiance I would very much like to feel.

Instead, I had Domino, who was coercing me into breaking wind and, of course, I declined his offer in front of such esteemed company.

Soon, we found ourselves back in our seats again for part two of the *Doune School Historical* (or hysterical, as Domino put it) *Special Event.*

Anita stood back on her plinth waiting for everyone to get comfortable. She reminded me of the Statue of Liberty, only much prettier. I looked outside. It was a bit of a dull day really. Slate grey.

'Right, ladies and gentlemen and ma dear pupils, Doune castle itself has a very interesting history.'

Really? I thought. I was always told it was just a merchant castle of little significance; although, according to my mother, it was the epicentre of all great global battles.

'Doune castle is a medieval stronghold situated on a wooded bend where the *Ardoch Burn* flows into the river Teith. It was built in the 13th century, damaged in the *Scottish Wars of Independence* and was rebuilt in its present form in the 14th century by Robert Stewart, *the Duke of Albany,* son of King Robert II of Scotland.

'In 1425 Robert Stewart was executed for treason. In 1361 Robert Stewart had been made '*Earl of Menteith'* and was granted the lands on which Doune castle now stands.' A few pupils and adults alike frowned at the sudden wave of information.

As Miss Anita Ferguson paused to let all the information sink into the young and older minds alike, I commented to Katie that I hadn't known that and a new respect for Doune castle rose in me. I was really enjoying my proud Scottish day and spared a thought for my mother. Maybe she hadn't been telling such tall tales after all.

'Now, then, children, can any one of you tell me what very famous personage stayed at Doune castle on many occasions?'

'Andy Stewart!' volunteered a spotty little boy in the group. Here we go again!

The whole classroom flooded with cackling laughter and even I couldn't stop. The image of him singing 'Donald whaur's yer troosers?' from the battlements was just too much to contemplate. Even Katie was wiping away her tears of absurdity.

'I wasnae thinkin' sae recently, actually,' Anita commented drily.

'No. It wiz Mary Queen o' Scots. Is that no something? That oor wee castle hoosed such a luminary (whit?). Doune wiz held by forces loyal to Mary during the short civil war, which followed her abdication in 1567 until 1570. A messenger was caught, interrogated and tortured right here in Doune in October of that year. He was found with letters to Mary Queen of Scots on him. Just imagine that!'

'I think ye need tae be tortured yersel,' the wee boy next to Domino said to him and Domino just tutted and looked round at me, embarrassed. I just nodded to him and winked.

Well, it seems that my mother was telling the truth and that Doune castle didn't play such a minor role in history after all. In all these years, I never knew that Mary Queen of Scots had ever stayed at Doune castle, let alone on many occasions. Or about all the battles. It was all very impressive indeed.

'Whit else Miss,' a young girl asked, sitting upright with interest.

'Well, King James VI visited Doune on occasion and must have stayed at Doune castle. It hardly would have been the Woodside!' She laughed so enthusiastically at her own joke that others joined her in sympathy and raised eyebrows. She was really letting herself go. *Oh, miss Ferguson!*

'...and in 1593 a plot against him was discovered and the king surprised the conspirators at Doune castle.' (One can just imagine the bloodshed).

'Whit else, miss Ferguson?' a chubby black-haired boy asked, holding his ruler like a sword and swishing it in the air.

'Yer aye makin' me werk fer ma money the day!' Anita commented, but didn't mind because she found it such an interesting subject and got the blood pumping in her veins.

'Well now, the castle played host to military action during the *War of the Three Kingdoms* Clencairn's rising in the mid-17th century and during the Jacobite risings in the 17th/18th centuries.

'So ye see, children...and youse elder children at the back,' (titter) she added, indicating the parents, 'yon castle was not always as quiet as it is the noo and coming forward a few centuries, for a wee bit o' fun, ye may all be very interested to ken that the fillums '*Ivanhoe*' and '*Monty*

Python's Holy Grail' were both filmed at Doune castle. '*Ivanhoe*,' which was made in 1952, starred none other than Elizabeth Taylor and Robert Taylor. (It was hard to imagine Elizabeth Taylor walking down Doune Main street!)

'…and, of course, all youse children will ken who was in the Python fillum.

'So thank you very much for coming, everyone. I hope that you wee 'uns and big 'uns have enjoyed this '*History of Doune*' session and that you now look upon oor wee village in a different light. And remember, Doune isnae small. It's just modest. Thank you.'

There was a big, loud round of applause and all the parents scraped their chairs and stood in genuine appreciation. Naturally, the pupils stood there hooting and making other silly simian noises and movements; all clamouring for attention. There was a great cacophony of sound as more chairs and desks were pushed aside and people chatted away ten-to-the-dozen and doors cracked open.

Katie, Domino and I finally managed to catch up with Anita back in the playground. She was surrounded by a group of children and adults alike, but not for long, because the parents wanted to 'gie away hame fer lunch.'

As we walked up to Anita I saw a little girl with frizzy hair pulling on Anita's dress and heard her asking if it was true that Doune had fairies of its very own.

'Och, aye,' asserted Miss Ferguson, 'In a place ca'ed '*Ternishee*' near Doune Lodge and fairy dancing parties have been seen on the '*Fairy Knowe*,' a hillock on the Ardoch, aboot half-a-mile frae Doune centre. Tell ye what, Fiona, why dinae ye draw me a picture o' a fairy and bring it in tae me in the mornin?'

The girl smiled shyly and ran to her mither, I mean mother.

Finally we had Anita's attention and I told her how much I genuinely loved the session and that I had always thought my mother had been telling tall tales about Doune castle.

I then told her I was very interested in the history of Doune and perhaps she would like to have dinner with me one night to discuss it further. What a prat!

'Oh, I'm awfy sorry, Mr. Garland, er, Luke, but I am going away for a few days to visit a sick relative. I would have loved to have come. But maybe next time, eh?'

I think she was genuinely sorry that she couldn't make the date. Well, I needed to believe something to feed my ego. On the way back to Katie's house, Domino was teasing me by saying:-

'When I get home I'm going tae eat an apple; then Anita sandwich, then Anita banana then Anita humble pie!'

Oh, yes, Domino. Hilarious. So very hilarious.

***

-1965-

One temperamental morning I woke up and was really looking forward to going and meeting my cousins to play. So I dressed hurriedly, accidentally kicking an *'Oor Wulllie'* annual under the bed, while my mother prepared a breakfast of fried eggs and sliced sausage for me. I gulped it down as if there were no tomorrow and rushed down the stairs to the street door.

'Dinnae be late back!' my mother shouted after me and I replied that I wouldn't. But what did late mean? It was still daylight up to around 10pm in the summer up here.

I sauntered up Castle Hill to where my cousin Nigel lived and went through the side door of the house, welcomed by a lingering smell of fried food and wet laundry. I shouted '*Hello! Hello!*' as I walked through the empty kitchen into the sitting-room and suddenly encountered my aunt, who was standing in front of the big windae, holding up a pair of adult underpants to the light; which looked like one of those battle-scarred flags from a '*Battle of Waterloo*' documentary. My Uncle Billy had actually managed to blow three small holes through the material as parting shots to compliment the deranged briefs. To me, the screech marks in his underpants looked like the starting grid of a Formula One race track. My Auntie Maisie ignored my announcement. I noticed a pile of dirty laundry in a plastic cracked basket on the couch, before returning my gaze to the offending article.

'Will ye jist look at that! Jist look at all them shite streaks. I swear I'll have his guts fer garters, so I will!'

'It looks like they're already in his underpants!' I blurted out brazenly before I could stop myself. I knew it wasn't my place to comment on my Uncle Billy's underwear, but I was trying to fit in by being as crude as some of my relatives sometimes were.

I thought I was taking a risk and really didn't understand what guts and garters were in those days, as I had led a sheltered life; but I thought I could get away with it with my aunt. I blushed furiously, as I thought I had crossed the line. But it was just a spontaneous comment and I always liked to amuse people with my humour; even if it sometimes backfired as much as my Uncle Billy's rear end did.

Luckily my aunt ignored my hilarious comment and just grimaced into the light.

'I've a bloody guid mind to let him wash his ane undies,' she commented, enwrapped in her household thoughts. As I stood there waiting, I spotted her red-and-white carpet sweeper, which was all the rage in the sixties. I played with it once, riding it like a horse, but it didn't run very well. The first time I had seen a carpet sweeper, I thought it was a very strange appliance and didn't know what it was, as we had hoovers in London.

'I came to see if Nigel wants to come out,' I explained, tentatively, as I sensed she was not in a particularly good mood.

My psychic aunt looked directly at me, squinting through her sharply upward-sloping glasses and fag in her mouth. She was wearing one of those pinny things.

'He's no 'ere, Lukie. He's helping his da on the building site. If yon school's nae feenished, there'll be nae educatin' the young 'uns!' and she cackled at her own humour, which, even I, as a child didn't really find very funny or, to be honest, didn't quite understand it. But I pretended I did and laughed along with her; especially to cover my faux-pas. Ho-ho-ho! So funny.

'Oh,' I groaned disappointed, 'That's a shame. Okay. Please tell him I'll see him tomorrow.'

'Right ye are, Lukie. Tell yer mam to come roond tae tea wan o' these days,' she suggested, still looking at the offending underpants and tutting to herself, lost in a world of her own.

'I will, Aunty Maisie!' I shouted, as I tore out the door to next door.

When I burst into Aunty Hattie's kitchen, she was standing over the sink peeling potatoes with raw, red hands under running cold…no, freezing…water and looking out the window at the birds on the lawn. She had given them the remnants of some *Mother's Pride* bread. What a waste! I spotted a fresh loaf lying on the kitchen table. Even when I was in a hurry I noticed food.

'Can Ryan come out to play?' I asked hopefully.

'Och, I'm sorry Lukie. Ryan's gone to Stirling for a dental appointment. I dinnae ken when he'll be back. How are ye, son? Are ye faring fine?'

'Yes, thank you Aunty Hattie. Maybe I'll catch him tomorrow. Can you tell him I came round?'

'Oh, I will, Lukie. Dinnae ye worry aboot that,' she assured me with a very motherly smile.

So there I was out in the streets with no-one to play with. There seemed to be no-one about. Not even any silly little girls with their dolly prams. Okay, the weather wasn't perfect and there were heavy purple clouds looming about like great sperm whales in the sky. But that usually didn't deter children, as they seldom took much notice of the weather. I supposed everyone was just busy doing other things. Though I couldn't imagine what. It was just one of those negative days.

I roamed around the village to see if there was anyone about, but all was as dead as the contents of a coffin. I went to Moray park but, apart from some old wifeys and an ancient relic of a craggy bent old man walking their dogs, there was nothing else happening. I didn't bother going to my cousin Rae's house in Queen street because I knew she was on holiday somewhere in Lancashire visiting relatives who had moved down south. I wished I were in Lancashire with her.

I naturally seemed to roam further and further away from Doune and soon found myself on the fringes of the Wood of Doune. I wasn't really interested at that age in country walks, but I thought that perhaps the Wood of Doune would be quite interesting to explore, as I thought I might find some hide-outs or whatnot and what-have-you. I had heard some stories of ghosts and hauntings deep in the woods and I didn't really believe them; yet was too frightened not to. I just decided subconsciously to carry on through curiosity and not go too deep in.

At the entrance of the wood was a lea spread out with a fine carpet of yellow, orange and rusty-red leaves to welcome all who came to visit and I liked the feel of the foliage scrunching under my feet and I stomped heavily for more sound effects. I met a man with a lovely Labrador and stopped to pat it with my podgy, soft hand. The dog must have thought it was a sponge.

I then carried on into the fringes of the wood and looked up dreamily at the great graphite-grey shafts of light streaming down from above. Even a child can be impressed by nature and I curiously imagined all sorts of things going on. I could hear a sweet cacophony of birds twittering away to their hearts' content; all vying for centre stage and I noticed many things like mushrooms amongst the wet grass and moss growing on the trees; the trees which stood so massive, tall and proud while not moving; just watching and biding their time. Looking for the English coming over the hill. Nature's sentries.

I picked up a stick and started waving it around, imaging that I was *Zorro* or some Caribbean pirate and prodded the naked air with it to grunts of my invisible foe. After a while I felt a bit silly doing that, so I carried on, just looking around for anything interesting to see or do and I didn't notice how temperamental the weather was getting.

I then followed an earthen path which led to a bird-watching refuge by the lake and went in there, pretending to fire my stick-rifle at enemy German soldiers. For a short while it was fun, but then it got boring doing it all on my own because I couldn't see the reactions of my friends. I leant on the window-pane and puffed away in boredom. Even the ducks had ignored my bullets. As I turned around to look around the inside of the hut, for anything of interest discarded, I noticed some graffiti which read *'Get Stuffed'* and was shocked out of my naïve world by its sense of aggressiveness and rudeness. Even though I did not know what it actually meant, I sensed it was negative and wondered whether or not it had something to do with taxidermy. I thought it must be something naughty and made a mental note to ask one of my pals what it meant exactly. Though it wasn't directed at anyone in particular, apart from society itself, I felt it was directed at me.

I gladly left the hut and, inevitably, went deeper into the woods in search of someone to play with. Even the friend of a friend of a friend would have done. But there was absolutely no-one about and it was as if everyone had flown to the moon. It made me realise that it didn't matter where in the world you were, as long as you had your friends around you.

I trod on the mulch under my feet and could hear insects scuttling away in the undergrowth; which rose my hackles. Blowing leaves made me feel isolated, lonely and depressed and the dark canopies of verdant foliage made me feel hemmed in. I kept tripping on the tree roots on the ground and that made me more frustrated and I tutted at life and wanted to cry. Were there slimy frogs about? Unlike other schoolboys, I didn't like slimy frogs and was becoming very wary and I felt the darkness closing in so as to entrap and engulf me in its amorphous and infinite body.

As I walked further and further into the woods, it got darker and darker and this was not only because the denser trees were blocking out the sunlight, but because the sky itself had become very dark, threatening and brooding, huffing and puffing until the purple-bruised, pregnant, bloated clouds suddenly disgorged a sea of water, Nature's amniotic sac, down onto the woods and me.

The rain suddenly shot down with a vengeance, sending ultra-fine elongated spears of spiked ice-cold darts of water piercing through the trees, the leaves, the foliage, the flowers, the mushrooms, the toadstools, the moss and onto my head so that, in a few seconds, my shirt had turned from a light blue to a macabre black from the effects of the downpour.

Although the trees at first tried to shelter me as best they could, they were no match to the power of mobile nature and they began to wave their arms about in a windy panic as, suddenly, thunder roared and lightning cracked with an electrifying bark and struck with silvery metal fingers, feeling their way down to the ground; searching for victims. Like me.

The tree branches appeared to jerk towards me as if suddenly brought to life like Frankenstein's monster; as if they wanted to grab hold of me, kill me and devour me. They were dancing about as if under the influence of some terrible sorcerer's evil spell in an attacking ecstasy…the rain pelted me with watery bullets, which stung me on the face and hands. I looked up at the sky and then down at the ground. I didn't know where to go nor what to do and I wanted my mother.

'Oh, my God!' I thought. How had this happened so suddenly? I held my arms up to try and stave off the offending elements as I tripped and stumbled along, like some stupid romantic woman in one of those melodramatic television period dramas and I felt like a big girl's blouse. And, for me, it would have had to have been a very big girl's blouse indeed.

I also felt lonely, sorry for myself, sad and started to whimper. The thunder was roaring above me and the lightning was crashing its evil tentacles upon me and I thought of my family and of how I just wanted to be with them. Friends didn't matter now. I just wanted to go home. To my mother's bosom and the pantry.

I started to turn. I was all over the place and it was obvious I had never been a boy scout. Mild panic started to set in as the wood wept and roared around me, accompanied by the sound of huge globules of rain smacking against the leaves like soft punches, to a maniacal orchestral sound: the thunderous drumming of rain.

I really didn't want to be in the woods any more and was desperately trying to find my way out. But everywhere I turned, all I saw, through the blurriness of rain and running water were trees and other obstacles.

But then I suddenly spotted a little yellow glow in the deep darkness, like a static firefly and wondered what it could be. I headed for it, gingerly, because I thought it might be one of the tinkers and they could be scary at times. But it was my only point of reference in this miasma of misery and so I headed for the only life-ring I knew.

As I got nearer, out of the gloom emerged what looked like a ramshackle, dilapidated, makeshift bivouac-of-a-hut put together like *Oor Wullie's* shed and the rain pattering on it was astoundingly loud. So loud that I thought it must wake the whole village. On making my final descent, I heard someone or something shuffling about inside and felt like Hansel and Gretel approaching the witch.

But it is like in one of those horror films where the main victim just keeps on walking into danger out of sheer stupidity and so I slowly moved aside a remnant of hessian, which was acting as a flimsy doorway.

To this day I don't know why I didn't just call out a query of who was within but, nevertheless, I suddenly saw a figure sitting on an inverted bucket by a rickety old table, casting a long shadow behind it. I was never so happy to see another human being in all my life.

'Opie! What are ye doing here?'

'Eh? Whit? Whit are ye daein' here? Can a man no get a bit o' peace?'

'But what are you doing here, Opie?' I asked, delighted to see someone I knew with a friendly face.

'Come on in, laddie,' he ordered me upon seeing how soaking wet I was. 'Yer aye drookit. Jist like a dug.'

So I went in to the little hovel and saw that the light I had seen was from a little fire that was flickering away on the ground; providing quite a nice little bit of heat to boot. I quickly further observed that he also had a kettle, tin cups, tea bags in a beaten-up, old rusty tin and dirty, brown-clogged sugar in a jam jar sitting on a quite expertly nailed table shoved up against the bivouac wall.

'But what *are* you doing here, Opie?' I persisted, looking around the inside of his refuge with disbelief. I felt a bit sorry for him because he was all on his own. Like I sometimes was.

'This is where I come to get awa' frae a'body else. They aye tease me at teems.'

'Oh, Opie,' I said, suddenly realising and feeling very guilty and sorry for him, 'they're only having a laugh. They don't mean anything by it. Everyone likes you really. You are popular in the village, you know.'

'Aye, weel. That's as may be. Onyways, come in and sit yersel doon. Fancy a brew and a pie?'

What a silly question.

When I had surprised him, I noticed that he was sitting quietly by the table with a pair of glasses on, reading a newspaper; though his glasses were sitting quite askew. I hadn't thought about it before, but, for some reason, I hadn't thought he could read. Or that daft people needed glasses.

Opie and I spent the next part of two hours chatting away about nothing really and having a good laugh. It was the first time I realised that he had feelings. Feelings very much like I had about lacks of confidence and being teased and feeling stupid and from that day on I saw a different Opie; though didn't always remember it.

The rain stopped gradually and you could only hear the odd drip of water off the leaves and bare-back branches smacking on the ground with a dying effort.

'C'mon then. We'd best get ye hame son.' The way he said '*son*' filled me with humility.

Of course, I wasn't his son, but his familiarity and affection gave me a warm, grateful feeling and we were soon walking out of the woods and onto the sodden lea. It was quite late now and the twilight twinkled around us with relief. Stars were coming out.

Then out of the gloom, I saw a big limping figure approaching.

'Don!' I exclaimed. I had never seen Don MacFairlane out from behind his counter, let alone out of his shop. A bit like a dog off his leash; a sweet out of its wrapper.

'Yer mammy was aye afeart fer ye, laddie, so I shut the shap and came lookin' fer ye. You alright son?' he asked with a kind smile, which extended to Opie Bopie, as I sometimes called him. Opie just stood there looking slightly ill-at-ease. Too many people made him nervous. Especially adults.

'You shut your sweetie shop just to come and look for me?' I asked, flabbergasted. I could not believe anyone would do that for me.

'Aye, weel, it was just ten minutes early,' he grinned and winked at Opie, who didn't really catch the implication.

So, with Don MacFairlane's hand on my shoulder and Opie trotting alongside us like a faithful dog, I walked out of the Wood of Doune feeling like a man…well, what I thought a man would feel like anyway and I thought Opie and Don were my best friends ever. I couldn't wait to tell my brother and mother how valued I was.

Chapter Nine

Should auld acquaintance be forgot
And never brought to mind?
Should auld acquaintance be forgot
And auld lang syne?

For auld lang syne, my dear
For auld lang syne
We'll tak a cup o' kindness yet
For auld lang syne
-Robert Burns-

-1997-

And now I had to go and do what I had been putting off ever since the day I came back to Doune. I had to go to the quarry, or rather, the site where it had been. It was now like the dentist; it was a place I dreaded to go to, yet one I had to go to out of respect for those who are now gone and to face the ghosts left undone, if I ever wanted any closure and any future peace in my life. I had left it for far too long and was fed-up of being a wimp. We can always put things to the backs of our minds, but they will eventually rush forward with the unstoppable power of a tsunami unless we find ways of calming the waters.

That is why I felt a bit wary of coming back to Doune and that, through my own guilt, expected everyone to stare at me and comment about me when they saw me in the street. It was true that a lot of people in Doune remembered the catastrophic events of that one day in the 1960s; but that was the older generation and the younger people were less bothered about it and newcomers, who had moved in more recently knew not of it.

The emotion of it had subsided. It had not been my fault anyway, even though I had always felt guilty through association. Like all good Catholics, I was brought up to always feel guilty about everything and anything.

Everyone said it had not been my fault. But still… survivor guilt.

As I was now nearing the end of my little holiday in Doune, a wee holiday in a wee village, I thought it was the right time to go and get it over with. I simply had to go; especially as I might never return, with the future being so unpredictable these days. There was no question about it. It would have been like coming to Doune and not visiting a very close dying relative. It would have been unacceptable to avoid it; and not practical.

So I walked up the village, turned left into Moray street, walked passed Northlea, wondering what Katie was doing and wanting to visit her instead of having to go to my other destination. But I walked on a bit - a dead man walking - and stopped and stood there, a silent witness, waiting for the imagery to hit me in the face.

-1965-

It was a very dour, grey day, with a heavy silence in the air and, thinking back on it, it didn't feel right. There was negativity in the atmosphere. Prescience. Things were out of kilter, but a child does not notice these things as much as an adult does because they don't have the maturity of mind to notice it or cope with it. Or worry about it.

Anyway, that was the atmosphere that day and my playmates and I were especially bored. It was one of those days where no-one was around; adult or child alike and my usual friends, apart from Ryan Mallone, were not to be found. Luckily, Ryan was at home and I got him to walk down to the sweetie shop with me, to eat out of boredom. Ryan was quite willing and smiled his usual happy grin, being such a placid lad.

As we came out of Don MacFairlane's, we bumped into Patrick, who was a bigger and older lad than we were and his wee neighbour's son, Callum McCulloch, who sometimes hung about with us, when he was allowed to by his mam.

I have mentioned him before when he clung on to our group as we did the rounds of the village. He reminded me of '*Wee Eck*' from the '*Oor Wullie*' annuals. He was only about five or six to our ten and eleven. Patrick was twelve and was considered quite the grown-up of the crowd. He wasn't often in our crowd, as he was that much older and bigger (big for his age too) and I was a bit wary of him. He had a football face, big boiled-egg eyes and a haystack of menacing black hair around his head, which made him appear more feral. He was fine, but I felt an underlying current of aggression in him and there were stories that he had had fights with other boys from time to time. So I never gave him a reason to be aggressive with me. I was always so nice to him and used humour as a defence. He wore a big patterned jumper that made him look twice the size he already was. Big ship in the harbour.

We started to walk aimlessly about with me in my dungarees, (which I loved because it made me feel like *'Oor Wullie'* and had big pockets which I could keep my sweets, Scotch pies and Corgi toys in) and unkempt long hair (which my father would have killed me for, if he had seen it); Ryan in his jeans and checked shirt and wee Callum in his little red trousers and brown shirt sticking out at the back like the flap of a tent. Patrick showed us his cigarettes and matches and said 'Let's gae tae yon quarry. No ane wull see uz there.'

I had no idea what it was he wanted to do there, but obviously it was something naughty, like smoking a cigarette or maybe burning some newspapers. So we all went. I never would have refused because it would have been very un-cool of me. Children, especially, never refused a suggestion, as they did not want to be the odd ones out. They wanted to be accepted in their clan. Up for anything, game for a laugh. Whit ye dae, I'll dae.

Anyway, I was interested in going to the quarry, which was deserted now as it was the holidays, as I had got to know it when I was having all those lorry rides and used to be driven around it. It was a great big muddy mess when it rained. A child's perfect over-sized sandpit.

As we turned into the quarry, confirming that there was no-one about, Patrick lit a cigarette and we all stared at him in admiration; though I really can't imagine why.

He puffed away like a politician and threw his chest out with self-importance. He made Ryan and I take a puff each, but it only reminded me of the *Capstan Full Strength* I had had with Rae in that field behind her house. I didn't like the taste of those horrible things.

'It's like breathing in the fumes of a car's exhaust pipe!' I commented.

'Wheesht! Dinnae be such a Jessie! Are ye afeart o' a wee bi'o' baccy?' Patrick mocked me.

'No, I'm not,' I countered, taking another puff just to be tough. (Stupidity knows no bounds).

Patrick then tried to give Callum a puff and both Ryan and I stopped him by saying he really was too young and that he would get into so much trouble if Callum's mother smelt nicotine on his breath. Thankfully, Patrick didn't argue the point. Instead he lit and flicked the matches ahead of us and, luckily not at us. You see, Patrick wasn't a bad boy, he just sometimes did anarchistic things because he was bored. He craved attention.

I spotted a big, brown Rover P5 parked near three lorries and knew exactly what make it was because I loved cars so much and was always studying them. A bit like train-spotting. This was the car which the British Government used for their politicians in Downing street and they were big and boxy and impressive with a massive square grill on the front.

The row of lorries, which was parked-up by one side of the quarry, looked very exciting for exploration and I thought that maybe we could play in them. There was an *AEC* and two *ERF*s. All tipper trucks. One of them was the blue one I think I had had a ride in at some time.

We climbed up and tried to open them, but they were locked, so we spent some time just hanging onto them like monkeys, enjoying the view. Callum even made monkey noises and giggled with his little mind, as Patrick laughed along with his own little mind. But then Callum got scared and he was helped back down by Ryan. When Ryan and I eventually jumped down, on this quiet day, with no-one around, Patrick was standing by the side of the lorry with the matches in his hands. He was fiddling with something and Ryan asked him:

'What are ye daein?'

'I'm gonnae open the fuel tank spout and put a match in it,' he announced daringly.

'Yer, whit? Are ye aff yer rocker? Ye want to kill us a'?' Ryan asked, flabbergasted.

'Dinae be sae stupid, ye great stookie! I'll no allow it.'

Anger, shock and disbelief had given Ryan the bravado to challenge Patrick like that. But the alternative was unthinkable and the trouble we would get into was potentially monumental.

Luckily, Patrick ignored Ryan's insults and just stood there with the cap of the fuel filler in his hand. He put it on the fuel tank.

'Dae ye dare me?' he asked brazenly.

'No, we don't!' Ryan and I both replied in unison. I was more worried about being caught for being naughty than anything else. I had visions of my father's ire and it was not a pretty sight; not because I feared him, but because I respected him so. I'd always felt bad when I was bad. Apart from that, I was not a very brave child and didn't want to get hurt in any way.

Before we could say anything more, Patrick dropped the lit match down the filler tube. I screamed and dashed away in an almighty sprint with Ryan not far behind me.

I wanted to leave the area, not only for my own safety, but also to discourage Patrick from doing anything bad or stupid and I thought that if he didn't have an audience, he would give up and go home.

I had expected a fire or some burning. But, when we turned around, breathless, we saw and heard Patrick laughing his head off with little Callum standing beside him grinning away while not really knowing why.

'Yer aff yer heid!' shouted Ryan, shaking with rage and fear. Ye'll start a fire!'

'No ah'll no!' Patrick shouted back. 'Did ye all like ma trick?' He was laughing so much now, he couldn't stand up straight.

'Yer baith looking' aye shoofly!' he shouted at us, between laughing his head off almost uncontrollably.

'You're mad!' I shouted back, still running away towards home.

'Come on, Ryan, let's go home,' I suggested as we walked further away, still looking back at Patrick and wee Callum, to see what they were doing. Calum was now playing with a little stick and following Patrick around. With relief, we saw them walking away from the trucks, so gave up our entertainment for the day and continued to walk towards home, calling it a day.

But then suddenly there was an almighty roar, a deafening explosion (actually what seemed like multiple explosions all in one and an almighty jolt) which threw us to the ground; like the most violent thunder you've ever heard in your life, right over your head.

I lay there for a few seconds, which seemed an eternity, not understanding what had just happened. I was confused and couldn't understand where I was. I was aware of all the birds suddenly bursting up into the sky in a grey swarm smudge and flapping away madly, like a swarm of locusts, there were so many of them. Everything slowed down to a crawl. There were echoes in my head and a lot seemed to have happened at once. I felt sick and got up in a stagger. Ryan was already up and staring back at the scene of carnage in deep shock and total disbelief. What had happened to suddenly make this world so disorderly?

'Christ almighty! Oh, no, no, NO!' he uttered to himself and he started to run back to Patrick and wee Callum. I instinctively ran with him because I needed moral support and didn't want to be left alone; apart from wanting to see exactly what had happened. I couldn't hear properly and everything was muffled. The silence was very eerie. Like when you suddenly turn down the volume on a TV that had been blaring and can still see the action. It was like watching everything in slow-motion. Action-replay.

As we got closer, I saw a spectacle of utter devastation. It was like a war-scene after a big battle I had watched on TV or at the cinema many times. Some of the trucks were still on fire; the Rover was a burnt-out shell, all grey, black and bare-metal-brown; there was debris everywhere; things were still fluttering down from the sky like dead birds or confetti; there were huge palls of acrid black smoke pumping into the placid blue celestial sky and drifting away, dead.

Dead.

And then we saw them.

One was a big, black beetle on its back, with its legs and arms in the air, as if reaching for salvation in its last-ditch death throes, like a victim of Pompeii.

Patrick.

Stiff as a board. Hard as concrete. Rigid as steel. Harder than he had ever been in his life. An immobile non-entity now, frozen in still-death and the other one nowhere to be seen. Ryan and I both stood there in our own little worlds, completely immobile and just stared at our Armageddon, knowing what had happened, but completely traumatised and not knowing how it had happened, barely able to take it all in. After all, he had done this party trick many times before, apparently. It was a bit like a sword-swallower forgetting not to bow.

Gradually, we saw adults running to the scene but had absolutely no interest in them whatsoever. Everything circled around us. We wanted our Patrick and our Callum. That is all we wanted.

Someone came and put an arm around me. I have no idea who it was. Someone told me my Uncle Benny had also come running when he had heard the explosions, as he was driving back into Doune from a carpentry job in Bridge of Allan. But I don't remember seeing him there.

What I do remember, is something I wish to God I had never witnessed and it will stay with me for the rest of my life. It was a man walking up to a flat piece of boarding, that had come from God knows where, maybe the shed behind where the vehicles were parked.

He lifted up this board and, as he did so, I saw what looked like a plastic doll lying on its stomach. It was pink and black and smoking. When he lifted up this board, long strands of what looked to me like melted mozzarella cheese sticking to the underside of the board, stretched upwards, coming from the 'doll's' body.

The doll twitched and I wondered why he wasn't doing anything to help it. Instead, he immediately gasped and put it back down. It was Callum McCulloch and I was later told they all knew he was dead. It had just been an involuntary spasm. A death spasm. A last, hopeless, fleeting, jolting nerve-grasp at life.

At five and a half years old.

This had been my first glimpse into Hell, made worse by its association with fire. My hard lesson in life, my vision of unadulterated horror, of terror undiluted, the waking nightmare which I would never be able to shake off. This scene of utter destruction, misery, sadness and woe.

At that moment, even as a child, I simply could not understand how God could allow that to happen to two of his children. I wondered in later years if God and the Devil were one and the same entity; both good and bad, just like Mankind. Doctor Jekyll and Mr. Hyde. It would explain a lot about all the horrific happenings in the world. I thought that if He were truly the Almighty, then He wouldn't let the devil influence these events.

Construction or destruction. Make up your mind.

Were they different, or one and the same? Two sides of the same coin? Two sides of the same creature? Two sides of the same mind? For a long while I went off religion and have never really been back.

Ryan and I were guided away from the site as the fire brigade, ambulances and police arrived. Our statements would be taken later. After all, it wasn't as if we had committed any crime.

It just felt like it.

There were sirens and blue flashing lights everywhere and a great hubbub of activity. Anyone would think it was carnival-time in Doune.

It was as if Doune had suddenly become a dingy city. It was so gratifying to walk away from a death scene. I didn't want to see any more and I just had to tell my mother. Everyone else had to know to take the pain off me. Share the burden.

Ryan Malone became my best friend that day and we have formed a bond which has not broken to this day; for we had both shared an experience and a secret; my brother-in-arms, even though a couple of years after this event Ryan threw himself in front of a train at Stirling railway station because he couldn't cope any more with the images which kept flashing up in his mind and tormenting him like Chinese water-torture and he had always blamed himself because he hadn't gone back for wee Callum; to take him out of harm's way. But he didn't know about the harm's way.

Patrick's death was bad enough, was sad enough. But he was older, tougher and he was the one who had caused the explosion and catastrophe in the first place, by deciding to put a lighted match into the petrol tank of the Rover P5. Not diesel.

Big car - big bang.

Apparently, he had scared many local lads and lassies with his lighted-match-into-a-diesel-tank trick. In later years I read that diesel will not ignite to a lighted match as it is not as combustible as petrol and has a higher flash point.

Not enough evaporates that will make a fuel/air mixture that will burn.

Did Patrick not realise that there were different types of fuel? Obviously, he wouldn't have done it on purpose. He just got carried away. Maybe he had wanted to see the difference between diesel and petrol. Maybe he just didn't think before he acted. Maybe.

Some people were just born stupid and if it had only been him, I don't think it would have affected Ryan and I so much, as there was no love lost between us and Patrick.

But it was Callum. Such a poor, innocent little boy who only wanted to hang around and play with us in all his naïve, angelic innocence. One who followed us around for wont of nothing better to do. One who put his trust in us. One whose mother tried to watch over him as best she could in her single-parent position.

She had allowed him out to play because she had needed him out of the way so that she could get on with all her busy packing, as she and wee Callum were due to fly out to America the following week to start a new life there with her brother who had found a good job for her. Well, who wanted to go to America now?

My mother had not come running because she was a bit indisposed that day and still wobbly on her feet when we all walked through the front door of my Grandpa Hock's house above the Co-op.

Aunty Joan came running up and looked me straight in the eye and asked if I was alright. I was alright physically, but never emotionally or psychologically ever again. I had nightmares for a week and kept waking up to my own screaming and my brother and sister were crying through the fear of not knowing what was happening to me and my mother kept fussing around me like an old, staggering hen. How macabre.

We curtailed our holiday in Doune, to get away from the area and went back to London, where I had begun to believe it had all been a dream and had on occasion asked my mother and siblings if it had all really happened.

No. Not a dream. A nightmare. A real nightmare.

A psychiatrist told my mother that I was suffering from post-traumatic stress-disorder and survivor-guilt but that, because I was a child, I would soon learn to put it in the past and get on with my developing life; being so easily distracted at such a young age by other sensations obtained through my five senses. My mother was grateful to the psychiatrist but wished he could speak plain English. Whit?

I had felt guilty about running away from the scene. But this is instinctive and a survival tool within us. In later years I often heard the saying *'Many times you run away to fight another day.'*

'If' is the biggest word in the English language and I had to agree. If only I had pulled poor wee Callum away and taken him with us when we started to run away.

If only.

If.

Only.

The aftershock of the explosions had brought down the Catholic church bell in the kirk with an almighty bang when it hit the floor. It had been in need of repair as the wooden struts were cracking and rotting away religiously and were due to be repaired in a couple of weeks' time. Seems God was a bit impatient to get the work done. Is that no' right son?

***

I jolted back into the present day and stood there now, much older and at times wiser, with tears flowing down my cheeks. For a while I had not noticed that I was crying, so deep were my thoughts and so rapt in the abhorrent memories was I.

Luckily, there was no-one about as it was a very quiet time of day. I rubbed my face with both hands as if I were washing it, dried my face with a hankie, calmed down, turned around and walked away to continue my difficult journey through Life. Sometimes too difficult. It was to be the last time I would go to what used to be the quarry and just wanted to get on with other things. Still, that guilt never goes away. I had to go the once though, to pay my respects to Callum McCulloch and to let him know that I had not forgotten him. Would never forget him. Ever.

The disaster helped me in a crazy sort of way, because, whenever I felt sorry for myself, I would just remember Callum McCulloch and thank my lucky stars that my plights in life were nothing compared to what he went through. Because of it I appreciated every day I had on earth. Even the bad ones and the sad ones.

I walked away from my quarry reverie, glad to be free from the oppression of its memory. I had felt I had to pay homage to Callum McCulloch and bury the ghost; but now I felt as if I had dug them all up again. I would never forget him or the catastrophic incident which had so horribly engulfed us all in its fireball and I didn't have to be there to be reminded of it. It was branded on my heart. Just like in the kirk: you didn't have to be there to worship God or to pray.

I gladly popped in to say goodbye to Katie, to distract me from my super-incumbent mood. Katie knew the full story. So, when I went in I simply said 'I've just been up to the quarry,' even though it was there no longer and she immediately understood. As I sipped her offered cup of tea, she sat beside me with her arm around me, slowly rubbing my back. She didn't refer to anything, but just rubbed my back. Sometimes words are not needed. Sometimes they can spoil things. Like lyrics encroaching on an instrumental song.

'When are you next coming up?' she had asked quietly, hopefully.

'I don't know,' I shrugged, 'You know life: it always gets in the way of our intentions.'

We embraced by the front door as her daft dog danced around us goofily. She was sorry to see me go and had a little tottering tear on the edge of her bottom eyelid. I had one in my heart, where no-one could see it.

I asked her to say 'goodbye' to her lovely husband for me and, as I walked down to her gate, I smiled to myself, as I remembered having said to him the first time we ever met: *'Ahana Hini Huni,'* as his face took on the most painfully-confused expression I have ever seen, as he tried to work out what region of Scotland the phrase came from. But it was simply my own gobbledegook. My attempt at sounding Gaelic. Funny how everyone could see through me. Story of my life, really.

I walked down Main Street on my way back to the Woodside Hotel and looked across at 'The Highland.' It was correctly called 'The Highlands Hotel,' but everyone referred to it as the former, as it rolled off the tongue better; like the smooth-flowing waters of the river Teith.

Seeing the hotel, where we never stayed, but only had High Tea, I was reminded of the sad time we had my mother's wake there, not that long ago. I remembered meeting my dear cousin Rae when she suddenly introduced me to her son. Son? This was a fully-grown young man! Where had all the years gone? It made me feel wistful.

Be that as it may, I, for some reason, didn't speak to her for long (probably too many people there) but I do remember her commenting: 'Ach, I was sae sarry t' hear of Aunty Anna's passing; I wonder hae'll be next?'

Well, that was very prophetic because the next person to be next was her and that was a great shock to me. I had always meant to go up and see her in Perth but never got around to it and I thought it seemed like yesterday we were smoking in the fields behind her house, during those incredibly care-free days. The years just flapped on top of each other like rubber mats in quick succession.

It had only been a simple blood clot. Small clot, big body. David and Goliath. There you go. I thought about how, at one point, I believed I was going to join her; until the doctor had set me free for now.

After Rae died, I got an obituary card from Aunty Macasa and I had written back to her, saying that I would keep it on my bookcase forever; and I have.

I trod on past the hotel and quickly found myself staring up at my dear grandfather's house above the Co-op and a lightning-image of a memory flooded my mind of when I had been told that my mother had been found dead. Not 'your mother has died,' but 'your mother has been found dead,' which implied mist and mystery, shattered your nerves and sent a sharp shiver right down the centre of your spine. No wonder some people collapsed when told of the death of a loved one.

My mother had been a whisky alcoholic and she had been found at the bottom of the stairs leading down to the coal bunker. In her drowsy, drunken state, she had stumbled like a loosely-strung marionette before crashing down them and collapsing in a dead-weight heap, having hit her head quite forcefully on the metal banister and opening up a fair-sized bleeding gash.

She had not been badly injured by the bump per se, but, having been a chronic alcoholic for over fifty-three years, over half-a-century, (good God!), the part of her brain which controlled balance had atrophied so much, like sand being washed away by the sea, or blown away by the wind; that it could no longer command her body to get up; and, because alcoholism also stops blood from clotting, she simply lay there on her back, growing cold and not just from the cold, until she perished.

All alone, all abandoned, completely isolated, losing consciousness and finally bleeding out. The blood had pooled out around her like a cape and flowed out like a running tap, a cascade; never-ending and ending only when her life-force lay beside her, yet not keeping her warm.

You reap what you sow.

There is nothing lonelier than an alcoholic, who drinks, not only to get away from it all; but mainly to get away from themselves, which is as hopeless as trying to get away from a Siamese twin. But, in the end, the alcohol just ends up floating their boat on the most treacherous of seas. Her potation was the death of her.

The police even went as far to say that they at first thought it was a murder scene. Maybe she wasn't murdered; but my feelings for her certainly were.

So she had simply lain there and died, with no-one to hear her muffled, drunken cries for assistance. My grandfather had died many years previously and she had thus been living on her own, hiding away. So there was no-one there to save her.

In a village, especially the one she had been born and brought-up in, some people had commented that it was highly unlikely that no-one had realised she had gone sooner and they all mooched about feeling guilty. But the truth of the matter was that she had alienated herself from her fellow-villagers so that she could pursue her highly-enjoyable pastime of drinking behind closed doors like a naughty little schoolgirl.

Secreting herself away, in the furthest corners of society and debauchery, gulping and guzzling in private where she had all the whisky she ever wanted to herself, she shoved it down her throat in buckets and waterfalls, no doubt.

The villagers had kept their distance from her as well, truth be told, because she was always pestering them for money to purchase *The Devil's Juice*, while explaining it was for anything else under the sun; her pride and dignity having been flailed away long, long ago. It had been eroded away by the power of the whisky sea.

She had died a lonely old, abandoned, dribbling, pathetic, worthless, addled, ghoulish wreck, which no-body wanted to bring back to the surface. Not even on God's mind. A simple imprint of the human being she had once been. Everyone had finally turned their backs on her, including her closest family, because she had unintentionally caused everyone so much pain and heartache throughout her adult life. She never understood the pain and frustration people felt at not being able to help her; the pain of her neglect; the pain of seeing her act so foolishly and the pain of seeing her stumble about like someone in the throes of Parkinson's disease.

No more pain.

Dead and gone.

Sigh of relief.

Amen.

I carried on to the Woodside hotel, my wee home-away-from-home and watched someone in its car park struggling to get a set of golf clubs out of his hatchback. It was nice to see something mundane and normal in life again. I had forgotten there was a golf course hereabouts; especially as I don't play.

As I walked into reception, my surrogate mother told me she was sorry to see me go. I thanked her for her sweet sentiment and added that I was also sorry to be leaving, but that life had to go on; albeit, sometimes, at a grind.

***

All good things come to an end and thus, all too soon, I found myself packing my bags in my room. I had so many positive memories of the Woodside hotel because I had spent many happy times there when I was a child; always going there for some treat or other.

Summer…school was out with no teachers to worry about. But it wasn't only that. It was because part of my roots were there and because it and Doune hadn't changed at all in all the intervening years and so was even more easily identifiable.

Tomorrow morning I would be leaving and it was certainly a bitter-sweet feeling, to say the least. But before going there was something, actually, two things, I wanted to do first. I could come back to Doune for a longer holiday sometime, God willing, but, to be honest with you, a week is enough. Because then you get a bit bored; and you never know what's going to happen in life. You should leave a place before you start taking it for granted. That way your bond with it remains stronger.

No doubt apprehensive about leaving, I awoke in the middle of the night; got out of bed in the dark; threw the curtains aside; flung the window open and just stood against the cold window-frame, looking down at the village slumbering happily away while standing rigid with the cold.

I sensed the stillness of the night and smelt its rich life-force emanating through the earth. The few street-lights threw orange shadows across a lone cat that was stalking someone or something or other or imaginary. Silver sheens sparkled off moonlit surfaces and the cat's shadow was ten times its own size, reminding me of *Nosferatu*. Nothing else moved and not even the buildings were breathing. It was as if I were looking at a photograph…

…a painted ship upon a painted ocean…

Blank inertia filled my senses as I drank in the cold and sharp intoxicating peace and quiet that this little baby village exuded so naturally. Silence can speak volumes and it can often tell you exactly what you want to hear. I felt very protective towards Doune, like a night sentry. Also, you know my mother…

I got back into bed and felt I had done something deliciously naughty (like…oooh…cream in the doughnuts to a diabetic) and then slept the sleep of kings.

***

In the morning I leapt out of bed with great verve and vitality, as if my bottom had just hit the raw end of a bed-spring and I very consciously stopped myself from singing out aloud: *'The Hills are Alive with the Sound of Music!'* I wasn't happy because I was going, but because coming to Doune had put me in such a positive frame of mind and because I had had such a fantabulous time here.

As I brushed my teeth over the cracked and well-lived-in bathroom sink I imagined I could already smell that stupendously-delicious fried breakfast creeping up the stairs to get me with its greasy talons. It was a bitter-sweet expectation. Sweet for the taste and bitter because it was going to be the last one; just like the Last Supper.

Nonetheless, I bounded down the old wooden staircase like an overgrown puppy and calmed myself down enough to walk into the breakfast-room with some form of poise and dignity (even though I was as chirpy as a bird) and… tripped on a ruck in the carpet. It was only a momentary blush quickly quelled by the happiness I felt at finding out I was not seriously ill after all. So I didn't really care if the patrons saw me acting like a twelve-year-old.

A new lease of life is what I now had and I was going to make the most of it. I could now go back down to London with a new and reinforced agenda and blood-flow, as clear and fresh as the river Teith.

Obviously, Morag was not as elated as I was, for she had not had any earth-shattering good news lately, but she still greeted me with a warm smile and chirpy small-talk.

'God bless ye, Luke. Yer a very guid person. You look efter yersel'' she advised me sincerely.

I was very touched by this kind gesture of hers and didn't know if I deserved such an accolate. The knowledge of good health and a compliment overwhelmed me and my eyes wet.

Obviously, she didn't even ask me what I wanted for breakfast, as I had had exactly the same thing every single morning. And, do you know, she seemed genuinely sorry to see me go. It could have been because I was an easy customer, but I don't think so, because we had developed such a great rapport together. Even though she was gay, I believe she appreciated my attributes. Certainly more than Claire had done. This now reminded me of the time I had asked Claire what she thought my best feature was and she had replied: 'Your absence.'

Ah, yes. Very rum I must say. Its nice to feel wanted.

After my fodder-feeding I sailed out of reception on a breeze and told the lovely lady owner that I would be back shortly to pick up my bags, but that I had to go somewhere first. She smiled back at me and said *'certaaiinlay'* in her broad Scots accent and turned back to a new arrival.

'Great hotel!' I told him. 'The best!'

I disappeared outside, turned up George Street and headed towards the Mercat Cross once again, as I wanted to see Doune castle one last time. Not only did I have a renewed interest in it since the pep-talk by that Doune school mistress, but I also felt the need to be surrounded by big, wide, open spaces; as big as my heart felt now, to feed the largess my spirit felt now. Whit?

As I stopped momentarily to look at the fabled Mercat Cross, I couldn't imagine how many people had walked up and down its few steps throughout its history and lifespan; even in such a small village. I thought of all the various tradesmen and characters and imagined romantically that I would have liked a lot of those people. Still, whimsicality is not practicality, so I moved on.

Lead on MacDuff.

With renewed interest I looked at all the shops along Doune Main Street and felt a great affection for them. I have always been a supporter of the underdog and hoped that they would always do well. Better than a faceless, granite conglomerate any day.

My mother had long-since passed away, but I could still see her in my mind's-eye, walking along and standing on every street corner, as if waiting for me. Waiting for me to what? Forgive her?

Yet when I saw her while in a positive mood it was not with sadness or regret or a feeling of waste, but rather with the reluctant acceptance of a life sadly lived.

I passed our church, brown against the green, where my mother's funeral service had been held and remembered it with a philosophical and sympathetic smile. When my mother died, I did not cry, though I admit I did have wet eyes, whose tears were trying to swim away from them. Still, I did not let a tear drop, like a brave soldier, perhaps the Scottish soldier she wanted me to be; perhaps the grandfather in me.

Though I had emotions of anger and frustration and no matter how much you tell yourself that you don't care about someone, if you know them for a long time, then you cannot help but be affected by their death. Because at those delicate moments in time, your spirit comes out and shows itself and it knows. You don't know, but *it* does.

Luckily, on the day of my mother's funeral, the organist had not turned up, so we were not subjected to wallowing in a sea of evocative and heart-wrenching dirges and heavenly bellows. Less traumatic for everyone else, I had thought philanthropically.

But today was not a day for slate-grey melancholia. It was a day to celebrate Life, and death would just have to take a back seat for the time-being.

So I carried on to the castle and, upon glimpsing it through the trees, could feel God's spirit there and rejoiced as though it were an old family friend or pet dog. I walked up the gently-rolling hills around the castle proper and never felt so at ease with my soul.

It was a quiet time of the day (so what else is new?) and there was absolutely no-one else around. I stood on one of the higher hills, with the castle looking over me as if protectively and drank in the scenery and smell of Scotland with all my might and my delight. Earthy and wet, fleshly and fresh, budding and beautiful. Pungent in its patriotism.

The visions of the rushing, tinkling, clinking river Teith; the vast canopy of the sky, like an inverted metal bowl; the gently swaying trees waving back at me; the yellow and reds of the flowers, the proud purple and green of the heather and thistles ever-present and the seductive fingering and tickling of the day's gentle breeze teasing the nape of my neck, brought me such peaceful joy. It was the simple things in Life which really mattered. Don't get embroiled in it, just embrace and enjoy it for what it is.

As there was no-one about, I slowly held my head back, closed my eyes with my lashes fluttering shut and spread my arms out like Jesus Christ on the cross. It was that freedom of airing my armpits, of blowing away all Life's cobwebs that I loved so much; and, because I was so relieved at having been granted a reprieve from the *Pearly Gates* or *Satan's Knocker*, I began to sway slightly to what I imagined to be nature's rhythm, nature's pulse, nature's beating being, the ley-lines of life; its life-core. Now I had been set free.

Momentarily overcome by my happiness, I began rotating around the hills and running a few steps here and there on the deeply luscious grass as I watched red, pink and bordeux shades and shadows from behind my closed eyelids, spinning by. It was dream-like.

Then I opened my eyes and watched with rejuvenated glee as the sky and the trees and the sun and the upper walls of the castle spun, spiralled, rotated and rolled around my head in reckless abandon; the vista sliding and slipping by at breakneck speed. I felt like an insect on a spinning-top. I felt so light (a miracle for my weight) and began dancing and prancing to nature's silent music, the only true music, which only the deliriously-happy can hear.

Shortly thereafter, before I brought all my breakfast back up, I calmed myself down because you can always have too much of a good thing and, after all, I was now a responsible adult and no longer a child; though the child lived within me still, protected; put aside for now. Still wanting its mother.

As I weaned myself off my self-inflicted bout of possession, I opened my eyes properly. All the motion subsided like water after a ripple, the calming of a shunted bowl or the end of an avalanche and I quickly became aware of a plump white-haired wee wifey in a woolly coat and gold brooch looking on at me with raised eyebrows and tittering to herself as she held the lead to her little Scottie dog. I went as bright-red as a sun-blushed tomato or lobster Thermadore and spluttered to explain, suddenly feeling twelve years old again.

'Isn't Life wonderful? I'm sorry. I'm just enjoying it.' I explained my behaviour as incoherently as Hugh Grant in one of his bumbling comedy films.

'Och aye. Ah ken Whit ye mean, laddie. Sometimes it can be aye wonderful and ye shid niver apologise to Pope nor peasant for that, big man!'

I did not know this woman, yet still felt a bond with her, even though she had called me 'big man!' My mother had known many people just like her. In that instant I hoped she wasn't struggling in real life and was moved to say: 'Thank you madam. I hope you have a good life yourself. My mother was from here.'

'Ma condolences!' she threw back teasingly as she laughed enthusiastically at her own joke and winked.

'C'mon Hettie,' she suggested to her wee dog, as they both trotted off to the continuance of their lives. Doon the brae and far away.

I stayed on a bit longer, grasping the end of my holiday firmly; thirsty to quench my love of the scenery and sat on the banks of Bonnie Doune, glorying in the moment like a seal basking on a rock in the sun. It was a day to remember.

A simple day to remember and one that others wouldn't have noticed at all. And though, as a freelance writer, not all my work was accepted, I wrote a few lines to mark the occasion anyway.

Here I am cavorting around Doune Castle
Down by the river Teith
It is amazing how Life can be so farcical
For you never know
What really lies underneath.
Only God can call Time
But, I am grateful to the doctor still.
Though now I cannot dither
As it's time for me to go
Back over the border
And far away over the hill.
-DRG-

Chapter Ten

Ye Hielan's and ye Lowlan's
O, where have ye been?
They hae slain the Earl of Moray
And lain him on the green.
He was a braw gallant
And he rode at the ring.
An' the bonnie Earl of Moray
O, he micht hae been the king!
O, lang may his lady
Look frae the castle Doune,
Ere she see the Earl of Moray
Come soundin' through the toun.

-Bonnie Earl of Moray-Anon

As I walked back yet again to the Woodside hotel, I was beginning to feel a bit like a yo-yo: to Moray park, back to the Woodside; to Doune castle, back to the Woodside; to Katie's, back to the Woodside; to Stirling, back to the Woodside; to my grandfather's house above the Co-op near the Callander bus-stop, back to the Woodside; to Deanston, back to the Woodside; to Callander, back to the Woodside and so on, ad infinitum. But this time it would be the last time. For now, until I came up North again; if I ever did.

I don't like long goodbyes. So I blew into reception, got my cases, paid my dues, hugged the lovely owner, pecked both her cheeks, (who, like a puppy, I wanted to take home but whose impracticality allowed me not to do so), thanked her for being so kind and attentive to me, threw my luggage into the car and farted off in a cloud of blue smoke towards Stirling. Really must get this car serviced one day.

I could feel the pull of Doune like a familiar lover as I tore myself away and turned right towards Deanston cemetery. One more duty to perform before I headed back to the daunting South.

When the car crunched up to the graveyard, with my wheels spitting gravel everywhere, I looked around as I was in no particular hurry to go and noticed the small and incongruous industrial estate opposite it and thought what strange bed-fellows they made.

The odd couple.

Life and death. Both silent, humbly ploughing their trades.

It was obvious that the industrial estate had no respect for the cemetery, or else it wouldn't have been there. Still, life goes on, I suspect; or rather, it doesn't when you are looking at the cemetery.

Standing there at the gates, about to go in, to take the plunge, like someone on a very high diving-board, I was reminded of an uncle of mine telling me once how he had gone there to visit his late wife soon after her death and of how he had been a 'bit put out' to see a car parked right bang in the middle of the entrance, causing an obstacle and inconvenience of itself.

But that how, on further investigation (basically sticking his big honker right up to the window) had discovered that, not only was there an occupant in the driver's seat and not only was he dead, but he had also blown his head off over a failed love affair. Over a woman dumping him. Or was he trying to tell everyone that's where he wanted to be buried? No, I mustn't be flippant; it's not a good quality.

I walked in and began to feel the butterflies taking off in my stomach.

I just did not like cemeteries nor visiting the people in them. Everything tightened and I was very tense. It was hard to look at people who had hurt you.

My mother had been one of the few people on this earth who brought out the raw emotions in me and I very much resented her for that. I never liked showing my weaknesses to anyone.

My feet scrunched violently on the scree and set silence fleeing away like a startled bird as they trod over the uneven gravel path. It made me wonder what was coming up from the ground.

I hated announcing my arrival; so I just concentrated on swiftly finding her headstone so that I could pay homage to it and quickly leave. God knows why I came; it was a pull. I walked on the spongy, bouncy and velvety rich green grass, which was laid-to-lawn, or laid-to-mourn (as the cynics would say) and noticed the contrast between it and the dull, sometimes bright-grey, headstones: the new recruits. Rural meets urban.

My grandfather is buried here somewhere without a headstone and I don't know why. He was most certainly more deserving of one than my mother ever was. Obviously, no-one wanted to spend the money on it or didn't have it at the time. But if only they had asked my side of the family, we would have forked out. Anyway...

Looking down on her light-grey headstone with my hands in my pockets, the stone not yet having had time to discolour, rot and decay, unlike her, I began to analyse the affect my father and mother had had on me.

My father had been stalwart, strong, understanding, intelligent, positive and demanding of respect, while at the same time being soft-hearted, kind-hearted and fair; whilst my mother had been whimsical, negative, daft, crude, patriotic and off her head with alcohol.

My father had been moral and very correct and instrumental in teaching my siblings and I the best of manners and decorum, while my mother had been idiotic, spiteful, nasty while drunk, confused and unconditionally-loving. She was an enigma. I even blamed her for my bad handwriting as I felt she had shaken my very soul and aura to the core; vibrating my whole being through trauma and right through to my hands. She had turned me into a vibrator of nerves.

But unconditional love cannot always salvage the severe rips and tears and jagged lacerations of alcohol abuse and my mother's love for whisky washed away any remaining love I ever had for her an ice-age time ago. I regarded her with more disdain than a bin-full of sinners. We all have to pay for our actions in life.

What a waste.

What a tragedy.

What a betrayal.

As I stood looking down on her, I wore my grief like an old familiar overcoat, weighing me down on the shoulders.

I sagged.

Though I never felt it myself, people have told me that I am intelligent, logical, with good reasoning and a lot of common sense. But my mother shattered my confidence into a thousand crystal shards and neglected to teach me how to prepare for this world; and she bestowed upon me an incredibly negative attitude in life that I have been fighting to this very day.

Something doesn't just happen with the effect eventually going away. The effect lasts like a stubborn stain forever. This resulted in me saying things to myself like: 'Why should I apply for that job? I won't get it,' or 'What's the point in asking that girl out, she'll only say no and put me in deep rejection,' or 'How can I go on a diet when I know I won't lose any weight?' or 'What's the use in writing a story when they won't publish it anyway?' and so forth.

People would tut and tell me to get a life, but you can't help the way you feel. She ingrained that negativity in me so deeply, like a cigarette-butt trod into a floor, that there isn't a submersible in the world that can get to it. So I missed out on many opportunities that I could and would have exploited had I had a more positive and assertive character. Had I felt I had more worth.

And I resented the way she had neglected me, always being *'indisposed'* with her silly, infantile alcoholic experiments; while she should have been bringing me up properly. The one who had meant to be nurturing me, guiding me and protecting me was the one rolling about on the floor in yet another drunken stupor, crying out for my dead father.

Do you forgive someone so readily just because they're your mother? Was she so wrapped up in herself that she didn't realise the subtle, penetrating and chronic suffering she caused to others around her?

Because I was so young I could only stand there and watch. I was not meant to be looking after her. It was the wrong way around. A mad axe-man could have walked into the room and chased me around, hacking me to pieces and my mother still would have been rolling and lolling around the room in her tumble-dryer, alcoholic-stupor- mind, crying out for my father, someone who wasn't even there.

Long gone.

My mother should have been there when she was not. She should have been encouraging me when she did not and she should have been guiding me through life, when she was not; instead of tossing the potent alcohol down her throat, *glug, glug, glug,* as if she were someone dying of thirst in the desert.

Everyone kept telling me that it was a disease. But it was not a disease; it was a life-choice and a self-inflicted addiction that she could have fought off if she had even bothered trying.

How can anyone choose between a bottle of foul-tasting liquid over the flesh and blood of their own child; their own creation? The world is full of mysteries and that is certainly one of them. An unselfish person would not want to hurt others.

I thought of the first stanza of the famous Scottish mother's poem I had learnt by heart long ago, wishing my mother had been like her.

Hush, my bonnie bairnie
Dinnae greet sae sair
Mammie noo has dune her best
What can she dae mair?
If my wee lass will be quiet
Or try to sleep a wee
When she rises, oh, so gran'
Will oor housie be!
-Anon-

And the other one which also came to mind:-

In an old Scottish home that is dear to my mind
Lives an old Scottish mother, so gentle and kind
Trouble and care may have wrinkled her brow
But with thoughts sweet and tender
I think of her now
-Anon-

I was so sorry that I could not think of *my* mother with those sweet and tender thoughts. I stared at her gravestone as if I had never seen it before; so alien was the idea that she was down there and I half-expected it to come alive and reveal hidden secrets like an oracle.

In my mean mood I sarcastically thought it a good job she had not been cremated because the crematorium would have exploded like the *Hindenberg,* with all the alcoholic fumes which surrounded and snaked around her; and further mused that, if she were dug up in a thousand years' time, she would still look the same as the day they buried her; perfectly preserved in alcohol.

I had always felt a veil of obtuseness about me, which I have always suspected had damaged my brain; being caused by her copious drinking while I was in the womb.

I suspected and still do, that all her drinking had really affected my cerebellum physically; especially at my developmental stage. Although I was intelligent, I would say stupid things without thinking and while most people are guilty of that I especially seemed to come out with some very silly things indeed and some simple information received would go right over my head. Sometimes I felt a haze in my mental faculties.

Maybe I panicked through lack of confidence. Because sometimes I knew something or other was not quite right, but went ahead and did it anyway, just to complete the task; a bit like a lemming. And another thing: I seemed to suffer from a regular attack of mental blocks. I was beginning to feel very weighed down by my self-pity.

It was at this stage of my musings that I remembered a piece I had done for a quarterly magazine, pertaining to the dead:-

As you stand by the graves of the Dead
Do not forget to remember the Living
For one day they, too, shall be Dead
And they may not be so Forgiving
-DRG-

But all this moribund pensiveness was getting a bit much for me and I didn't want to make the rest of my life miserable. Nor was it practical nor constructive. I was now happier in life, especially after my good news; so I looked up to break the spell of the moment. I bored easily.

I looked around the graveyard and took in two young yews standing erect to attention; sentries to the dead; with a larger, older one, acting as a protective umbrella to the tombstone-contents underneath.

I noticed all the headstones standing-to-attention like soldiers on parade, some listing with fatigue, while some were upright and proud like true Scots and came to realise that I was not alone.

There was a man with his back to me, near the far-end wall, looking down. I watched him for a while and came to realise that I knew this person, even if I could not name him straight away. There was something incongruous about him, yet he was very familiar to me…

'Bloody hell!' I thought to myself, 'It's Opie Cameron!'

Somehow, I had never pictured anyone who was mentally deficient, standing in a cemetery and I was even more surprised when he made the sign of the cross like any other good Catholic and normal human being. I was ashamed of my ignorance and my benightedness.

So, curious, I slowly walked towards him. Slowly out of respect for him and where we were and also a bit out of wariness. As a child I never felt he was one you could startle, as people like that can be quite unpredictable.

I managed to get as far as being able to read the headstone inscription he stood in front of, before he half-turned on sensing another.

'Agnes T. Cameron 1921-1992 R.I.P.'

'Your mother?' I asked Opie gently.

'Aye,' he confirmed.

'I'm sorry Opie. My mother's buried over there,' I added, pointing behind me.

After a few respectful seconds, I asked him:-

'Do you remember me, Opie?'

'Aye, Lukie, af carse ah dae. Ye wer thon fat boy in thae dungarees that ran aboot wi' untidy hair and a pocket full o' cash. Frae doon Sooth.'

I was quite taken aback by the sharpness of his memory, perception and awareness and felt quite ashamed of myself for having looked upon him in such a haughty way. It prompted my next remark.

'You're a poor lonely wee soul without any friends, aren't you, Opie?' I commented without sarcasm, criticism or malice.

He looked at me with those sharply-penetrating clear grey eyes of his, as clear as a dew-laden Scottish dawn, before tapping his left temple.

'They're a' aye in 'ere,' he told me, as if he were a member of a secret club, reserved for the few. Maybe he was. For a moment it was as if he were insinuating that he was not as stupid as he looked. And maybe he wasn't. For a moment.

'Ma Mammy,' he told me again as he looked back down at the grave.

'Aye, Opie, yer Mammy,' I agreed as I put a hand on his shoulder instinctively; not only in empathy, but in silent apology for the way I had looked upon him in all the years gone.

We both smiled at each other for a few seconds before he made the thousand-yard-stare into oblivion and, thinking of my own mother and feeling tears well up behind my eyes, those bitter tears of loss and pain for what could have been, I quickly broke off and told him that I had to go.

'Have a good life, Opie, and just be happy,' I advised him as I took and shook his hand. To any stranger it would have looked just like two ordinary men meeting. But to me it was much more than that. It was an understanding. An acceptance. An apology from my soul.

I walked slowly back down to the car, with my head down under the weight of sadness and regret; not wanting to disturb the peace and the dead and was in deep thought about my mother and my meeting with Opie Cameron. Maybe this was God teaching me some humility. And about time too.

I slid into the car and turned the engine over and was so preoccupied that I didn't notice that she wasn't firing. Just like an incompliant lover. I let out a sigh. Now even the motor was dead. Seems the cemetery had its influence on others too.

I really couldn't be bothered to get the hammer and chisel out of the boot, so I got out and shouted over to Opie Cameron, who was now creeping towards the entrance with a crab-like gait, a victim of his mushy mind. I went back to meet him and handed him a tenner.

'Here, Opie, that's for you. Give us a push, would you?'

He looked curiously at the brown note and grinned lopsidedly, shoving the folded paper money into the top outside pocket of his sports jacket. He then put his hands on the back of my car as if I were about to frisk him. I noticed he had a tear in the seat of his pants. No-one to darn it for him now.

I got back in the car, released the hand-brake; the only thing keeping me in the area now, and it soon rolled quite quickly. Opie had always been known for being quite strong as madness knows no bounds. I let out the clutch in second gear and the engine reluctantly coughed into life, as if to say it hadn't had enough of a rest. I revved the engine to encourage it and drove away.

As I watched Opie Cameron receding in my rear-view mirror, I waved back at him and I just had to laugh, because I had engulfed him in a thick cloud of black-and-blue smoke. I had expected him to turn and dart off like a gazelle. But he just stood there waving back at me or perhaps waving the smoke away. What a lonely character. We were all like Opie Cameron in our own different ways.

'God bless you,' I thought, as I realised I was crying. This was not especially for Opie Cameron or for my father or my mother or for leaving Doune or for the tragedy of the quarry or for Rae or for Nigel or for the relief at my being illness-free or from all the ups and downs in life and the pressures of it. It was simply a build-up of everything and sometimes the pressure cooker needs to blow its value and revel in the sweet release.

As I drew further away from Doune, I could feel all the memories unfurling behind me like leaves in the wind: the Mercat Cross and Nigel; Uncle Billy and the river Teith; Grandpa Hocks and the Co-op; Opie Cameron and MacAlpine's bakery; Doune castle and the kirk; Uncle Benny and his toupee; the Woodside hotel and Morag forever lost to me like a ship that passes in the night; the quarry and Callum McCulloch. Especially Callum McCulloch.

I drove through the day like a demon possessed; engulfed in potent memories and bitter happiness.

When I finally turned into my little London street at around 10:00pm, I saw Claire sitting on the steps outside my house, leaning forwards, fists on chin, surrounded by her bags and all her worldly goods as if she were a bag lady on the streets and my happiness grew even more.

I realised how much I had missed her and of how sorry I was for our break-up. My holiday in Doune had done me the world of good and I realised how true it was that absence does make the heart grow fonder, after all. I was so inwardly happy to see her that I grinned as wide as the front grill of my car.

She shuffled up to me like a shy little puppy and hugged me very tightly, laying her head on my chest, with me feeling my heartbeat pumping into her ear when I stepped onto the pavement.

She didn't have to say anything.

Her hug did that for her.

She didn't even look at me.

Her stance did that for her.

Maybe she was too ashamed to do that yet. But I love people who show their feelings, so it didn't matter one iota.

I let her go into the house first and turned back to look at the car. Normally this was a security habit but now it was out of nostalgia. I pictured it back in the Woodside Hotel car park and at Loch Ness.

Memories.

I just needed a few moments to myself.

To some, memories seem insignificant. But when you have experienced them yourself, they are giants.

I saw the doctor's happy face in my mind's eye reflecting my own and flashes of my Doune visit whirled around in my head like fireworks over the river Thames, as when your life flashes by before your very eyes; when you are in danger of death.

Perhaps the visit to my mother's cemetery killed the ghost.

Perhaps.

'I'm Anna's boy,' I said under my breath, 'I'm Anna's boy,' as I smiled to myself and shut the door.

Cast of Characters

GRANDPA HOCKS (Maternal Grandfather)
MRS. WALLIS (Grandpa Hock's 'girlfriend')
LUKE GARLAND (Main character/Narrator)
CLAIRE WESTMORLAND (Girlfriend)
ANNA GARLAND NEE HOCKS (Mother)
DIANA GARLAND (My sister)
JUAN GARLAND (My brother)
ALEC MACANNISH (Sister's boyfriend)
MACGREGOR (Sausage)
AILEEN LOHERTY (Mother's cousin)
ARCHIBALD MCKENZIE (Local man in angling scene)
DON MACFAIRLANE (Sweetie-shop man)
JOAN PLUMLY (Mother's childhood friend)
OPIE CAMERON (Village idiot)
AGNES T. CAMERON (His mother)
DONNACH LUAG COLQUHOLN (Boy killer)
BILLY HOCKS (Uncle)
MAISIE HOCKS (Aunt)
NIGEL HOCKS (Cousin)
BUNION HOCKS (Cousin)
BENNY HOCKS (Uncle)
MACASA HOCKS (Aunt)

RAE HOCKS (Cousin)
MORRIS MCCRACKEN (Grandpa Hock's friend)
FATHER ALEC DRUMMOND (Catholic Priest)
GORDON MCKENZIE (Drowned boy)
MATT MALLONE (Mother's cousin)
HATTIE MALLONE (His wife)
RYAN MALLONE (His son)
LUCINDA MALLONE (His daughter)
PATRICK (Quarry misfit)
CALLUM MCULLOCH (Little quarry boy)
STEWART ROBINSON (One of the gang)
CONALL MACGILLIVRAY (Another one of the gang)
CUTHBERT CATTENACH (Smallholder)
KATIE (Cousin)
JANET (Cousin)
BELLA (Her daughter)
DOMINO (Her son)
MORAG (Woodside owner's daughter)
BRODIE MACAVOY (Cheery coalman)
FIONA ARBUTHWAITE (Butcher's daughter)
RABBIE (Cat)
HETTIE (Little white Scottish terrier)
DOCTOR OVERWRIGHT (London GP)
DOCTOR LOMAX (Doune Village GP)

About the Author

Derek Ghirlando was born in Tripoli Libya in August 1955 and is the son of a Scottish mother and Maltese father. He and his family had to leave Libya after the revolution of 1969 when Gaddafi took over the country and thus came to live in England. Derek's mother was actually born in Doune, near Stirling, in 1927 and it is through her patriotic enthusiasm and promotion of her homeland that this book was inspired.

Lightning Source UK Ltd.
Milton Keynes UK
UKOW04f1805041117
312145UK00001B/10/P